TRUE BLUE MYSTERIES • BOOK ONE

BLUE PLATE

Special

AWARD-WINNING AUTHOR

SUSAN PAGE DAVIS

Scrivenings
PRESS
Quench your thirst for story.
www.ScriveningsPress.com

Published by Scrivenings Press LLC
15 Lucky Lane
Morrilton, Arkansas 72110
https://ScriveningsPress.com

Printed in the United States of America

Paperback ISBN 978-1-64917-096-5

eBook ISBN 978-1-64917-097-2

Library of Congress Control Number: 2021933538

Cover by www.bookmarketinggraphics.com.

1

Telling her father what happened was the worst thing about going home.

Campbell pulled up at the small brick ranch house. Her father had moved here near the end of her first year of college. She'd never lived in the house but had visited on school breaks and vacations. His car wasn't in the driveway, but that wasn't surprising. He was probably at his office. She should have called ahead.

Just to be sure, she walked up to the front door and rang the bell. No answer. She had a key but didn't like to go into his space until she'd at least talked to him. It would be different if he still lived at her childhood home.

She walked over to the garage door. Shielding her eyes from the sun's reflection, she peered in through one of the small windows. No car. Dad definitely wasn't home. She went back to her loaded Fusion and backed out of the driveway. Next stop, her father's storefront office, True Blue Investigations.

The only car out front was a Jeep—not her dad's. Great. He was probably off on a stakeout somewhere, and that jerk Nick Emerson was most likely inside the office. The kid was good-looking, but that didn't cut any ice with her. Although he was only a couple of years her junior, she still thought of him as the brash kid who chafed against authority. The tattoo of a skull and crossbones on his arm didn't help.

But Nick spent a lot more time with her dad now than she ever had. That made her a little uneasy, but she refused to consider that she might be jealous.

She pulled in a deep breath, determined to treat Nick as she would a wisecracking student in one of her freshman comp classes.

"Well, well, well, Campbell McBride. Long time, no see, Professor." Nick gave her his annoying grin as she walked through the doorway.

"Hey. Where's Dad?"

"Not sure." Nick leaned back in his desk chair and locked his fingers behind his head, so his elbows stuck out on either side like elephant ears. "You been to the house?"

"Yeah."

Nick arched an eyebrow. "Well, I haven't seen him today, but he called me last night and said he was picking up a new case."

"What is it?"

"Dunno. He said he was meeting a client and he'd see me today. But he hasn't shown up yet."

"It's almost noon," Campbell said.

"Yeah." A slight frown puckered Nick's brow.

Her father didn't like to be called when he was out on a job, but enough was enough. Campbell took out her phone and punched the speed dial buttons for her dad's number.

"This is Bill McBride of True Blue Investigations. I can't take your call right now, but leave a message and I'll get back to you."

She sighed and waited for the beep. "Dad, it's me. I'm in Murray. Call me when you get this, okay?" She ended the call and sat down in her father's chair. The desktop was neat. One file folder lay on the left side. Her dad's coffee mug sat empty on a square of memo paper. A few other sheets lay beside the computer keyboard. She shuffled them. Phone numbers. Only one had a name.

Nick seemed to be hard at work on his computer, but from all she could tell from this viewpoint, he could be playing a video game.

Okay, that was a little snarky. True, she'd never liked him much. Nick had been a teenager struggling through his last year of high school when her father had left the Bowling Green Police Department and moved here. The young man had been ticketed for speeding right outside Bill's office. A few weeks later he'd been picked up for running a red light.

By then, her dad had made friends with several local cops, and one of them had confided that Nick was his cousin's boy, and he was concerned about him. His father had abandoned the family, and Nick had been in trouble for several infractions. Nothing huge—one count of underage drinking was the worst. But he showed a general disregard for the law at that point, and his attitude was steering him for bigger problems.

For some reason, her dad had taken a shine to Nick. Maybe he thought he could be a mentor and help him straighten out his life. Avoid jail. Bypass the drug scene. Become a useful citizen. Campbell stopped short of drawing a connection to the fact that Bill had never had a son, just a bookish daughter.

He looked up and caught her staring. "What?"

"Nothing." Campbell picked up a ballpoint pen and clicked it on and off.

Her father probably saw himself as a positive role model for Nick, and there was nothing wrong with that.

But hiring him as an assistant investigator? He'd given Nick a job as soon as he turned twenty and paid for his P.I.'s exam the next year.

"Right." He turned back to his computer screen.

Campbell studied his rugged profile. Maybe Nick had grown

up over the past three years. She hoped so. He'd been impetuous and easily distracted, and her father had worked on helping him focus and take responsibility. Still, she couldn't imagine he was the ideal employee.

He worked for a few minutes and looked over at her again. "So, you're off for the summer?"

"Yeah." She frowned. The summer and the rest of her life. Dad wouldn't be happy.

"You look upset."

She blinked. "My dad is missing, and I just got fired. Wouldn't you be upset?"

"You got fired?" Nick sat up a little straighter. "How come?"

"Oh, not fired exactly. The university's budget was slashed, and they're downsizing. I'd only been there two years, so I got cut."

"Wow. That's rough."

"Tell me about it." She picked up the memo squares and stared at the top one. She'd have to start job hunting right away.

"You didn't see it coming, huh?" Nick asked.

"Well, I thought it *could* happen, but I hoped it wouldn't. I did put my name in at some other schools, but nothing's opened up for me yet."

"Did you try Murray State?"

"Yeah, that's one of three I sent my resumé." She should be home sending out more job applications. She scowled at the small square of paper on top. "So, who's Darrin?"

Nick's brow wrinkled. "Darrin? The only one I know is Darrin Beresford, but you don't mean him, do you?"

"I don't know, do I? There's a phone number here, and it says *Darrin*. Who's this Beresford guy?"

"Oh, he's the town crackpot. He walks all over town and asks a million questions."

"So?" she said.

"He's nosy and annoying. He's got a scanner in his house,

4

and he goes to every fire or car accident. He used to call the police at least twice a week to tell them something he thought was important, but it was mostly his imagination—that and rumors. Finally they told him never to call them again unless he had some concrete evidence of a crime to show them."

"Did he stop?"

Nick shrugged. "I guess so. Now he calls the newspaper all the time instead."

"Why?"

"To give the reporters little tidbits he's sure will lead to their next big story."

"And you know this, how?"

"I have a friend at the paper. Nobody there can stand Darrin because he's such a pest, but once in a great while they find him useful, so they tolerate his calls."

Campbell considered that. "How is he useful?"

"Sometimes he'll hear about something newsworthy before the newsroom does. Like things that happen in the middle of the night. He tips them off, and they look into it to see if it's worth doing a story."

"So how do we know if this phone number is his?" She glanced at the memo sheet again.

He sent her a look that clearly said she was stupid.

"I guess I could call it, huh?" she asked without enthusiasm.

"Bring it here. I can probably find the number online."

"Even if it's a cell phone?"

He wiggled his eyebrows at her. "Zee private detectives have zee methods."

"Riiight." She got up and took him the piece of paper.

Nick was already typing on his keyboard. After a moment, he took the note from her and pecked in the number.

"Yeah, it's his."

"Okay. So why would my dad call him?" Campbell asked.

"Who knows. Maybe Darrin called first and your dad took

the message off the voice mail and wrote down the number. Although, Darrin's never called here before, that I know of."

She nodded slowly. It made sense. "Have you checked the messages today?"

"Yeah, first thing this morning. There was nothing from Darrin, but if your dad took it, he probably erased the message."

She sighed.

"Hey, are you hungry?" Nick asked.

She was. Hours had passed since her sketchy breakfast on the road.

"They have pizza and sandwiches at the convenience store on the corner." He closed a couple of programs on his computer and stood. "Come on. My treat."

NICK BOUGHT HER LUNCH, which made Campbell feel a little better, but her dad still hadn't returned when they got back to the office. She sat at his desk and tried his cell phone again.

"Nothing?" Nick asked.

"Nope." She put her phone down. "Pretty quiet around here."

"Well, I'm working a diligent search, and we've got one case for a lawyer's office. Your father may be working on that."

"I guess I expected some people to come in."

"We get most of our cases through connections with insurance companies and lawyers, not from walk-ins."

"Oh." Dad's job was more boring than she'd thought. Watching insurance claimants to see if they were faking their injuries. Yawn.

Nick worked for several minutes without speaking. The desk phone rang, and Campbell snatched it up.

"Hello? True Blue."

"Hi, this is Dr. Aiken's office. Is Mr. McBride in?"

"No, but this is his daughter." Campbell's heart raced. Was there some sort of medical emergency?

"Could you please tell him that his reading glasses are ready? He can pick them up anytime."

"Sure. Thank you." As she lowered the phone, she noted the number on the display. She checked the memos on the desk and sighed.

"What's up?" Nick asked.

"Eye doctor. Dad's new glasses are ready. And one of these phone numbers Dad wrote down matches theirs."

"That's one mystery solved. How many numbers you got?"

"Besides Darrin's, two more."

He stretched out a hand, and she took them over to him.

A minute later he said, "This one's for the garage Bill uses. I think he had something done there yesterday. Oil change? Anyway, I doubt it's significant. This other one … Oh, that's for Riverside Insurance. We work for them off and on. I did a surveillance job for them a couple weeks ago."

"So, maybe they called and gave Dad a new case?" she asked.

"Maybe." Nick got up and took a canister of coffee from a small cupboard.

"I can do that," Campbell said.

"It's okay."

"No, I need something to keep me busy."

Nick hesitated then surrendered the carafe. "Look, your dad's a smart guy. He's okay."

"You don't know that." She carried the carafe into the tiny bathroom and filled it with water at the sink. When she came out, Nick was working again. She poured the water into the coffeemaker and measured the coffee grounds into a new filter.

"I'm calling that Darrin guy." She hit the BREW NOW button.

"Sure." Nick didn't sound as if he even paid attention to what she'd said.

Campbell sat down, picked up the desk phone's receiver, and

punched in the number from the memo sheet. It rang, but no one answered.

She puttered around the office while Nick worked on his diligent search. After checking her email, she searched a regional site for job openings. Maybe she could get something temporary for the summer. But most of the openings she qualified for in Murray, even with her master's degree, paid minimum wage—which was pitifully low in Kentucky.

Around three o'clock, she tried her father's cell for about the tenth time, but again, all she got was voice mail. She walked over and stood in front of Nick's desk until he looked up at her.

"It's time to call the police."

"Good luck with that," Nick said drily. "They won't do anything yet."

"That forty-eight-hour rule is hogwash." Campbell scowled at him. "They can start looking for a missing person anytime they think it's warranted."

"Sure," Nick said, "if there's evidence the person is hurt or in trouble. But Bill is an adult. He often stays out all night on the job. They won't start looking for him yet."

Campbell clenched her teeth. "It's been nearly twenty-four hours since you heard from him."

"How about we try to find Darrin and ask him if he's talked to Bill lately." Nick rubbed his eyes and then refocused on her. "It shouldn't be hard to find him. I'm pretty sure he eats supper at the Barn Owl Diner every night."

She thought about that for a few seconds, surprised Nick had offered to help. It was better than nothing. "Okay, let's go."

The Barn Owl was a small, family-owned restaurant off Highway 641, with a gambrel roof and red siding. Inside, they asked for Darrin.

"He's not here right now," the waitress at the cash register said. "Were you supposed to meet him?"

"No," Nick replied. "We just thought we might catch him here."

"Well, he'll be here for sure by five o'clock. He's always here for an early supper."

"We'll come back," Campbell said.

They walked slowly out to Nick's Jeep.

"I might as well go home." Campbell shot him a sidelong glance. "To my dad's house, I mean."

"Didn't you live there before you went to college?" he asked.

She climbed in and buckled up. "I grew up in Warren County. Dad decided to move over here after my mother died about six years ago. He gets more clients here than he did where we were. Less competition."

"Yeah, that sounds about right. We're the only P.I.s in Murray. Sometimes Bill tells me stories about when he was a cop." Nick steered back toward the office. "Why don't you go home and unpack? He may have been there sometime today."

She nodded, but doubted she'd find her father there. "I can unpack some of my stuff, I guess." The night before, she'd crammed everything she could fit into her car and left two cartons of books and her microwave with a friend. "I'll meet you at the diner at five, okay?"

"Yeah," Nick said as he parked next to Campbell's car, the only one in the lot in front of True Blue. "I'll call you if Bill shows up or calls in."

"Thanks." She didn't bother to go into the building, but got in her ten-year-old Fusion and drove the mile and a half to her father's house. It sat on a quiet street of unpretentious homes.

She let herself in and wandered through the small brick ranch house. Empty, as expected. Mostly neat—her dad couldn't stand clutter. No pets or house plants. Only one piece of art: her own face smiled at her from a framed photo on the living room wall, taken in her cap and gown the day she'd graduated with her master's two years ago.

In the small second bedroom he used as a den, she dropped her suitcase and purse. On visits, she always slept on the hide-a-bed there. His orderly desk held a computer, a mug full of pens, a blank notepad, and a photo of her mom in jeans at their old house in Bowling Green.

"Dad, where are you?" She went back to the kitchen. He'd obviously planned to return home last night. A small package of hamburger sat on a plate on the counter. The moisture under it told her he'd left it out to thaw. She stuck in the refrigerator. A small mudroom led off the kitchen to the back door, and she went out there, opened the washing machine, and wrinkled her nose.

"Okay, you left a load of wash that needs to be dried?" Something was wrong. Why had she listened to Nick? She pondered her options as she poured soap and started the washer again. She'd unpack her clothes and then meet Nick at the Barn Owl. But if they didn't get any satisfaction there, she'd go straight to the police.

At FIVE, Nick drove into the diner's parking lot and Campbell got out of her car, where she'd been waiting ten minutes. She walked across the pavement toward him.

"Anything?"

Nick shook his head. "Let's see if Darrin's here."

At least he looked worried, too.

"Hey, Shari," Nick said to the hostess. "Is Darrin Beresford here?"

"Uh…" she looked around. "I guess not. He's usually here by now. Orders the blue plate special every Tuesday."

"What's that?" Nick asked.

"It's an old-fashioned term for the special of the day."

"It goes with your retro décor." Campbell smiled.

"Do you want a table?" Shari picked up two menus.

"Yeah, sure," Nick said.

Campbell followed him, looking around as she walked. The diner held six booths along one side and about a dozen square tables. On one wall, a large, stuffed owl held pride of place, and she shuddered. The rest of the decorations included rural antiques, old signs, and a couple of primitive paintings. Could be worse.

A waitress approached the table.

"You want to order?" Nick asked.

"I'm not that hungry." Campbell shrugged. "But I guess we should get something."

Nick ordered a burger and a beer.

"Beer?" Campbell almost shrieked. "We're on business. You don't know what we'll need to do tonight, and you're going to drink?"

"Make that a Coke." Nick rolled his eyes.

The waitress nodded and wrote on her pad. "Together or separate?"

"Separate," Campbell said at the same moment Nick said, "Together."

"Fine," he said. "Separate."

"I'll have a BLT and unsweet tea," Campbell said.

"Okay. I'll be right back."

She brought their drinks, and Campbell moodily sipped hers while studying the other patrons.

When the waitress brought their sandwiches, Campbell asked, "Do you know Darrin Beresford?"

"Sure, he's a regular."

"Would you tell us when he comes in, please?"

"Okay."

"I know what he looks like," Nick said.

Campbell ignored him and ate her BLT without tasting it. When their food was gone, Nick ordered lemon meringue pie and coffee, but Campbell just had a refill on her iced tea. She checked the time on her phone every few minutes and made a trip to the restroom.

At a minute to six, she frowned at Nick. "We've been here an hour. He's not going to show."

Nick sighed. The waitress came with his change from his bill and Campbell's receipt.

"Excuse me," Campbell said. "Is the owner here tonight?"

"Ray? Sure, he's out back."

"I'd like to see him, please."

"Okay. Is everything all right?"

"Yeah, it's fine. I just want to ask him something."

"Okay." The waitress looked doubtful as she headed for the kitchen.

"You scared her," Nick said.

Campbell only scowled. Nick was probably right, but she wouldn't admit it. Her dad's unexplained absence had her on edge.

A plump, fiftyish man wearing a white apron came out of the kitchen and approached their table.

"How's everything, folks?"

"It was good," Nick said quickly.

"Yes, very good," Campbell said. "We were looking for Darrin Beresford, but he doesn't seem to be here tonight."

Ray took a quick look around. "Doesn't seem to be."

"And that's unusual?" Campbell asked.

"Yeah, he comes in almost every night. He's usually sitting right over there about this time." He pointed to a table near the front window, now occupied by a couple in their twenties.

"Was he here last night?" Campbell asked.

"Yeah, definitely."

She nodded. "I'm Campbell McBride. My father is Bill McBride, of True Blue Investigations. Do you know him?"

"I know who he is. Comes in here once in a while."

"Was he here last night?"

Ray shook his head. "I don't think so, but then, I'm in the back a lot. But I don't recall seeing him."

"Who else was here while Darrin was here?"

He frowned. "Uh ... Brock Wilson ... Dr. Exter ..." He lifted a hand and beckoned to the hostess. Shari came over and eyed the boss questioningly.

"You were on last night. They want to know who was here while Darrin was in. All's I remember is Brock Wilson and Dr. Exter."

"Hmm," Shari said. "Professor Neilson and his wife were here, and some college students. The Barnes sisters came in for spaghetti."

"Right," Ray said. "Well, I've got to get back to work. Help them as much as you can, Shari. Come in again, folks." He turned and went back toward the kitchen.

Shari took an order pad from her pocket and flipped to the front. "I only serve the beverages, but—oh, yeah, there was a large party after the ball game. Out-of-towners. And I served Mary Innes, the woman who owns the new thrift shop. Gary West—he's a regular. There were lots of other people, but I didn't know them all. There were three waitresses working."

"Thanks a lot," Campbell said. She slipped a ten-dollar bill into the woman's hand.

"Thanks." Shari looked at her wide-eyed.

Campbell walked toward the table where Darrin had sat when he ate his last meal in the diner. Two women sat at it now, talking and laughing. The table had a good view of the parking lot, she noted, and a couple of businesses across the street. The real estate office and the equipment rental store were both closed for the night.

She walked back to their table and Nick rose.

"Come on," he said.

"Where are we going?"

"Darrin's house."

For once, she liked the way Nick was thinking.

TWILIGHT WAS FALLING as they drove to the house on the edge of town. Campbell had opted to ride with Nick. He pulled in slowly and parked in the driveway behind a twenty-year-old pickup with no tailgate. They got out and walked to the front door of the run-down frame house.

"You ever been here before?" she asked.

"No. Looks like a dump." He knocked.

As they waited, Campbell looked around the yard. No flowers that she could see, no vegetable garden. The grass was long and unkempt. There was no garage, but off to one side some sort of cages stood a few yards from the house. She caught a glimpse of white moving inside one.

"I guess he's not home," Nick said.

Campbell followed the path beaten through the grass to the rectangular cages. Four of them, about three feet by five, were raised off the ground a couple of feet on two-by-four legs.

Rabbits.

Their dishes and water bowls were nearly empty, and they looked hungry. One black-and-white-spotted bunny stood on its hind legs with its front paws against the wire mesh and sniffed at her.

She walked a couple of steps into the overgrown lawn and pulled two handfuls of grass. She poked the blades through the small holes in the mesh, and the spotted rabbit and its cage mate fell eagerly on her offering.

"What are you doing?" Nick was standing right behind her.

"The rabbits are hungry. They look healthy otherwise, though. If he normally takes care of them, would he let their food and water get so low?"

"Maybe he's been gone all day."

"Yeah." Campbell stooped for more grass. "And he missed his regular dinner stop."

While she pulled more grass and stuffed it into the other cages, Nick wandered off toward the back of the house. After she was sure all the rabbits—seven in all—had something to nibble on, Campbell followed him.

The unmown back yard was full of junk. An old bucket, boxes, a bike with one wheel, a hose that was so deep in the grass she could barely see it. She looked around and saw building debris, parts of machinery, and several cans and bottles.

"Disgusting," she said.

"Yeah." Nick ambled to the back door of the house, which hung a bit crooked in its frame. He knocked, waited two seconds, and turned the knob.

"Hey," Campbell said, but it was too late. Nick was already inside.

Hesitantly, she mounted the creaky step and looked in. Nick fumbled along the nearest wall in the dark. He found a light switch and flipped it. A bare bulb in the ceiling fixture lit up the kitchen—or at least, Campbell supposed it was the kitchen.

Food containers and dishes littered every flat surface. The table was only identifiable because of its legs and the two chairs sitting near it—both of which were piled with magazines, newspapers, and empty cereal boxes. One plastic trashcan overflowed with rubbish, and another contained an open sack of rabbit pellets. The place reeked of spoiled food and mold.

"Darrin?" Nick called. He got no answer, but that didn't stop him from turning sideways so he could fit between piles of trash and enter the next room.

"Nick, we shouldn't—"

A loud expletive from Nick cut her off, followed by, "Call the police."

Campbell felt as though she'd been standing on one of Darrin's rickety chairs and someone kicked it out from under her. She edged into the living room doorway. Nick was kneeling beside a prone form on the floor. For a split second, she wondered if that was her dad, lying there in this filthy place. But that didn't make sense.

"Is it Darrin?" she asked.

"Yeah." Nick looked up at her. "Call 911 now. He's dead."

2

"**D**on't touch that!"

Too late. Nick obviously didn't think Campbell's orders carried any weight. He'd already picked up the cell phone that lay on the floor beside Darrin's body and was clicking buttons. Some detective. She punched in 911 while Nick went on snooping on Darrin's phone.

"What is your emergency?"

Campbell gulped. "My friend and I found a dead body." Okay, so Nick wasn't technically her friend, but explaining what they were doing in Darrin's house would be too complicated. She hung up after telling where they were, even though the dispatcher said not to, and looked back into the living room. "They want us to stay until someone gets here."

"That's standard."

"Yeah. What are you doing?"

He was scrolling on Darrin's phone, that much was obvious.

"He didn't have a password, so I'm checking his recent calls. Looks like he called Bill last night—probably while he was at the Barn Owl eating supper. He also called another number immediately before that." Nick looked up at her. "It's the police station's non-emergency number."

"What?" Campbell took a step forward, avoiding looking at the corpse and the dark pool of blood that seemed to have come from the poor man's head. Her stomach churned, and she turned away. "He called the police and then he called Dad?"

"Yeah. Maybe it was like I told you—the police brushed him off, so he called Bill, hoping for some cred with him."

She glanced around the dimly-lit room, noting more clutter including several empty food containers and a chair with only three legs—but a large-screen television mounted on the wall opposite the sagging sofa. She wondered what Darrin had hit his head on.

"We should go outside," she said.

"Yeah, maybe." Nick slowly rose to his feet.

He put down Darrin's phone, and they sidled their way to the back door. Stepping out into the fresh, clear night Campbell pulled in a ragged breath. The stars were gleaming now, and a light breeze ruffled her hair. The entire situation felt unreal, but she knew it was true. She and Nick had just found a dead man.

Lord, what have we gotten into?

The unspoken words shocked her. How long since she'd prayed? Far too long. She added another silent petition—*God, keep my father safe.*

They waited on the driveway, both wrapped in their own thoughts. After a couple of minutes, she heard a faint siren. The wailing grew louder. "That was fast."

"Well, we're not that far from the station," Nick said.

They walked a few yards to meet the patrolman as he climbed out of his squad car. By the time they'd explained the situation, an unmarked car and an ambulance had pulled in.

"You won't need the ambulance," Nick told the officer. "You'll need a hearse."

They waited outside while the police did whatever they did.

Campbell gave the rabbits more grass. After about ten minutes, the EMTs came out of the house empty-handed and left. The detective emerged next. He walked over to them, his expression sober and his eyes alert and considerate.

"Thanks for staying, folks."

As if we had a choice, Campbell thought, but she appreciated his supportive manner.

"I'm Detective Fuller. How do you two know Darrin Beresford?"

"Everyone in town knows Darrin," Nick said.

Fuller took out a pocket notebook and flipped it open. "And you are?"

"Nick Emerson. I work for Bill McBride at True Blue Investigations. I think we've met before."

"I think you're right." He made a note then quirked his eyebrows at Campbell.

"I'm Bill's daughter, Campbell. I teach at Feldman University, and I just arrived today to visit my father."

"I know Bill." Fuller's nod seemed favorable, which soothed Campbell's nerves a bit. He asked for their phone numbers and home addresses.

"I'll be at my dad's." Campbell gave her father's address and her own cell phone number.

"And how did the two of you come to visit Mr. Beresford?"

Campbell glanced at Nick and decided to take the lead. "My father hasn't been to his office all day, and I don't think he went home last night, either. Nick talked to him early yesterday evening, but that's the last we've heard from him. We found Darrin's phone number on my father's desk, so we thought we'd ask him if he'd talked to Dad recently. But now this has happened, and I want to make a missing person's report on my dad."

Fuller's eyes squinted a little narrower. "So, Bill McBride is missing?"

"Yes," Campbell said.

"It's over twenty-four hours now," Nick said. "We're both concerned."

"Hmm. Bill's known to stick to a case for days sometimes."

"Yes, but he always checks in with me," Nick said.

Campbell nodded. "And the way things were left at the house, I'm sure he intended to come home last night." She explained about the thawed meat and the composting laundry.

"Okay. Well, Bill's a capable guy. Let's take care of business here first. We'll have a lot of processing to do here." Fuller looked toward the street, where a sedan was pulling in. "Oh, there's the M.E. Listen, if Bill hasn't checked in by morning, then we should probably get him on the missing persons list. I agree with you there. Why don't you check his house again? He may have just put in a long day."

"Yeah," Nick said. "So, are we done?"

Fuller nodded. "I'll contact you if we need anything else. But stay in town."

"Do you know the cause of death?" Campbell asked.

"Not yet. The medical examiner may be able to tell us something tonight, but the autopsy report probably won't be available for several days. Thanks for calling it in."

Nick started walking toward his Jeep, and she followed.

"What now?" she asked when they reached it.

"I hope we can get out past the M.E.'s car." He frowned. "I think we should sleep on it."

"Well, you can if you want," Campbell said. "I'm going to talk to some of those people who were at the diner last night. Maybe somebody saw Dad there."

Nick turned to face her. "Campbell, you're exhausted, and none of the staff remembered Bill being in the diner. We know Darrin called him from the diner. Your father wasn't there."

"Right, but maybe he went over there afterward."

"Probably not. Shari was the hostess on duty. Don't you think she'd have noticed if Bill joined Darrin at his table?"

He had a point, but Campbell wasn't willing to let it go. "I just think someone may have noticed something the staff didn't. They were busy, right?"

"Okay." Nick heaved out a sigh. "An hour. No more."

She got in his Jeep with him. Nick knew a couple of the patrons Shari and Ray had mentioned. They managed to track down Mary Innes, the thrift shop owner, as well as the Barnes sisters, but none of them were much help. They did confirm that Darrin had arrived at the diner at his usual time the previous evening and ordered his meal. He made at least one phone call, and he left without finishing his supper, which Jerusha Barnes deemed unusual.

"Oh, yes," her sister Paula said. "Darrin always orders dessert."

"I wonder if he left the waitress a tip last night," Campbell said.

Back in the Jeep, she buckled up and looked over at Nick. "Maybe we should have told the detective about Darrin leaving the diner early."

"Too late now." Nick didn't argue this time, but his mouth was set in a grim line as he drove back to the Barn Owl.

Shari was still on duty when they arrived. When she saw them come in, her expression looked a little pained, but she greeted them cheerfully.

"I just had a quick question about Darrin for the waitress who served him," Campbell said. "Is she on tonight?"

"Yeah, I checked on it after you left. It was Lily."

Shari called over a college-age girl, and Campbell asked, "Did Darrin leave you a tip last night?"

"No, he didn't."

"Funny," Shari said. "He's not much of a tipper. He usually

gives a quarter or two, but we all understand he doesn't have much money, and we're glad he eats here regularly."

Lily glanced at her then said, "Last night, he left half his meatloaf and no tip. He dashed out of here in a hurry. I kept his plate for half an hour or so, in case he came back, but he didn't."

"Thanks," Campbell said. "We'll let you get back to work."

She and Nick walked out into the parking lot.

"Maybe that professor is home now," she said.

"It's getting late." Nick shook his head. "We should call it a night."

"But—"

"Go home." Nick stopped walking and faced her squarely. "Maybe Bill's there now. If he's not, go to sleep, and in the morning, we'll file that report."

"I'm worried."

"I know. But there's really not much we can do tonight. We can't keep bothering people who have to get up early in the morning."

For a long moment, she stared into his eyes. They were nice eyes, blue with a little smoky cast. If he wasn't so annoying, she'd notice that, but she didn't want to notice anything favorable about Nick. Especially not tonight. Not when her father was missing and Nick didn't want to do anything about it.

She looked away. Perhaps she'd been unjust to Nick. He was acting like an adult now, she had to admit. "Okay, but I don't know if I can sleep."

"Warm milk," he said.

"Ick."

Nick smiled. The little dimple near his chin and the five-o'clock shadow didn't help her determination to dislike him.

"Chamomile tea, then. Whatever you find restful. I'll see you in the morning."

NOTHING HAD CHANGED at the house, except Bill's laundry needed drying. Campbell stuck it in the dryer then showered and made up the hide-a-bed. By then the clothes were dry. She hung up her dad's clean shirts and folded the rest.

The only tea in the cupboard was full of caffeine, so she skipped that and went to bed, but sleep eluded her. Her father was out there somewhere, maybe injured or dead, and here she was trying to drift off to dreamland. She punched the pillow.

To be honest, Nick had been helpful today. He'd done the legwork with her and called on his contacts for information. But he was still reluctant to search too hard for Bill, as if he were afraid of stepping on his boss's toes.

After an hour or so, she got up and rummaged around until she found her dad's password list. She got into his home computer, an up-to-date laptop, but she couldn't find anything useful. The most recent emails were business related.

There was one from Mart Brady, his old buddy from the police force in Bowling Green. Before Bill took early retirement, Mart and Dad had worked together for years. Campbell opened the message. Mart wanted to set up a fishing date. It looked like her dad had replied, so she checked the sent box.

'Busy this weekend but soon,' was all he'd said. Had Mart retired, or did he simply have Saturday off? She'd ask her dad when she had the chance.

If she had the chance.

If not, she'd contact Mart. In fact, she would get in touch with him tomorrow, no matter what. Why hadn't she thought of him this afternoon when she was killing time at True Blue?

If her father hadn't turned up in the morning, she doubted Mart would be able to tell her much, since he lived a hundred and thirty miles away, near where Campbell grew up. But she should let him know his friend was missing, and it was just possible her dad had checked in with Mart.

She went back to bed and lay there trying not to imagine all the horrible things that could have happened to her father. If he'd gone east of Land Between the Lakes, he could have called Mart for a place to spend the night, and that comforted her enough to allow her to doze off.

<hr />

THE NEXT MORNING, she called Nick at seven.

"Hey." He sounded sleepy. "Anything from Bill?"

"Nothing. Are you going to the office?"

"We usually open at nine."

"Well, I'm going to the police station," she said.

"Now?"

"Yes."

"Okay. Why don't you come to the office after? We can do some strategizing."

"Right." She hung up trying not to be mad at him. What was wrong with that man? This was her father they were talking about! He ought to be willing to pry himself out of bed at seven and get over to the police station.

She dressed quickly and ate cereal with the last of the milk and a banana that was beginning to get brown spots. Better pick up a few groceries today. A fleeting thought of Darrin Beresford's hungry rabbits crossed her mind.

The young officer on the front desk at the police station had a fresh, military-short haircut and a crisp uniform shirt. His nametag said FERRIS. He nodded when she gave her name, as if he was familiar with it.

"Are you here to see Detective Fuller?"

"If he's here," she said, "but mostly I came to file a missing person's report on my father."

He looked surprised at that but shuffled some paper and passed her a clipboard. She sat down on a plastic chair and filled in the blanks. Name. Address. Age. Description. Vehicle. She didn't know the license plate number, or even the model year, of her dad's blue Toyota. Should've checked with Nick. Surely it was on file at the office.

Oh, well, she was sure the police had access to information like that. She wrote down the names of a few of her father's friends, but most of the ones she knew didn't live in Murray.

When she got to the question on when the person was last seen or contacted, she wrote down the time of his call to Nick. Thirty-seven hours and counting.

She took the clipboard back and passed it across the counter to Officer Ferris.

"Okay." He glanced down at the form. "I told Detective Fuller you're here, and he'll be right out." He frowned. "Bill McBride is your father?"

"Yes. You know him?" Campbell asked.

"Sure. He comes in a couple times a week and checks the log, and I see him around town. He's missing?" His eyes skipped down the page. "I'm sorry to hear this. He's one of the good guys."

"Yeah, he is."

KEITH FULLER WALKED down the hallway and opened the door behind the front desk. His gaze settled on her right away. Her hair was a shade lighter than Bill's deep brown, but she had his green eyes. "Ms. McBride, step on back."

"Thanks." Campbell nodded at Ferris and walked down the hallway with Keith.

He automatically did a quick physical assessment. Five-eight, a hundred and thirty pounds. She was prettier than he'd realized last night, but that didn't matter. At least it shouldn't. He'd learned over the years not to let a person's attractiveness or lack of it affect his reactions and assumptions.

They walked through the duty room, where the patrol officers did some of their work and wrote up their reports, and he showed her into the detectives' office. Most of the desks were empty, but the civilian secretary was typing at one.

"I'm sorry to hear your father's still missing." Keith waved Campbell toward a chair and sat down behind one of the desks.

"Thank you," she said. "Did you find anything at Darrin Beresford's house that might indicate Dad had been there?"

"Nothing yet." He didn't mention the coffee mugs in the sink. If Bill McBride's prints turned up on them, he'd notify her then. He didn't want to raise her hopes.

"I'm sorry. I mean, it would have been nice to know more about where Dad's been, but it's a relief in a way."

"Sure." Her mother must have been lovely, he decided. She didn't get that bone structure from Bill.

"It seems Darrin left the diner in a hurry last night."

She held his gaze, which he found a little distracting. People he interviewed often tried to avoid looking at him squarely.

"I wondered if he ran out of there to meet Dad for some reason," she said.

Fuller studied her face for a moment, thinking about how much to reveal. "Nick Emerson said Bill called him that evening about a new case."

"Yes, but he didn't tell him what it was."

He nodded. "Bill's call to Emerson was about a half hour after his call from Beresford. Do you think there's a connection?"

"Don't you?" Campbell asked.

"It's possible. But Darrin has a reputation for trying to get attention. Chances are his reason for calling your father wasn't important."

"You can't know that."

"No, I can't." He huffed out a breath. "You seemed pretty diligent about following up on your interviews at the diner."

Her eyes widened as she realized he'd looked into her activities the day before. Her lashes fell, covering the green eyes. She probably figured he'd tell her next to let the professionals handle it.

"As far as I know." She raised her chin. "Darrin and Nick were the last people to speak to Dad before he dropped off the radar. Nick talked to him on the phone for about thirty seconds. I want to know if Dad met Darrin face-to-face."

"Sure." Keith couldn't blame her there. If it was his father, he'd feel the same way. "The case he mentioned to Emerson could have been totally unrelated."

"Yes, it could." Campbell pressed her lips together.

"Is there something else?" he asked.

"I thought about it a lot last night. After seeing Darrin's house, I'd say he wouldn't have much money to hire a private detective. If Dad *was* interested in what Darrin told him, it wasn't because of the fee he thought he'd get from him."

Good thinking, but Keith didn't say so. Campbell McBride was as intelligent and as direct as her father. After a moment, he stood. "Will you look closely at your father's files and call me if you find anything suggesting he may have met with Darrin?"

"Of course." Campbell picked up her purse and stood. "But I did some looking yesterday. If he only got the call from Darrin Monday evening, I doubt he had time to make a file, and Nick didn't seem to think Dad had done any business with Darrin before."

"Okay."

Campbell hesitated. Genuinely concerned about her father, Keith waited. Bill was a nice guy and did his best not to get in the way of the police when he was working on a private case. When he uncovered evidence of a crime, he brought it to the department. Keith hoped he'd turn up, and soon, before his daughter reached the panicky stage. But his job was to find Darrin Beresford's killer, not to hunt for Bill.

"Is there something else?" he asked, trying to be patient.

"The rabbits," she said.

He arched his eyebrows in question. "Rabbits? You mean at Beresford's?"

"Yes. They were hungry, as if they hadn't been fed all day, and their water dishes were almost empty. I know you have work to do, but I kept thinking about them."

Keith nodded, relieved it was a topic on which he could offer reassurance. "Don't worry. The M.E. thought Beresford had been dead at least twelve hours when we got there, probably longer, but he needed to do some tests to pinpoint it closer than that."

"So, someone fed the rabbits?"

He smiled. "One of our officers gave them water and pellets last night, and we called the animal control officer. They're sending someone to pick them up this morning."

"And they'll give them to good homes."

"I guess so."

Campbell pulled in a slow breath, frowning and staring at the floor.

"Do you like rabbits?" he asked.

She looked up and smiled for the first time. That made it much harder to ignore her appealing features.

"Not that much," she said. "But they shouldn't suffer. I'm glad someone's seeing to their care. You're going to find my dad, right?"

"I'm investigating the homicide. Someone else will probably be assigned to your father's case, unless we find a link between it and Beresford, but you can bet I'll stay interested."

"But the phone call—"

"Yes, that's something. But it's not much. Come on. I'll walk you out."

She was disappointed, he could tell. She'd hoped he'd handle her father's case, but the homicide was urgent, too, and he probably couldn't do both well and solve either case quickly.

In the lobby, Ferris was talking to a fortyish woman whose face was streaked with tears. Keith waited until Ferris had sent her to a chair with a clipboard and asked, "Who will be handling the McBride case?"

"Oh, Ms. McBride." Ferris tossed Campbell a perfunctory smile and looked down at the papers on the desk. "I got your father's license plate number from the DMV, and we've put out a BOLO on his car. We'll send a patrolman out to talk to his neighbors and coworkers."

"His only coworker is Nick Emerson, and we already know his last contact with my father was a phone call Monday evening. I wrote it on the form." Campbell spoke slowly, as though trying hard to keep her voice neutral.

"Right." Ferris sent a floundering gaze at Fuller.

"I'll be keeping a close eye on this," Keith said evenly. From the sound of things, none of the detectives had been assigned to the McBride case yet. He handed Campbell a business card. "Call me if you hear from your father."

"Thank you." Her shoulders slumped as she left the police station.

Keith watched until the door closed behind her, then let out a sigh. He'd hoped to run out to his folks' place on the lake after his shift, but he had a feeling he'd be working late. And he wouldn't feel right relaxing with a killer on the loose in town and a good man missing.

CAMPBELL COULDN'T STAND the thought of going back to her dad's place and hovering in the empty house, so she drove to a coffee shop and then went to the office. Nick's Jeep was in the lot when she pulled in at ten minutes to nine. She carried her coffee inside.

"Hey."

Nick was already on the phone. He nodded at her and grabbed a pen, listening. Checking messages, Campbell guessed. He punched a few buttons and scratched a few notes, then hung up. She just looked at him, waiting.

"Nothing from Bill, but I've got to call back a couple of people. A lawyer we work with sounds like he's got a new case for us, and the insurance company wants an update."

"Okay."

"How'd it go with the cops?" Nick asked.

"They're on it. They're looking for his car, and an officer will probably come around here later to check in."

"Good." Nick leaned back in his chair, frowning. "Look, do you think I should take this new case for the lawyer—assuming there is one?"

"Why wouldn't you?"

"Well, until we clear this up about your dad..." He couldn't hold her gaze.

He thinks Dad may be dead. She clenched her teeth, refusing to go there. "What do you think Bill McBride would do in your situation?"

Nick hesitated only a second. "He'd take the case."

"Can you handle it if Dad's not back, say, by tomorrow?"

"It depends on what it is."

"Maybe you should find out." Campbell looked pointedly at the phone.

"Right." Nick picked up the receiver and hit some buttons.

Campbell sat down at her father's desk and woke up the computer. The first item of business was one she should've thought of yesterday. She did a search for any mention of Darrin Beresford's name in any of her father's Word files. Nothing. Then she looked for an email contact with either Darrin or Beresford in the addresses. Again, zilch. But then, Darrin probably had an address like Superman1 or rabbitsRgr8. Nothing logical.

She stood and went to the file cabinet. Nick was deep in conversation. He sounded as though trying to project confidence and almost succeeding.

"Yeah, yeah, I'll talk it over with Bill. If he's good with it, one of us can meet with you tomorrow. ... Oh, okay. Three o'clock, then. Got it, Mr. Lyman."

He hung up. Campbell didn't ask him anything as she rifled through the file folders again. One drawer seemed to be all expenses and office-related files.

The two below it held client files, alphabetized by last name or corporate name. She paused on the one labeled LYMAN & NESMITH. A quick glance showed her it was indeed a law firm, and several sheaves of paper were clipped together inside the folder. A repeat customer. It looked as though her dad had worked with the firm since shortly after he opened his office in Murray.

She went back to the desk without anything to show for her rummaging. What was left of her coffee was cold. Nick finished his second call and laid down his pen.

"So. We've got plenty of business lined up for the next two weeks, assuming Bill shows up."

"If not?" Campbell asked.

"I don't know." He frowned and eyed her uneasily. "What happens when your boss disappears? How long should I go on working as if everything's normal?"

Campbell let out a long, slow breath. She didn't want to think about those questions. Should she reassure him by letting him know she was her father's sole heir? But even if the unthinkable happened and she inherited the business, she wasn't a P.I. She was a college professor. At least, she had been until two days ago. Maybe she should call the schools she'd applied to and assure them she was very interested.

"Listen." Nick leaned forward, clasping his hands on the desktop near his keyboard. "I really don't want to think something bad has happened to Bill, but—"

"Neither do I."

"Right. But maybe you should prepare yourself. I mean, he's never stayed out of contact for a whole day before, let alone two. If he had to be out of the office all day or made an overnight trip, he always checked in with me by phone or email. No exceptions."

Campbell's chest tightened. She nodded slowly. "I understand. We've got to find him."

3

C ampbell went out to get lunch and spent fifteen minutes sitting in the restaurant's parking lot, on her cell phone with Mart Brady while waiting for the takeout order. Mart was dismayed at the news of Bill's disappearance, but he couldn't offer her anything but sympathy.

"I'm so sorry," he said. "Call me if he doesn't turn up. Maybe I could come over for a day or two and help you."

"Thanks," Campbell told him. "The police are on it, and Nick and I are doing our best, but we just don't know where to look."

"Just follow up on every little crumb you get."

"I will. Thanks for being there, Uncle Mart." She went back to the office with Chinese in white take-out boxes.

She and Nick sat on either side of his desk to eat, making small talk and not mentioning her father. When she was done, Campbell cleared away the trash and wheeled her chair back to her dad's desk.

"Give me something to do. I've gone through Dad's address file and called everyone I remotely thought might have heard from him."

She hated feeling helpless—anything she could do now would feel like progress.

"Maybe you should take a look at Kentucky's requirements for private investigators," Nick said.

"Why?"

"Why not?"

Campbell leaned back in the chair, locking down on that thought. If her father didn't turn up right away, she'd certainly want to keep looking for him. If she had a PI's license, she could work alongside Nick. But that would probably take a lot of training. Former law enforcement officers could get a license easily, she was sure, but English professors?

She didn't have time to think about it right now. She needed to find her dad and apply for a few more teaching jobs. Surely someone needed an English professor. She pursed her lips, regretting her major, even though she'd loved it. If she had a math or science degree, she could have a job within hours.

Halfheartedly, she searched for and opened the website for Western Kentucky University, in her hometown of Bowling Green. She really had no desire to go back there, did she? It felt like a regression. Still, she opened the tab on jobs available. Nothing in her field. She didn't want to start applying for secretarial jobs. Not yet. And she didn't want to move that far away until she knew her father was all right.

Nick had plunged into his workload once more, and she envied him. At least he had some clear direction on what to do next.

Maybe she should actually consider what he'd said. If Bill didn't turn up soon, she might need to stay here longer than the few weeks she'd planned on.

A search on the computer came up with the Commonwealth's statute. In seconds, she was looking at a file titled 'Become a Private Detective through Training and

Certification in Kentucky.' She scrolled to the section on minimum requirements.

- Must be at least 21 years old. *Check.*
- Be of good moral character. *Check.*
- Be a U.S. citizen or lawful resident alien. *Check.*
- If you have any felony convictions, 10 years must have passed since the completion of your sentence. *Not applicable.*
- No convictions for crimes involving dishonesty or moral turpitude within the past five years. *Check.*
- If you are a military veteran, you must not have been dishonorably discharged. *No problem there.*
- Be of sound mental capacity. *Check—despite what Nick might say.*
- No misdemeanor or higher convictions within the past three years for crimes involving controlled substances. *Check.*
- May not have been enrolled in a facility or program for substance abuse in the past three years. *Check.*
- May not chronically or habitually use alcohol or drugs. *Check.*

"Okay, so I researched the law for private investigators in Kentucky." She looked up. "I meet the minimum requirements."

"Great." Nick stared at his screen.

She read on and found she easily met the education requirement. "So, for a few hundred bucks I can apply for a license." Something farther down caught her eye. "Oh, wait. Do I need the liability insurance?"

"The agency covers that if you're working for True Blue."

She nodded and read on. A few minutes later, she sat back. "Sounds like I could put in the application right away and send permission for them to see my medical records. Who does the background check and fingerprinting?"

"They do. And then you take the test."

Still not certain this was the way to go, she nodded. "I do expect to find another teaching job."

"Then you don't need to worry about the PI's test."

Campbell sighed. Joining her father's business had not been on her list of possibilities when she drove away from Feldman. Right now, she wasn't sure what she wanted to do, except find her father. Was she seriously considering this? Maybe it would be wise to apply, just in case she found herself the owner of the agency. A wave of nausea hit her. Why was she even thinking that? She clicked firmly to close the website.

Time to think about something else. Something constructive. She opened her purse and rummaged for the notebook where she'd jotted down information they'd gleaned when they interviewed diner patrons.

"I think I'll try to contact some more of the people who were at the diner last night," she said.

"Who's left?"

Campbell frowned over her notes. "Several unnamed college students, a Dr. Exter, a Brock Wilson..." Since she had both a first and last name there, she decided to start with Wilson.

To her surprise, he wasn't hard to find online. He worked at an auto parts store on Twelfth Street, a main thoroughfare running past the university's stadium and southward toward the Tennessee border. Several shopping centers clustered along it. She debated calling Wilson's store but decided to drive over there.

"I'll see if I can get five minutes with this guy, Wilson," she told Nick. "Call me if anything important comes up."

Nick said nothing, so she shoved the notebook in her purse and went out to her car.

She didn't want to disrupt Wilson's workday, but it turned

out he was the store manager. A clerk called him to the counter. He looked about forty, dark haired, had crows' feet at the corners of his eyes, and carried a few extra pounds on his tall frame.

"Sure, I remember Darrin being at the diner Monday night," he said. It seemed everyone in town—at least, everyone who frequented the Barn Owl—did indeed know Darrin Beresford.

"Did you speak to him?" Campbell asked.

"No."

"Did you see Bill McBride?"

"Who?"

Campbell grimaced. "Bill McBride. He owns True Blue Investigations."

"Don't know him," Wilson said.

"Okay. Well, did you notice anything unusual about Darrin Beresford while he was there or when he left?"

Wilson frowned. "I read in the paper that he's dead."

Of course, it had hit the *Ledger & Times* this morning. "That's right," Campbell said.

"Are you a cop?" Wilson asked.

"No, I'm Bill McBride's daughter. My dad hasn't come home since that night, and I think Darrin phoned him from the diner."

"I did see Darrin talking on his cell, but I don't know anything about the other guy. Your dad. I'm sorry about that."

"Thanks. I don't suppose you heard any of Darrin's phone conversation?"

Wilson squeezed his lips together and squinted. "I don't think so. Maybe ... hmm, at one point I did hear him say, 'I'm sure it's him. I don't care how long it's been.' Or something like that." He shrugged. "I have no idea who he was talking about."

"I'm sure it's him," Campbell repeated slowly. She jotted the words in her notebook. She was certain Darrin had something to do with her father's disappearance. When Brock Wilson overhead him, was he telling her father he'd seen someone of interest?

That statement sounded like something he would tell an investigator. Darrin was known for calling the newspaper and the police with tips he thought were important. But how could she find out what—and who—he was talking about?

"Do you remember who else was there?" she asked.

"Well, I was there with Paul Exter."

Campbell looked down at her notes. "*Doctor* Exter?"

"Yes. He's a dentist."

"Good to know." She scribbled "Paul" beside the "Dr. Exter" she'd written while interviewing the diner's owner.

Wilson glanced toward the door as a customer entered, but the clerk hurried forward to help the man. The manager leaned over the counter toward Campbell.

"Now that you mention it, there *was* something funny. Paul and I had been talking about playing golf together, and all of a sudden, he seemed distracted. I turned around to see what he was looking at. Darrin was yakking on his phone and I didn't see anything weird. But then Darrin got up to leave, and that's when Paul said he had to go."

"Right after Darrin left?"

"Yeah."

"Would you say he followed Darrin out?"

"Uh, I don't know. He threw two twenties on the table and said, 'Tonight's on me. I'll call you.' And then he left. Very sudden."

"Did he call you?" she asked.

"Yeah, the next day. We set up a golf date."

"Did he tell you why he left the diner in such a hurry?"

"No, I don't think it came up again. We're playing golf on Saturday. I can ask him."

"Do you guys eat at the Barn Owl often?"

"Who, me and Paul?"

She nodded.

"I do once in a while, maybe a couple times a month. I don't think Paul goes there much. Look, I've got to get back to work."

"Here's one of my father's business cards." She turned it over and wrote quickly on the back. "That's my cell phone number. Please call me if you think of anything else. And thanks for your time, Mr. Wilson."

"No probs."

Campbell drove back toward the office thinking over what he'd told her. Maybe she could talk to Dr. Exter, but he probably wouldn't like to be interrupted while he was working on patients. She decided to give his office a call later and try to set up something. On a whim, she turned toward the police station. When she stepped inside, Ferris was at the front desk.

"Ms. McBride," he said with a polite smile as she stepped up to the glass barrier.

"Hi. I was wondering if I could look at the police log."

"Sure. Come around through that door. He pointed to the side opposite where she'd gone with Fuller that morning. Ferris opened the door for her and led her to a small desk with a ledger lying open on its surface.

"This is where our dispatchers log calls. Later they're put in our computer log with more detail if it's appropriate."

Campbell was surprised to see the handwritten notations.

"If you have any questions, I'll be right over there." Ferris pointed to his usual station.

"Thanks." Campbell sat down and eyed the open book. The left-hand page was only about half full of calls that had come in over the past few hours. A barking dog, a stolen purse, a collision with a deer on Route 94. So, this was how the reporters got their tips on local law enforcement. And how her dad did it when he came in to see what was going on that might be of interest to him.

She flipped back a page. One day's entries ran right into the next, and she was able to back up until Monday evening. She puzzled over the page for several minutes then stood and walked over to Officer Ferris. At the moment he wasn't talking to anyone, and he turned toward her.

"May I help you?"

"Yes," Campbell said. "I was looking at Monday night's log. I expected to see a call from Darrin Beresford, but I couldn't find it."

"Darrin?" Ferris's face went blank.

"Yes. I understand he called the police before he called my father. It was a 'recent call' on his cell phone. But there's no record of a call from him that evening or all day, in fact. I even checked back as far as Sunday morning."

"Okay, let me check who was on duty that night." Ferris clicked a few strokes on his keyboard and consulted the computer screen. He punched in a phone extension. A couple of minutes later, another officer came into the room.

"This is Patrol Sergeant Andrews," Ferris said and turned away to speak to a woman who had come to his window.

"May I help you?" Andrews asked.

"I hope so." Campbell introduced herself and explained she knew Darrin had called the police station's non-emergency number Monday night between 5 and 5:30 p.m. "I couldn't find a record of the call in the police log. Officer Ferris said you were on duty then."

Andrews hesitated. "Yes, I was the one who took Mr. Beresford's call."

"But it's not in the log." Campbell waited for him to respond.

The sergeant let out a quiet sigh. "It was a nothing call. Darrin claimed he'd seen someone who used to live in town a long time ago."

"Why would he think that was worth a call to the police?" Campbell asked.

Andrews said carefully, "The person Darrin claimed he saw

was a suspect in a crime several years ago, and the case is still open."

"So, why isn't that in the police log?"

Andrews's face reddened. "Did you know Darrin?"

"Not personally, but I've heard things."

He nodded. "That guy called here all the time. He was a bit of a crackpot, but don't quote me on that. We didn't really take Darrin seriously. If we did, we'd be out on wild goose chases all the time. One day it's a cat up a tree, the next day he's seen a mafia boss in town. Next time, it will be a UFO."

"Okay." Campbell wasn't sure whether to push harder or not. She didn't want to antagonize the police, but she wouldn't learn any more if she didn't.

"My father is missing," she said. "Darrin made the call to you, and right after he hung up, he called my father. I'm guessing that was because he didn't get any satisfaction from the police department."

"It's possible, but—"

"Don't you have to take *every* call seriously?" Campbell asked.

Andrews dropped his voice. "Generally, that's true. But due to experience, we had to ask Darrin to stop calling."

That tallied with what Nick had told her. "So if you told him not to call, but he did anyway, wouldn't you think maybe it was really something this time?"

Sgt. Andrews didn't seem to have an answer to that. Campbell didn't know the man, but his cheeks looked a little flushed, and she could swear he was holding back whatever he wanted to say.

"Detective Fuller is investigating Mr. Beresford's death," she said. "We think it's connected to his contact with my father."

"I'll touch base with Detective Fuller." Andrews seemed almost relieved that she'd taken the conversation in a different direction.

"Thank you." It was all she could hope for, she supposed. She nodded and strode out to her car. Better check in with Nick. She headed for the office.

"You got something?" he asked as Campbell breezed in. He was clicking languidly at his keyboard and sipping coffee.

"Maybe. Remember how Ray, at the diner, said a Dr. Exter was in there Monday night?"

"Yeah, vaguely."

She plopped her purse on her father's desk. "Well, Brock Wilson was eating supper with him. Paul Exter, D.M.D. And it seems he got up and left in a rush right after Darrin Beresford left."

"Really?"

"Yeah, really. So, I was thinking—"

Both desk phones rang. She glanced at Nick and picked up the one on her father's desk.

"True Blue, Campbell McBride speaking."

"Ms. McBride, it's Detective Fuller. We've found your father's car."

4

C ampbell leaned in, as though getting closer to the phone would bring her closer to her dad. "You found it? Where?"

"It's parked off Gabriel Road, out in the county. Would you be able to come out here?"

"Yes. Sure. Just give me directions. No, wait just a second." She pushed the mute button and turned eagerly toward Nick. "They've found Dad's car. Can you go with me to Gabriel Road?"

"Sure."

She pushed the button again. "Could you please tell Nick where it is? He's more familiar with the area than I am."

Nick picked up his receiver and jotted a few notes. "Thanks, Detective. We'll be there in about twenty minutes."

Before they'd reached the city limits, Campbell wished she'd driven her own car instead of letting Nick take her in his Jeep. Now she was at Nick's mercy when it came to returning to the office or pursuing some lead. She swallowed hard and kept quiet. *Next time, think, Campbell!*

They drove several miles from the office, and the

countryside spread around them. The grass was lush, and oak trees were in full leaf. They passed a farm with a thriving field of wheat, then one of half-grown corn. Detective Fuller was waiting for them, his unmarked SUV pulled over at the side of the road behind two sheriff's department cars. She didn't see her dad's car until Fuller pointed it out, parked off the road under a big sycamore. The nearest house was a quarter mile away.

"You think Dad left his car here?" she asked. "I mean, why on earth would he park here, in the middle of nowhere?"

"We don't know," Fuller said. "I hoped you two could help us out."

"Is anyone in the car?" Nick spoke casually, but the implication made Campbell's stomach heave.

"No," Fuller said. "It's locked, though."

"What about the trunk?" Campbell asked.

"We haven't popped it yet. I wondered if you'd have keys. We decided not to jimmy the door until you got here."

"I don't, but Dad's a big believer in hide-a-keys." Campbell looked toward the Toyota. Her father had insisted on making extra keys the day she bought her first car and had shown her where to place the little magnetic box. "If he's true to form, it should be on the frame behind the driver's door."

Fuller crouched beside the door and felt along the metal underneath. He smiled and held up the key box.

"Your dad's a careful man," Nick said softly.

"Sometimes it might be better if he wasn't so predictable." Campbell frowned, watching Fuller open the driver's door and wondering if her father's habits had somehow made him an easy target.

The detective took a cursory look inside the car and then walked to the back. He turned the key in the Toyota's trunk and lifted the lid. Nick and a couple of uniformed officers crowded in beside him to look. Campbell held back and pressed her hands to her face.

Fuller was silent as he surveyed the interior, then he turned to her. "It's all right, Ms. McBride."

She stepped over beside him. The trunk held the spare tire, a jack, a wool blanket, a small red toolbox, a folding shovel, and a quart of oil.

"That's Bill for you," Nick said. "Ready for emergencies, but always neat."

Campbell let out a breath. "Okay. So he was healthy when he left the car here."

"That seems probable," Fuller said. "I haven't seen anything so far to suggest otherwise. The car was spotted by one of the sheriff's deputies, and we're working together now. I'll make a more thorough inspection of the vehicle." He turned to the deputies. "You spread out from here and look for signs of Mr. McBride."

The deputies started out, one on each side of the car, pushing through brush and into the woods.

"He may very well have gotten into another vehicle," Fuller said.

"You think he met someone here?" Campbell hadn't considered that.

"It's possible. And he's not close enough to a house or a business to do an effective surveillance from the car in that position." He opened the passenger door and then the glove compartment.

Campbell looked around and decided he was right. Two distant houses were visible, but there wasn't a clear view of either front door.

"The car's pointed away from the road," Nick said. "If he was doing surveillance, he'd have backed in, so he could get out quick and follow someone if he wanted to."

"You think it's odd that he parked nose-in?" Fuller asked.

"I wouldn't say odd, but not his usual style." Nick shrugged. "He taught me otherwise. It looks like he was more concerned about hiding the car than getting out quick."

Campbell felt a mild resentment rising inside her. Nick had worked closely with her dad for more than three years now. Dad had trained him. Nick knew his habits, his likes and dislikes better than anyone—including her. She didn't like that.

"That brings us to another possibility," Fuller said. "Someone else could have driven the car here and abandoned it."

WITH THE OFFICERS, Campbell and Nick searched the area for any sign of Bill but had nothing to show for it at the end of half an hour. Meanwhile, Detective Fuller lifted fingerprints from the steering wheel, door handles, trunk latch, armrests, and gearshift. He handed Campbell the key to her dad's car. "I guess you can take it home."

"So, there's nothing else you can do?" Campbell asked.

"I didn't see any signs of foul play." Fuller gave her a sympathetic smile. "Believe me, if we'd found anything suspicious, I'd have the car impounded."

"Isn't it suspicious enough that his car was abandoned?"

Fuller sighed. "I understand your concerns, Ms. McBride, but there's really nothing for me to follow up on. We'll check the fingerprints I took to see if anyone else was in the car. Beyond that..."

She nodded slowly. "Okay."

"Do let us know if you hear from him, won't you?"

"Of course."

Fuller went to his vehicle, and she turned to Nick.

"So what now?" Nick said.

"I want to keep looking for him. Ask at the nearest houses, that sort of thing." She looked around, trying to judge how far each of the searchers had gone. She could barely see the roof and top story of the nearest farmhouse. "He could be injured, lying out there somewhere in the bushes."

Nick looked doubtful. "If he was hurt, he wouldn't have gone away from his car. And his phone wasn't in it."

"Can we at least go to that house over there and ask?"

"Why don't you do that, and I'll go back to the office? Our client won't be happy if I don't get my report to him by five o'clock."

Campbell tried not to scowl. Nick seemed awfully eager to get back to work. On the other hand, it was probably a good idea for one of them to stay near the office phone.

"Okay." She watched bleakly as Nick walked back to his Jeep. Campbell felt as abandoned as her dad's Toyota. It had been two days since Nick's last contact with her father. Looking for him seemed critical, but no one else seemed worried enough to go on with the search. There may not be a point to hanging around this spot any longer, but she wasn't about to give up.

Nick drove away with a wave, and she headed for her dad's car, eyes on the ground. A few yards from the driver's door she spotted a cigarette butt. How could they have missed that? She bent to retrieve it. Her dad didn't smoke. She rummaged her pockets for something to put it in and came up with a clean tissue.

Great. Nick had driven off with her purse. She'd better not do too much driving without going back to the office to retrieve it. But she would make a stop at that nearest farmhouse. She drove cautiously down the road, trying to get used to the car's controls. Nobody answered when she knocked on the front door of the dilapidated house. She got back in the car and sat for a long moment fighting tears.

Dad, where are you?

CAMPBELL HATED GOING to the dentist. As a result, she'd become compulsive about brushing and flossing. Even though she'd never been to Paul Exter's practice, she shuddered as she walked into the waiting room Thursday morning.

The woman behind the window smiled at her. "May I help you?"

"I'm Campbell McBride. I called earlier to see if Dr. Exter could give me a few minutes this morning."

The receptionist consulted her computer screen. "Yes, I thought he might be able to take a quick look at you around ten."

"Oh, it's not a dental problem," Campbell said quickly.

She frowned. "No?"

"No, I just need to talk to him. It won't take long, I promise."

"Well … take a seat, and we'll see if he can fit you in."

Campbell sat down on a vinyl-covered chair in the waiting area. The magazines ran heavily to golf and fitness, but she did find an old copy of *Architectural Digest* with an attractive mansion on the front. She leafed through it, then set it aside and thought about the few clues she and Nick had found. Was she wasting her time here?

After twenty minutes, the door into the business part of the building opened, and a woman in scrubs said, "Campbell?"

She rose and followed the tech down the hallway.

"Dr. Exter will see you in just a minute. He's with a patient." She opened a door. "Just take a seat."

The room appeared to be a cubbyhole of an office, not an exam room. Campbell sat for a few minutes and soon found herself looking around for another magazine. Dr. Exter didn't seem to keep any in his office. She got up and studied the framed diplomas on the wall. She was looking out the window at a pair of grosbeaks in the plum tree a few yards away when the door finally opened.

"Ms. McBride?"

"Yes." She turned toward the tall, thin man.

"How can I help you?" He walked across the room and sat behind his desk, gesturing for her to plant herself in the chair she'd vacated ten minutes ago.

"I wanted to ask you about Monday night," she began.

He stilled all movement and gazed at her. "Monday?"

"That's right. I understand you ate dinner at the Barn Owl diner."

"Uh … I think that's correct. May I ask why you're interested?"

"My father is Bill McBride. Do you know him?"

"Is he a patient here?" Dr. Exter frowned.

He was on edge. Campbell could see that. Maybe he was afraid she or her dad was about to sue him. She made herself smile. "I don't know. But you see, my father went missing Monday evening."

"And am I supposed to have something to do with that?" He took off his glasses and blinked at her.

"I'm sorry. I'm just trying to gather information. I hope I can find my father, but so far I haven't been able to learn anything about what he did that night."

"What does that have to do with me?" His expression cleared. "Did he eat at the Barn Owl?"

"No, I don't believe so. But he received a phone call around 5:30 that night from a man named Darrin Beresford. Did you know Mr. Beresford?"

"I know who he is."

"Unfortunately, he died recently."

"I saw it in the paper," Exter said.

"Yes, well, the police think he died Monday night, not too long after he phoned my father. And he made that call while he was at the Barn Owl."

Exter gazed at her impassively across the desk.

"And you were there at the same time," she said.

"Oh."

"Yes. I've been talking to people who were at the diner. Several people saw you eating there. Did you see Darrin Beresford that night?"

He swiveled his chair toward the window and gazed into the distance. "Darrin might have been there that night."

"Did you hear any part of his conversation?" she asked.

"No." He turned toward her and focused on her face. "I think I did see him talking on his cell phone, if that helps."

"Your friend Brock Wilson was with you."

The frown was back.

Campbell went on, "He said you left immediately after Darrin Beresford left. You suddenly said you had to go, and you threw some money on the table and followed Darrin out."

After a long pause, Exter said, "I wasn't following him."

"Then why did you leave in such a hurry?"

"I just had to be somewhere."

She puzzled over that. "Brock Wilson thought it was odd."

"Oh? I'll have to call him and assure him it was nothing out of the ordinary."

"So, where did you go?" Campbell asked.

"Is that any of your business?" He eyed her keenly.

Campbell pulled in a shaky breath. Her concern for her father was becoming something like grief, and she determined not to break down in front of this man.

"No," she managed, blinking fiercely against tears. "It's just that I want very badly to find my father. Any little thing you saw or heard that night might help."

Exter's shoulders relaxed. "I'm sorry about your father. I hope you find him. But I assure you, I don't know anything about his activities on Monday evening. I don't even know him, and I doubt I would recognize him if I saw him." He glanced at his watch. "And now, if you'll excuse me, I have a patient waiting."

"Of course. Thank you for your time." Campbell rose and walked on wooden stumps of legs out to her car.

She unlocked it and crawled in. The interior was hot, so she started the engine and turned the air conditioner on high, but already she felt sticky. She shifted into drive and headed toward True Blue thinking about the dentist.

He was hiding something. She was sure of it. Maybe he really didn't know anything about her father, but he'd tiptoed around what she'd said about Darrin and his exit from the diner. She was certain about one thing: Paul Exter was lying.

WHEN KEITH GOT to the True Blue agency's office, Campbell McBride was pulling into the parking lot. He walked over to meet her as she got out of her car. She wore a green blouse, and her eyes picked up the color. He remembered Bill's eyes were green, too, but he didn't recall them being that intense a shade.

"Ms. McBride, I was driving by and I thought I'd stop and ask if you've heard anything from Bill."

"Nothing, unless Nick has heard something. And please call me Campbell."

Keith walked beside her to the door, and she opened it. Nick was on the phone.

She waved and whispered, "Anything?"

With a keen glance at Keith, Nick shook his head.

"Coffee?" she asked Keith.

"No, thanks. We did get a preliminary report on Darrin Beresford from the medical examiner."

She raised her eyebrows and waited.

"Blunt force trauma," he said.

Campbell sank into her chair. After a moment, she looked up at him. "There was a lot of blood."

"He had a severe blow to his left temple. His skull was

fractured. But there was nothing nearby that we like for the murder weapon."

"The poor man."

He could picture Darrin's body clearly, lying on his left side. Campbell and Nick had found him, and Keith was sure the image in her memory was a sharp as his. No doubt more traumatizing. They didn't get many violent death cases in Murray, but he'd seen enough to become somewhat desensitized. Still, it was always a shock—especially when the deceased was someone you knew.

"The examiner said it was probably almost instantaneous." He hoped that would be some comfort to her. "If you and Nick had arrived sooner, you couldn't have helped Darrin."

She nodded. Witnesses often tortured themselves with questions, imagining alternate scenarios where they'd prevented a murder or accidental death. He hoped Campbell wouldn't go that route. She had enough on her mind with her father dropping out of sight.

"Do you think he was killed in that room?" she asked.

"We think so."

"All that blood."

"Yes, and the medical examiner said there would have been even more if he hadn't died quickly."

"I guess that makes sense."

"So, what have you been up to?" he asked. "I know you're not going to rest until something breaks in your father's case."

Campbell leaned back and met his gaze. "You're right. I just came from talking to Dr. Paul Exter."

Mildly surprised, Keith said, "He's my dentist."

"Hmm. Well, he ate at the Barn Owl Monday night. He was with Brock Wilson, and he left abruptly when Darrin Beresford left."

"That's interesting." Keith's to-do list for the day included questioning the diner's staff and Monday night patrons. Campbell had beaten him to it.

She nodded. "I thought so, too. Dr. Exter says it was unrelated, but his friend thought he acted strange. And he claims he didn't hear Darrin's conversation." Her mouth twisted.

"You don't believe him," Keith said.

"Not really. He acted very wary when I mentioned Darrin and the Barn Owl. And he wouldn't tell me where he went when he walked out on his meal with Mr. Wilson."

"Okay, I'll touch base with Dr. Exter and see if I can rattle him a little more. Thanks."

"Oh, and I found this yesterday, near Dad's car." She opened Bill's top desk drawer and took out a folded Kleenex. "It's a cigarette butt. Probably nothing."

"Thanks. We found a few others. We'll test this." He hesitated. "There's one more thing."

He'd lowered his voice, and she was instantly alert.

"This hasn't been made public," Keith said, "but we did find some fingerprints at Darrin's house. Your father's were there, among others."

She caught a quick breath. "Dad's? You're certain?"

"Yes. His prints are on file, as are every P.I.'s in the state. He was there that night."

"Okay." After a moment, she asked, "So, what did he touch?"

"A coffee mug that was sitting in the kitchen sink."

"That's it?"

"As far as we know."

She nodded slowly. "So he did go to see Darrin after the phone call."

"That seems likely."

For a few seconds, she stared into his eyes before she spoke again. "You're not suggesting my dad killed him. I mean, if he did, he wouldn't have left the mug there. He's too smart."

"I think you're right. It looked like he and Darrin maybe had coffee together at the kitchen table."

"Those chairs were full of junk."

"Okay, standing near the kitchen sink."

She smiled wryly and picked up a pen from the desktop. "But Darrin cleaned up afterward."

"At least, he put the cups in the sink." Keith nodded. "I don't think Darrin was much for doing housework. The coffeemaker had shut itself off, but there was still half a pot sitting there."

"Who else's prints did you find?"

He cracked a smile. She was sharp, all right. "We're working on it. There were prints on the front doorknob on top of anyone else's. They're not in the system, though. We're asking people we talk to if they'll let us print them, just to rule them out."

"You can take my prints," she said.

"Actually, you're in the national database."

"Of course. When I was hired at Feldman University they required that. It slipped my mind." Her chin rose. "What about the prints from Dad's car?"

"His. Nick Emerson's on the passenger side."

"That figures," Campbell said.

He held her gaze for a moment. She was strong. She'd jumped right into the search for her father, and she seemed to be going about it systematically. But she was vulnerable, too, perhaps more than she realized. There was more to this investigation, but he couldn't tell her all he knew. He'd do anything in his power to protect her and find her father. A few hours could make a difference if Bill was in danger.

Gently he said, "You may want to back off a little in your investigating, now that we're sure Darrin's death was a homicide."

"I just want to find Dad." Her fist clenched around the pen. "Detective, I'm worried."

"I know." He glanced over at Nick, who seemed to be winding up his phone conversation. "Campbell, this isn't looking very good for your dad, and I'm sorry. We'll keep on it."

She blew out a shaky breath and nodded. "You're working on Dad's case now?"

"Yes. We know now that they're linked."

"Thank you. You'll—" Her mouth skewed.

"I'll keep you informed."

As Keith rose, Nick ended his call and stood. "So, Detective Fuller, what's the word?"

"Campbell can brief you. I need to get back to the station." Keith nodded to him and shot a glance at Campbell. "Good to see you both."

As DETECTIVE FULLER WENT OUT, Nick turned wide eyes on Campbell.

"Huh! So?"

"Darrin was murdered. Hit on the head. They don't have a murder weapon. But get this, Nick: they found my dad's fingerprints on a coffee mug in Darrin's kitchen."

"That's not good."

"Why do you say that?" Campbell wanted to slug him. "We know now that he was there."

"Did it move Bill to the top of the suspect list?"

"No. If anything, Detective Fuller is more concerned than ever that something's happened to Dad. Something bad."

Nick huffed out a breath and glanced toward his desk. "Okay, now what? I met with Mr. Lyman, and I locked down that new case for them, and I need to start a case file. They—"

"Nick! Stop!"

He stood staring at her like an offended idiot.

"I want to go back to that house closest to where Dad's car

was parked. It's getting toward suppertime, and someone might be there now."

"Come on, Campbell, I have to wrap up the file for Dunn & McGann so I can start on the new case tomorrow. We can't slack off on our clients."

"Do you hear yourself?" She scowled at him. "You're saying money is more important than my father's life."

"No, I—" He broke off and threw his hands in the air. "Okay, go. But you're the one who told me to carry on business as usual. I'll stay here and hold the fort and make sure your father's company doesn't tank while you're out there chasing rabbit trails."

She didn't bother to tell him she'd be chasing rabbits, not their trails—except there were no rabbits, other than Darrin's. Just criminals. She shook her head. "Come with me."

"You've got your phone, right? Call me if you need something."

"It would take you fifteen or twenty minutes to get out there." She took two breaths. Her dad's car had been found outside of town, at least ten miles from Darrin's house. Did he leave Darrin after having coffee with him and drive out there? Why? "Nick, I want someone with me."

"What, you think that's where Darrin's killer lives?"

"I don't know." A shiver ran down her spine. If she found something gruesome, she didn't want to be alone, but she hated to say that.

He looked from her to his monitor and back. With a resigned air, he let out a big sigh. "If I could ask Bill what to do, I know what he'd say."

"I'm guessing not the lawyer's file."

"Look." He shrugged. "I know you only saw your dad three or four times a year lately, but he loves you very much. And he wouldn't want you poking around by yourself when there's a murderer loose in this town. Let's go."

5

"We can take separate vehicles if you want," Campbell said. "Then if I decide to check out something else, you can come back here."

"Okay." Nick followed her out the door.

As she started her Fusion, she thought of her father's Toyota, now parked in his own garage. What had he been doing so far out of town after he left Darrin's house Monday night? Had Darrin told him something he'd decided to follow up on?

Twenty minutes later, she and Nick both parked on the farmhouse's gravel driveway and walked up to the porch together. There was no doorbell, and Nick knocked firmly on the door. They waited, looking around at the overgrown lawn. A magnolia and a redbud grew between the house and the road. The house's paint looked a little neglected, but this could be a nice place. Serene.

Nick knocked again, louder.

Nothing.

"Nobody's home," he said. "Maybe nobody even lives here."

Campbell sidled up to a window and peered between the drapes. The living room inside looked as though it hadn't been redecorated in at least fifty years, but she did spot a newspaper on the sofa and an ashtray with cigarette butts in it on the coffee table.

She turned at Nick's footsteps. He was walking down the steps.

"Where are you going?" she called.

He pointed to the detached garage set about ten yards back from the house. Campbell considered following but instead checked to make sure no one was driving by. Remembering Fuller's words about fingerprints on Darrin's doorknob, she lifted the hem of her shirt and used it to cover her hand while she tried the doorknob. Locked. She crossed the porch and looked at the garage. Nick was manually raising an overhead door. These people must be stuck in last century.

Even she could see the garage was empty except for an old push lawnmower and a few tools and hubcaps hanging on the walls. Nick closed the door and walked over to stand below her, where she leaned on the porch railing.

"There's nobody here, and I can't see that there has been for a while."

"There's got to be," Campbell said.

"Why?"

She didn't have an answer.

"Look," he said, "we could do a couple of things. We could go to the county courthouse in town and look at the property maps to find out who owns this house. Or we could go to the nearest neighbors and ask if they know the owners."

"Yeah," she said slowly. "Okay. But is there a back door?"

Nick's eyebrows shot up. "Oh, *now* you want me to do some breaking and entering?"

"You already opened the garage door." She shrugged.

He sighed and tromped off toward the back of the house. Campbell hurried across the porch to the front steps and ran down them. By the time she caught up, he'd gone around the back and was looking at some large stone blocks half hidden by grass.

"I guess there used to be a barn there." He glanced at her. "And you're right, there's a back door."

"Of course there's a back door." She followed him to it.

Nick stood there watching her expectantly.

"Maybe we should have brought gloves," she said.

"You are unbelievable." Nick laughed, reached for the knob, and twisted it. The door opened several inches, and he looked at her. "There you go. It's all yours."

She hesitated, then pushed the door open a bit more with her elbow.

"Hello? Anybody home?"

They both listened.

"I guess we already knew no one was here," she said.

"Well, we did find a dead body at the last house we broke into."

She couldn't come up with a scathing retort fast enough.

"Come on, let's go back to the office." Nick started down the steps.

"No, wait."

"What?" He was clearly annoyed now.

"I just want to check the fridge. See if there's any food in it."

Nick rolled his eyes skyward. "Be my guest, Ms. McBride."

She scowled at him but tiptoed across the linoleum to the ancient refrigerator and pulled the door open, using her shirttail again as a shield for her hand. Salad dressing, pancake syrup, a partially used half gallon of milk, Tabasco sauce, two cans of beer, and a small covered dish. The motor came on, and its humming sounded as loud as a biplane buzzing her.

"Someone's staying here, by the look of things." She closed the door and scurried back to Nick's side. "The milk hasn't expired. But it's minimal, not like a family that's been here for a long time."

"Let's get out of here."

He led the way around to the front of the house, and they paused beside Nick's Jeep. Campbell eyed him warily, her breathing a bit too shallow.

"You said something about property maps. Where do I look at them?" she asked.

"County courthouse."

"The big brick building on the town square?"

"That's the one." He fingered his keys.

"You go back to the office," she said. "I'll go ask them."

"Okay. If you're sure."

"Like you said, we need to keep the business afloat."

"Right." He hesitated a moment longer then nodded firmly and climbed into his vehicle.

Campbell hurried to her car and pulled out right behind him. Her breathing evened out as they turned off Route 80 and reached the outskirts of town. The road they followed turned into Main Street, and she realized they were on course to drive right past the courthouse.

They stopped at a red light at an intersection close to the building. Nick looked at her in his rearview mirror and waved. Campbell waved back, and when the light changed he turned off to go to the office. She turned on Fourth Street and found a diagonal parking space in front of the courthouse.

Inside the office of property valuation, a woman took her to a cabinet of shelves that held extra-large bound books. The county maps. She pulled one out and opened it for Campbell on the counter.

"There you go. You said Gabriel? It begins here, and if you need to continue it, go to the map listed here, at the bottom of the page."

"Thank you." Campbell took a moment to orient herself and study the map's legend. She concentrated on the roads in the outlying part of Calloway County and looked for intersections and landmarks. After a few minutes, she was sure she'd located the property with the old farmhouse she and Nick had visited.

It was marked *Timmons*, and it included a large parcel of land, nearly one hundred acres. The map indicated another parcel of about twenty acres had been sold from it, reducing the original farmstead. She was sure that smaller acreage was where her father's car had been abandoned.

She called over one of the clerks. "I know you're busy, but could you explain some of this to me? I'm pretty sure this is the property I'm interested in."

The clerk scanned the map and nodded. "The old Timmons place. I figured it would come up for sale sooner or later."

"And this used to be part of the farm?" Campbell touched the part of the map indicating the smaller parcel.

"Yes. Their son sold that piece after his parents died. He hasn't been around for a long time, and the house has stood vacant."

"Timmons, you said?" Campbell took out her notebook and pen.

"Yes, it belonged to Melville and Olive Timmons. Now it belongs to their son, Clark."

She jotted down the names. "And how long ago did they sell the twenty acres?"

"Four or five years ago. I think it was around the time Clark got married. If you hang on, I can look at the tax record and get you an exact date."

"I'd appreciate it."

Campbell wanted every detail she could get about that land. She recorded not only the date of the sale, but the new owners' names and the assessed value of both properties.

"What's this?" she asked, pointing to a mark on the Timmons property, several hundred yards behind the house.

"Hmm." The clerk bent over the map. "I'd say that was an old structure. There was probably a shed or something there years ago. I'd have to look back on older maps to be sure."

"It looked like there had been a barn right behind the house at some time," Campbell said.

"Yes, and that's gone now as well, but this would be smaller. Sorry, I can't help you with that without doing some research, and I really don't have time today."

"That's okay." Campbell closed her notebook.

"Come back another time and I may be able to work on it, if it's something you want to learn about."

"Thanks. I appreciate your help." Campbell went out into the muggy air and got in her car. After adjusting the air conditioning, she thought for a moment and then drove to the address of the couple who'd bought the acreage Timmons had sold. She found Lowell Halley, the new owner, but was disappointed in his response to her questions.

"Sure, I bought that piece because it abuts my big field. I planted soybeans on it for several years, and one year I put in winter wheat. But I'm getting too old for this. My wife wants me to retire so we can go into a senior complex. I'm thinking of selling that piece of land."

"So, you don't know anything about the car abandoned there Monday night or Tuesday?" Campbell asked.

"Nope. A detective came around and asked me about it yesterday, but I told him, I haven't been over there in weeks."

"Is it okay for me to walk over the field? I know the police searched the area near the car already, but ..."

"Go ahead," Halley said. "I didn't plant anything there this spring."

"Thanks." She started to leave but turned back. "Oh, do you know if there was an old shed or anything like that on the Timmons property at one time? Not the barn near the house, but farther back."

He frowned. "I think there used to be a cabin out there, early on. I think they let it go and it came down at least twenty years ago. And Clark hasn't planted anything lately. He could probably get someone to plant there on shares, but I haven't seen any activity."

Half an hour later she plodded back to her car. She'd walked over Mr. Halley's land, careful not to cross onto the Timmons property. She hadn't found anything other than the traces the policemen had made in their search. Standing by the car in the spot where her father had parked, she looked around again. Might as well try the only other house she could see from here.

Ringing the doorbell produced no results, though it looked like a working farm. She could see that the lawn was regularly mowed and the flowerbeds had been tended with care. A few toys were scattered about, and a large tractor sat near a barn, beyond which a field of soybeans grew.

She didn't want to go back to the office empty-handed. With a sigh, she started the car. As she pulled out into the road, she noticed something different at the end of the Timmons driveway. There was no traffic, and she rolled slowly up to it.

A for sale sign stood in the grass just off the gravel drive. That hadn't been there when she and Nick visited. She clicked a quick photo of the sign with her phone. A green pickup sat in the yard close to the house, and her hopes rose.

She drove in, knocked on the front door, and waited. After a minute's silence, she knocked again. Nothing. Maybe he was around the back. She stood uncertainly, wondering if she ought to go to the back door, as she and Nick had. Hands seized her from behind and snatched her backward into a choke hold.

6

"What are you doing snooping around here?" The raspy voice made her shudder.

She struggled for a breath. "Let me go."

He loosened his hold slightly, but kept her arms pinned to her sides.

"I'm looking for the owner," she gasped.

"You a cop?"

"No."

He let her go, shoving her toward the door. Against the frame, she caught herself and turned around. He loomed close to her on the porch, a lanky man in his thirties, wearing a plaid shirt and jeans.

"What do you want?" he demanded.

"Are you Clark Timmons?"

He squinted at her. "Who are you?"

"My name is Campbell McBride. My father is missing, and his car was found down the road on that land you sold a few years back."

"So?"

"I just wanted to ask people who live along here if they'd seen anything."

"No."

She frowned. "No, what?"

"No, I haven't seen anything. Didn't know about the car. Now, go away."

"Why?"

"Because this is my property and I'm telling you to leave."

She swallowed hard, her hand at her throat where he'd squeezed it. "I see your house is for sale."

"So? You want to buy it?"

"No, I—"

"Then you have no reason to be here."

She wondered if he ever blinked those flinty eyes. Her heart was pounding. Best not poke the bear, she decided. She walked slowly back to her Fusion and got in. Timmons stood on the porch glaring at her, so she started the engine and backed out of the driveway.

NICK WAS STILL at work when she returned to the office.

"Hi." He glanced up as she shut the door. "Find anything?"

"Maybe."

He sat back and gave her his full attention.

"I found out who owns the land where Dad's car was found, but they didn't know anything about it until the police told them."

"Okay."

"I also met the guy who owns that old house we went to. Clark Timmons." Campbell walked to her father's desk and flopped down in the chair.

"Clark Timmons." Nick frowned. "That sounds familiar."

"Well, he wasn't very friendly. In fact, he grabbed me from behind while I was standing on the porch."

"Yikes! He assaulted you?"

"Well …" She thought about it. "Maybe. I mean, I *was* on his property uninvited. He was pretty rude about it, though. The first thing he asked me was if I was a cop." She swallowed, still conscious of a little soreness near her Adam's apple.

"Oh, he did, huh? Like that's not suspicious. You ought to call Fuller and tell him. That guy shouldn't have put hands on you."

"I wasn't happy about it. But, hey." She looked up with a smile. "I maybe learned one useful thing. The house is for sale now."

"Oh yeah?"

"There's a Realtor's sign out near the driveway that wasn't there when we went earlier."

"Who's the agent?"

"Hold on." Campbell took out her phone and opened to the picture. "Pride and Calhoun."

"Their office is over on Twelfth Street."

Campbell's jaw dropped as she stared at the picture. "Yeah, isn't that the one right across from the Barn Owl?" Her gaze met Nick's.

He froze for a moment then reached for the phone. "You got the number?"

"I'd rather go over there."

He jumped up and grabbed his keys from the desk.

"What about the work you were doing?" Campbell asked.

"I'm due for a break. Let's go."

She jumped into the Jeep with him, and he wove through the tree-shaded streets, comparatively quiet now that the public schools and Murray State had ended their school year. He pulled into a parking spot across from the diner. Campbell climbed out and looked up at the real estate office's sign, then across the street.

"He could see the front door," Nick said.

"I looked out that window when they told us where he sat. But they'd have been closed, wouldn't they?"

"Let's find out." Nick strode up the steps, and she followed.

A woman of about thirty-five sat at the desk nearest the door. She rose, smiling.

"May I help you folks?"

She wore a red silk blouse with black pants, and her hair fell in a stylish shoulder-length cut. Flawless makeup. She looked professional, and Campbell wondered for the first time in days how she looked.

Like a professor? She doubted that. She'd thrown on jeans and a pullover top of cotton gauze that morning, figuring the heat would be simmering by noon. Like a private investigator? No, not that either. Right now she was nothing. Or in-between. Between professor and what?

"Hi," Nick said, stepping forward. "We're interested in the Timmons farm, out on Gabriel Road."

"Oh, yes, that's a new listing." She smiled and extended her hand to Nick. "I'm Nell Calhoun, and I'd be happy to tell you about the property. Will y'all have a seat?"

Nell's professionalism dropped a notch in Campbell's estimation. She was trying a little too hard to be Nick's buddy.

"I'm Campbell McBride, and this is Nick Emerson," she said before Nick could reply. He darted a glance at her but sat in one of the client chairs and allowed her to take the lead. "I was out there this afternoon, and I met the owner."

"Oh, Mr. Timmons." Nell's tight smile told Campbell her encounters with Clark hadn't been as chummy as she'd like. "It was his family's home for many years. He lives out of state now, and he's come back to settle things and get the place ready to sell."

"You've toured the house?" Campbell asked.

"Oh, yes. I took a lot of pictures, but I'll be up front with you: the place needs a lot of work."

"Is he going to make improvements before selling?" Campbell asked. She didn't think the agent would have already put up the sign if that were the case.

"I encouraged him to at least have some painting done." Nell frowned. "Buyers like to feel the house is ready to live in."

Campbell remembered the stark kitchen with old, drab wallpaper and cracked linoleum, but she wasn't about to admit she'd seen it.

"Of course," Nell went on in a more hopeful tone, "some people might consider tearing the house down and just using the acreage for crops. Mr. Timmons even asked me if it would be to his advantage to have the house pulled down, or to offer it to the fire department for a controlled burn."

"Really." Campbell found it hard to believe anyone would do that to their childhood home. But if he'd been away for years and didn't care—or if he had bad memories of the place …

"What did you tell him?" Nick asked.

"After some discussion, he decided to try to sell the place as is. He doesn't want to put a lot of money into it, and he felt that this way the buyer can decide what to do."

"Can we see the pictures you took?" Campbell asked.

"Sure. I was just working on posting them on our website, though I hate to in a way. You know, we try to present each property at its best." Nell turned her monitor toward them and made a few clicks. Campbell could see why she hated to show the interior photos. The house looked neglected and deteriorating.

"How many bedrooms are there?"

Nell gave her a quick glance. "Three upstairs, and there's one room downstairs that could be used as a bedroom."

"Was anyone else there when you toured the house with Clark Timmons?" Campbell asked.

Nell sat back in her chair, gazing pensively at Campbell. "Something tells me you're not interested in buying this property. Are you ... police?"

"We don't mean to take up your time," Nick said. "I'm a private investigator, and Ms. McBride's father is missing. His car was found abandoned near the Timmons place, and we were hoping you might have noticed something."

"I see." Her eyebrows drew together. "Where was the car?"

"Under some trees this side of the driveway," Campbell said. "It was actually on land that Mr. Timmons sold off the original farm a few years ago."

"Oh, yes. I'm aware of that parcel. We have to make sure potential buyers realize it's not part of the property we're selling."

"Well, the current owner led me to believe he might sell it again, if that helps you." Campbell shrugged. "But we wondered if you saw the car there, or if you saw anyone other than Clark Timmons around the property."

"I don't think so."

"When did you take these photos?" Nick leaned in and studied one that showed the garage and the side of the house.

"Tuesday," Nell said. "I went out there this afternoon just long enough to post the sign."

Campbell's hopes sank. Nell had been all over the house the day after her father went missing, and she'd seen nothing. Or at least, she'd noticed nothing. The car must have been there at the time. It had to be. If not, it had been left there a day or more after her father was last seen.

Nick looked her way, his eyebrows arched.

"So, when did Clark Timmons hire you?" Campbell asked.

"Tuesday morning. He left me a phone message Monday evening."

Campbell's pulse picked up. "What did he say?"

"That he had come by the office, but we were closed. He

wanted to make arrangements to sell the old farm, and he said he'd come in Tuesday morning. Which he did. We talked, and I went out to the farm with him."

Campbell nodded slowly. "Thanks. I guess we're done." She stood reluctantly, not wanting to leave without some promising clue, but that didn't seem to be happening. "Ms. Calhoun, will you call us if you remember anything that might be helpful?"

"Of course."

Nick handed her a business card and thanked her. Nell rose and walked with them to the door.

"You know, there was one thing," she said.

Campbell paused with her hand on the knob. She turned toward the Realtor, trying to calm her fluttering heart.

"It was when we went out back so I could take pictures of the land. That's the biggest selling point of the place right now, and I figure most potential buyers will care more about the acreage than the house."

"What did he say?" Campbell squeaked out.

"Nothing, really. It was just that when I asked him if there was anything else I ought to see on the land, he sort of hesitated. I mean, the original landowners had a cabin farther off the road, but it's gone now. I don't think it was very big. But they'd let it go, and he said it fell down when he was a child and his father cleared it away. I'm glad they cleaned it up. But ... I don't know. I felt like he was holding back on something."

"What sort of something?" Nick asked.

Nell shook her head. "I couldn't say. He'd told me about the water and the crops his father had raised there and the boundaries. Maybe it was nothing."

"WHERE DO WE GO FROM HERE?" Campbell asked in the Jeep.

"No idea." Nick blew out a big breath. "Maybe it's time to

talk to Detective Fuller again."

Campbell called him while Nick drove, and the detective offered to stop by their office again.

"I have a little news," he said fifteen minutes later, as Campbell put a cup of coffee in his hand. "Thanks."

"Anytime," Campbell said. "And so do we."

"Oh?"

"Yes. First of all, I visited the county courthouse this morning. The house nearest where Dad's car was found is owned by a man named Clark Timmons."

He nodded but said nothing.

"Nick and I went to his house this afternoon, but no one was home. He used to own the piece of land where the car was left, too, but he sold it off several years ago."

"I spoke to Mr. Halley yesterday." Fuller sipped his coffee. "He was very helpful."

"Yeah, he seemed very nice." Campbell half expected Fuller to tell her once more to stay out of it. Up until now she'd felt as if she was one step ahead of him. But he already knew about Halley, and probably Timmons as well. "You think Timmons is connected to this somehow?"

"I don't know, but I'll do my best to find out. You can be sure of that."

"Good." She poured coffee for herself and carried it to her dad's desk.

Fuller brought a chair over and sat down facing her. "And I had a chat with Sergeant Andrews."

"The one who brushed off the call from Darrin Beresford Monday night?"

He winced. "I'm afraid so. I asked him specifically what Darrin had said."

"He thought he saw someone. A fugitive," Campbell supplied.

"Not a fugitive, but definitely a person of interest." Fuller took another quick sip of his coffee and set the mug down. "Clark Timmons."

"We figured that out," Campbell said. "Nick and I just came from the Pride and Calhoun office, across the street from the Barn Owl. Apparently Timmons went there during the time Darrin was eating supper. He hoped to talk to one of the real estate agents about selling his family's farm, but the office was already closed. We think Darrin saw him out the window and called the cops."

"Yeah." Fuller let out a long, slow breath. "I wish things had gone differently that night. And I'd like to think there's no connection to your dad's disappearance, but that would be too much of a coincidence, in view of your father's visit to Darrin's house."

"So maybe Clark Timmons is connected to Darrin's murder?" Nick asked.

"We have no evidence of that."

"Oh, come on." Campbell sat forward in her chair and plunked her mug down. "Darrin sees Timmons, calls the P.D., and gets the brush-off. Then he calls my dad about it, and they get together and discuss it. Now Darrin is dead and my dad's missing." She pulled in a painful breath. "Do you think my father is dead, too?"

Fuller hesitated a moment too long. "I hope not."

She nodded slowly. "But every hour that goes by makes it more likely."

"I was planning to go talk to Dr. Exter, and I thought I'd go out to the Timmons farm afterward. Technically, that's in the county sheriff's territory, but I think it's worth a look. I've let them know I'll be out there later today."

"So you haven't talked to Clark Timmons yet?" Campbell asked.

"No. I stopped by his place after we found the car, but he wasn't there."

"Okay," she said slowly. "We figured out that Timmons was the guy Darrin was talking about on the phone. So what's Timmons wanted for?"

Nick, who'd been sitting at his desk tapping away at his laptop, said, "Got it. Clark Timmons was all over the news four years ago. His old girlfriend, Alana Shepherd, was murdered." He looked up. "I remember that. It was all people talked about for weeks, but it was before Bill hired me. And it was never solved?"

"That's right. Clark was the main suspect," Fuller said, "but we never could pin it on him. The D.A. decided to cut him loose until we could come up with more evidence."

"Which you couldn't do?" Nick asked.

Fuller shook his head ruefully. "He's not really a fugitive, but he's still a person of interest. It wasn't my case, but I was on the edge of it. I hadn't made detective yet, but I did some legwork for the detective squad. Clark Timmons is supposed to keep the police notified of his whereabouts, but he's not restricted from leaving Calloway County. Apparently he's been living somewhere else for the last three years or so."

"And you never learned who killed this girl?" Campbell asked.

"No, it's a cold case now. Timmons dropped out of sight." Fuller lifted his mug and took a big swig of coffee. "Look, I'll drive out there and see if anyone's around. I'll let you know what I find out."

"He assaulted Campbell when she went to his house alone earlier," Nick said.

Fuller stared at her. "What happened?"

"Nothing really." She waved a hand through the air.

"He snuck up behind her and grabbed her," Nick said.

"It was nothing." Campbell didn't want to deal with the complications and paperwork that would result if she made a big deal of it. "He said I was trespassing."

"Were you?" Fuller asked.

"I walked up to his front door and knocked. Is that trespassing?"

"Did he hurt you?"

"Not really."

He studied her face for a moment. "Sounds like you could press charges if you want to."

"I don't. I just want to find my dad."

"Okay. But I'm not going to forget about this. If he gets aggressive again, you tell me." Fuller looked at Nick. "You, too."

Nick nodded, and Campbell was sure Nick would report any further incidents, even if she didn't.

"I appreciate you keeping me up to speed," she said.

"Well, you do the same. And be careful, you hear me?"

Fuller held her gaze until she nodded and said, "I will be."

After he left, she looked around. What now? All she could see were loose ends, everywhere.

"I guess we can't blame Clark Timmons for leaving Murray," she said to Nick. "I mean, if everyone in town thought he was guilty. They probably shunned him. I expect some people said things, maybe even made threats. How much do you remember about it?"

"Not a lot," Nick said. "But since no charges were brought, I guess he had the right to move away. Skipping town makes him look guilty, though."

"Did you and Dad ever talk about that case?"

"Not that I remember. I was still in school when it happened."

Campbell frowned. "You know, Darrin saw Clark from the window of the diner Monday night. That's quite a distance when you're making an ID on someone you haven't seen for several years."

"It was still daylight," Nick said. "And besides, Darrin said he was sure."

7

That evening Campbell sat at her father's home desk in the den and typed up and printed out all her notes on the search for her father. She put them in a folder, mimicking the way her father and Nick organized their notes and reports in each investigative case.

She knew the value of a file backup from the time she'd lost an entire semester's final grades she'd worked out for her students. Her computer malfunctioned, and she'd had to go back to the exam booklets and recalculate scores for three hundred students. After that she'd backed up her work on an external drive every evening.

"Sometimes paper is best," her father had told her several times, and she could see the wisdom of that for something like the P.I. business. If her dad had started a file on Darrin Beresford's case, she and Nick might not be going through all this.

The notes amounted to less than a full page, and nothing jumped out at her.

"Well, Brock Wilson and Paul Exter were the most helpful," she said aloud. "Brock said that when Darrin got up and left without finishing his meal, Dr. Exter got up, too. He left money and said he had to go."

Still, Exter had denied her suggestion that he was following Darrin out of the diner.

She mulled over the small part of Darrin's phone conversation Wilson had heard—"I'm sure it's him. I don't care how long it's been." Wilson seemed to think his friend, the dentist, was interested in that. And they were quite sure now that Darrin was talking about Clark Timmons, whom he'd seen through the window. Why would Dr. Exter care if Timmons was back in town?

Feeling sluggish, she went to the kitchen. She didn't want to drink coffee now, but she poured herself a glass of juice. She hadn't slept well since her arrival in Murray. Every night, she woke up a dozen times, listening to the house's creaks and wondering where her dad was. If there was a chance of getting some restful sleep, caffeine would surely sabotage it.

More alert, she went back to the computer, still a bit at loose ends on where to look next. For lack of anything better to follow up on, she opened the local newspaper's website. Her father subscribed to the *Ledger & Times*, and at the time of Timmons's arrest, they'd run a lot of articles on the murder.

Nick had also mentioned the newspaper in Paducah, a larger city about an hour to the north. They might have a different perspective on the situation, but Campbell felt the local paper's reporters would be closer to the story and have a better grasp on the details.

Since her father was a subscriber, she was able to open the paper's online archives. Soon she was immersed in reports on the murder of Alana Shepherd, the arrest of her former fiancé, Clark Timmons, and his eventual release. Campbell scrawled notes on a pad of paper. Alana worked at a local clothing store and must have put away a good portion of her earnings. She had bought a shorefront cabin on Kentucky Lake with Timmons during the time they were engaged.

Apparently both their names were still on the deed when she died, although they'd broken up at least two years earlier. Campbell hadn't realized the pair had separated so long before Alana's murder. According to the news reports, she had a new boyfriend, and Clark had married a woman from Tennessee. Did he really still care enough about Alana to kill her?

After an hour's study, she sat back. The evidence against Clark looked pretty thin. Had he been a suspect of convenience, the obvious culprit? Had the police figured the breakup of their relationship was enough of a motive? Apparently, the district attorney had not. The breakup was old history when Alana was killed, and both had moved on to new relationships.

True, Clark's wife, Hannah, reportedly left him while he was in police custody. Were they back together now? Nick would know how to check on whether they got a divorce. She wrote a note to remind herself to ask him in the morning.

"I wasn't here at the time, but even I can see several other people they should've been looking at," Campbell said aloud. Some of the articles stated or clearly implied that Alana Shepherd had been at odds with her family before her death, and her boss didn't sound very chummy, either.

How deeply had the police checked into other suspects? It was possible they'd considered many people, but the results hadn't made it into the paper. Maybe Keith could tell her more. She closed the browser. Her mind kept coming back to what Darrin had said to her father—"I'm sure it's him." For some reason, those words set Paul Exter off.

What does that mean? Was Dr. Exter involved in Alana Shepherd's death? Maybe she should do some digging into Exter's background to see if he had any connections to the murdered woman. Was he ever even considered or asked for an alibi?

Campbell picked up the pen she'd been using all week to take notes. She hadn't really looked at it before. An image of a racehorse graced the barrel, the emblem for the Racers sports teams at Murray State. Her dad had always liked basketball, and he probably followed the local team.

She forced her mind back to the problem at hand. If Exter wasn't connected to the Shepherd case, in which Clark Timmons was a major suspect, why would he care what Darrin said and follow him out of the diner? It didn't add up.

Frowning, she stared at the calendar on the opposite wall. A possibility came to her, faint at first, then stronger. Either Paul Exter was somehow involved in Alana Shepherd's murder, or he thought Darrin was talking about a different case. Maybe the snippets he'd heard had prompted him to jump to conclusions—especially if he had a guilty conscience.

She yawned and blinked her gritty eyes. Time to sleep. She'd ask Nick to help her do a background check on Exter. Afraid she'd forget, she added that to the note about checking on the Timmonses' possible divorce. But Nick's regular investigative work could keep him busy all day. She could ask Keith Fuller about open cases. Older cases. Ones that would make Darrin say, "I don't care how long it's been."

Tomorrow would be a busy day if she looked into all the leads she'd found. Maybe now she could forget about it for a few hours and truly rest.

THE NEXT MORNING, Campbell arrived at the office with pastries she knew would tempt Nick. By the time he got there, she had a fresh pot of coffee waiting as well.

"Oh, wow, I ate breakfast," he said, but he reached for a doughnut anyway.

He seemed to be paying attention as Campbell went over the connections she'd made the night before.

At last she stopped for breath and eyed him expectantly. "Well? Does that make sense to you?"

"Yeah, it does. We need to find out what made Dr. Exter so interested in what Darrin was saying. And we also need to look into the Alana Shepherd case deeper and find out what was going on with her family."

"Right," Campbell said. "And her other relationships. And we need to find out why Hannah Timmons left her husband."

"Other than him being arrested for murder, you mean?"

"Well, yeah. I'm sure that would be hard on anyone."

"Okay, but I've got to finish this report on the insurance case and deliver it." Nick sighed. "Two hours tops, and I can do these things for you." He looked critically at the note Campbell had handed him with the searches she hoped he'd carry out. "I should start on the Lyman case today, but—"

Campbell scowled and almost snarled at him. Nick raised a hand in protest.

"Right. Bill is more important. But I do need to finish this one."

"You do that. I was thinking I might call Detective Fuller."

Nick considered that and shrugged. "Why not?"

She hesitated to bother the detective. He was no doubt putting in every minute he could on the Beresford case. Becoming too dependent on Keith might alienate him. He seemed like a good person and a competent detective, and she wanted to keep him on her side.

Although she wasn't a licensed investigator, she could do some things on her own. She went back to the online newspaper archives, looking for murder cases other than Alana Shepherd's, ones that might upset someone who overheard a conversation about them—someone with a guilty conscience. Unsolved homicides.

It took several tries at adjusting the keywords for her search to rule out accidental deaths and deaths by natural causes, but after a while she found a couple of items that seemed to qualify. She directed her laptop to send the articles to the printer in the corner. As the printer whirred and the pages spit out, she came to a decision and phoned Keith Fuller.

"Hi," she said when he answered. "I've come across a few things I'd like to discuss with you."

"Is it urgent?" he asked. "I'd be happy to talk with you, but we're really busy at the moment."

"Sorry," she said. "I guess it can wait."

"Okay, I'll be off duty at five, but I doubt I'll be free before then. There was a robbery this morning and a car wreck on 641. On top of that, we've had an incident at the middle school. Everyone's spread a little thin today. Could I drop by your office or the house when my shift ends?" he asked.

"Sure, but I don't like to cut into your personal time."

"I tell you what, I should be able to drop by after my lunch break," he said.

"Well, if you're too busy—"

"No, I can tell this is important. If I can't make it, I'll call you and we can set something up for later."

"Thanks." Campbell hung up feeling just a tinge of guilt. He did have other things to attend to. Truthfully, she wouldn't mind a bit seeing Keith on his personal time, but she couldn't tell him that. He was becoming the solid post for her to lean on, so far as her father's case went.

But other things that had nothing to do with it were creeping onto his schedule, too. Probably that was normal, but she still felt every hour—maybe every minute—might make a difference in her father's safety. She sighed and tried calling her dad's cell phone again. As expected, she got nowhere with that.

Questioning people connected to Alana Shepherd seemed like a very indirect way to learn anything about her father's disappearance, but she couldn't think of a better way to proceed.

Nick was printing out his report. "I need to run this over to the insurance company's office."

"Can't you just send it to them electronically?"

"Well, yeah, but they like us to present it to them and point out the most important stuff. And hopefully they'll give me a check if I'm right there in front of them."

"Okay." She supposed collecting the fee was a good thing—maybe even a necessary one. She had no idea how the business was doing, or when Nick was supposed to be paid. "I think I'll try to talk to Alana Shepherd's folks while you're gone," she told him.

He waved and was out the door. Campbell gathered her things, along with the folder containing the printed articles from the time of the murder, and locked up the office.

When she arrived in the Shepherds' driveway, a fiftyish couple was loading a cooler and some gear into the back of an SUV with a trailered boat hitched behind it. Probably heading for a day on Kentucky Lake. If she'd been ten minutes later, she would have missed them.

She got out of the car slowly, wondering how they would receive questions from a stranger about their daughter who'd been murdered four years earlier.

"Hello," she said with what she hoped was construed as a friendly smile. "I don't want to hold you up, but I thought maybe you could help me out. I'm Campbell McBride."

"Any relation to Bill McBride?" the man asked, pausing with a fishing rod in his hand.

"He's my father. Do you know him?"

"I've met him a couple of times. Seems like a decent guy. I'm Roger Shepherd. This is my wife, Wanda."

Mrs. Shepherd nodded and pushed back a lock of her short, graying hair. "How can we help you?"

"I'm looking into something that may have an indirect connection to your daughter's case."

"Rachel?" Mrs. Shepherd's eyes widened.

"Uh, no, sorry. Alana."

"Oh." Mrs. Shepherd looked at her husband.

"I don't see how digging up the past can help," he said.

"It's very painful to us." His wife stepped closer to him. "I don't really want to hash it over again."

Campbell could understand that—not wanting a stranger to intrude and stir up heart-wrenching memories. But part of her brain was spinning off in another direction. What was their daughter Rachel involved in that would make her mother think she had referred to her "case"?

"I'm sorry. I didn't mean to bring up unpleasant memories."

Wanda shrugged, set down the tote bag she was carrying, and turned toward their house.

"You'll have to excuse my wife," Roger said. "It's been a while, but she still gets emotional about it."

"I understand."

He raised his eyebrows. "So, was there something in particular you wanted to ask about? You said you're Bill's daughter. Is he looking into this?"

"Uh, no, not really. It's kind of a long story, and I don't want to keep you. I did wonder about Alana's relationships. I know she and Clark Timmons broke up, but—"

"Yeah, they broke up two years or more before she died." Roger shook his head. "We always thought he might've done it. I mean, he was the police's top suspect. But now I don't know. Clark didn't seem like the type to go and stab someone like that, especially someone he'd cared about.

"If it had been soon after they split up, I could see it more. But he's a quiet man, and he never complained or ranted about her that I know of. Who lets that kind of thing fester for two or three years and then kills the person?"

Campbell thought about that for a moment. "Why did they break up?"

"Kids." Roger huffed out a breath. "You know?" He eyed her sharply. "No, I don't s'pose you do. You're not much more than a kid yourself."

A smile tugged at Campbell's lips. "Did they give a reason?"

He raised his shoulders as though helpless. "It didn't pan out. They'd thought everything was fairytale land, I guess, but then reality set in and they realized they weren't made for each other after all."

"In what way?"

"Clark, he was a thinker. Quiet. Great at computers. Alana was more of a sparkly girl. Liked to go out with her friends. Liked to dance and go to parties." He frowned. "She was a little wild in high school. We had to ground her more than once. But Clark would just as soon stay home and watch a movie as go out. I guess she decided he was a stick-in-the-mud." He winced. "Now I'm making my daughter look bad. She was just more social than he was, that's all."

"So they sort of grew apart?"

"That's a good way to put it. And after they broke up, he quit his job."

"I didn't know that," Campbell said.

"Yeah, well, he worked for me in the family business. I'm an accountant."

Campbell nodded, realizing she'd seen billboards advertising the firm.

"Clark did all the IT work for us, and he was good at it," Roger went on. "We missed him after he left, I'll tell you. I tried to talk him into staying, but I guess he wasn't comfortable with that. Took me a while to find a replacement."

"What did Alana do?" Campbell asked. "She didn't work in your business, did she?"

"No, she wanted to get into fashion, so she went to work at

Bella's, downtown. After a couple years, she worked her way up to being Bella Chase's personal assistant. Alana didn't like Bella much, and she felt like staying in Murray was a dead end, but she saw her job at the store as a step to something bigger. She really wanted to get on as a buyer for some fancy store in a big city."

"Like New York?"

Roger shrugged. "Maybe. Nashville, at least, or St. Louis, Atlanta ... any place bigger than Murray."

"So, she wanted to get out of the small-town atmosphere? It wasn't personal with her and Bella?"

"Aw, she wasn't crazy about Bella, or Bella's family either."

"What do you mean?"

Roger glanced toward the house. "I prob'ly talk too much. I told the cops at the time, though. You know, they asked us if Alana had any people she didn't get along with. I told 'em she used to make remarks about Jared Chase—Bella's husband."

Campbell made a mental note of the name.

"Their son, too," Roger went on. "Can't remember the kid's name, but Alana thought he was a real jerk. He was a bit younger than her, but I think he had a crush on her in high school. She tried to treat him nice, but she got sick of him following her around, and I think she finally ripped into him. Told him to buzz off. He didn't hang around here after that. I heard later he went away to school."

Disliking someone wasn't a reason to put them on the suspect list, apparently, since Clark Timmons had retained his place at the top of that list, but this seemed like confirmation that Alana had issues with the Chase family.

Wanda came out of the house carrying a small beverage cooler and another tote bag. "Come on, Roger. It'll be hot by the time we get to the lake."

"Time to shove off." He gave Campbell an apologetic smile.

"Well, thanks for your time. I hope you have a great day on the lake."

"No problem," Roger replied. "We appreciate your effort of looking into things, but I just don't see what good it will do."

Campbell nodded to Mrs. Shepherd, got back in her car, and fastened her seat belt. The mother's attitude seemed odd to her. Didn't most families of homicide victims want justice for their loved ones at any cost? She'd seen many grieving parents on newscasts over the years, pleading for murderers to be found and punished.

Maybe it had been so long, the Shepherds had moved on. Mrs. Shepherd seemed to think talking about her daughter's death was the last thing she wanted to do. And Roger had implied that Alana got into trouble as a teenager. All of that had probably taken a toll on her mother, too.

Roger's references to Alana's job and her boss weren't very flattering. On impulse, Campbell headed downtown. There was time to take a browse through the high-end clothing store before lunch.

Her visit was brief, and she emerged from the store with a new lipstick and scanty information to add to her file on the Alana Shepherd case. A piece of paper stuck under her windshield wiper stopped her, and she leaned over to pull it free.

Keep out of the Shepherd case.

She stared at the message. Who on earth would leave this for her? She looked around, but shoppers were walking innocuously across the parking lot, to and from their cars and in and out of the store.

The plain white paper was half-sheet size, probably torn off a tablet. The words were written in block letters with black ink. Her pulse thudded in her ears as she got into her car. Should she take the note to the police? She glanced at the dashboard clock.

Nick was probably done with his report. He could help her decide.

As she drove back toward the True Blue office, Campbell wrestled with the idea that she was ready to accept advice from Nick Emerson. He still was not her favorite person, but in the last four days her opinion of him had changed. He'd shown a tendency to try to look out for her. She supposed that was good, but maybe he was only doing it for Bill's sake.

Okay, he cared about Bill, too. She tried to picture him as the younger brother she'd never had. Nope, not working.

8

"My dad is still missing, and you're playing a video game?" Campbell's anger spiked. So much for her elevated expectations of Nick.

"Oh, relax." He frowned at her with his whole body. "I delivered the report, got the check, and took it to the bank. Then I came back here and did some research. Now I'm taking a break, and if I do say so myself, I deserve it."

She shut the door and swallowed hard. "What did you find out?"

"No, you first." Nicked tipped his chair back and swung his feet up to the corner of his desk.

"Okay. I'll start with the last thing that happened, because it's the scariest."

He dropped his feet to the floor with a thud and sat up straight, immediately alert. "What do you mean, scariest?"

"This was under my windshield after my last stop." She walked to his desk and laid down the note.

Nick bent over it, his forehead wrinkled like a plowed field. "Well, that ain't good."

"My thoughts exactly." Except with better grammar. At least

he hadn't touched the paper. "Who do you think could have left it on my car?"

"Who knew where you were?"

She scrunched up her face, thinking. "It was an impulse stop at Bella's. I was inside ten or fifteen minutes, tops. Well, maybe twenty." She *had* paused to riffle through the dresses and tops on their clearance rack. "I suppose someone could have seen me go in and left it while I was talking to the employees."

"Or maybe someone was following you."

She didn't like to think that, or that she wouldn't have noticed a tail.

"But why would they leave this? And why would anyone follow me, for that matter?"

"I think the note speaks for itself. Someone doesn't like you poking around in the Shepherd case."

Campbell stuck both hands on her hips. "But it's a cold case."

"Exactly. And somebody wants it to stay that way." Nick looked down at the paper. "Who else did you talk to today?"

"First I went out to the Shepherds' house."

"Alana's parents?"

"Yes. They were getting ready to go boating, so we didn't talk long. In fact, Mrs. Shepherd pretty much blew me off. But her husband was nicer. Funny, though, when I mentioned their daughter's case, they thought at first I meant their other daughter, Rachel."

"That's weird."

"I thought so. But I guess after four years, maybe it seemed odd to them that someone wanted to talk about Alana. I did wonder if Rachel was in some kind of trouble, though."

"Hmm. Keith could find out."

The door opened and Detective Fuller looked in at them.

"You're right. We can ask him if she has a police record," Campbell said.

"Who?" Keith asked.

"There he is," Nick said more loudly than necessary. "You must have heard us talking about you."

Keith laughed and came further into the room. "What have you two been up to?"

"Well, Nick's been working on a case True Blue had before my dad disappeared," Campbell said.

"Finished it this morning." Nick nodded. "While Campbell was out getting into trouble."

"What kind of trouble?" Keith ambled toward them, his gaze riveted on Campbell.

"I went to see Alana Shepherd's parents this morning, and then I stopped off at Bella's—the clothing store."

Keith nodded.

"Well, when I came out of the store, this was on my windshield." She picked up the note by its edges and held it out to him.

Immediately his face darkened and his jaw tightened. "Looks like you've upset someone."

"Yeah, but why? I mean, it's an old case, and anyone can ask a few questions."

He fished a plastic bag from a pocket, and Campbell slid the note into it.

"Not if you've got something to hide. Word's gotten around town that your father's missing, and for some reason you're digging into old cases. Anyone Bill collected evidence on in the past would be unhappy about that."

"I didn't think about that." Campbell couldn't hold his gaze. "Am I messing up your investigation?"

"Let's just say you're adding to the things we need to look into."

She shuffled over to her father's desk and sank down into his chair. "I'm sorry."

"No, you're not," Nick said. He turned his attention back to Keith. "When you came in, we were just talking about Alana's sister, Rachel Shepherd."

"What about her?"

Campbell told him about the odd reaction she'd gotten when she'd mentioned the Shepherds' daughter without specifying her name.

"I think Rachel's been picked up for speeding a couple of times." Keith let out a slow breath. "Maybe something else. I can check." He focused in on Nick. "Didn't you go to school with her? She's about your age."

"She was a couple years ahead of me," Nick said. "Now that you mention it, she used to hang out with some of the troublemakers."

"Like you?" Keith softened it with a smile.

Nick barked out a laugh. "Well, I never dated her or anything, if that's what you mean. I was too young and insignificant."

"Right." Keith's smile broadened. "I'll look into her record, but I doubt it's anything to do with Alana's death."

Campbell pulled over an extra chair for him, and she recounted her visit with the Shepherds and the things Roger had told her.

"Yeah, I saw that Clark worked for the accounting firm when I went over the case file," Keith said. "Roger Shepherd has a thriving business. A couple other accountants work with him, and they have a receptionist and clerk, besides their IT person."

Campbell let that process through her mind. "Okay, what about Alana's job at Bella's? Her father said she didn't really like Bella Chase, or her family."

"J.J. Chase was in my class." Nick scoffed. "He's a piece of work."

"That would be Bella's son?" Campbell asked.

"Yeah, Jared Junior. Thinks he's a bigshot."

"Roger said he had a crush on Alana and drove her crazy until she told him to leave her alone."

Keith pulled out his notebook. "What does he do, now that he's out of school?"

"I'm not sure." Nick frowned and fiddled with his computer mouse. "He went away after our junior year. Word was his parents sent him to a prep school."

"To get him ready for college, or was he in trouble?" Campbell asked.

"I don't know. But not too many of us kids were sorry he was gone."

"Okay, another thing to check on." Nick wrote in his notebook. "I'll see if I can get his school records and find out if he's got a police file. Campbell, what exactly sent you to the store?"

"Roger Shepherd had said Alana didn't get on very well with her boss and was thinking about looking for a new job. So I went to see what the store was like and maybe catch a glimpse of Bella. She wasn't there, but I talked to one of the clerks who'd been there since Alana worked there. She said that as Bella's personal assistant, Alana wasn't out on the sales floor much. She did most of her work in the office area at the back of the store."

Campbell thought over the brief conversation and added, "According to this gal, everyone there seems to think Bella is a steamroller of a boss. The clerks didn't want to say much, but I got the impression that Bella doesn't suffer fools, gladly or otherwise."

"And she and Alana rubbed each other the wrong way?"

"I guess. But Alana held her position for over two years, so she must have known how to keep Bella happy."

"And she mustn't have been a fool," Nick said.

"Ha. Right." Campbell picked up her father's empty coffee mug and turned it in her hands. She'd been using it all week. She'd have to get another when Dad came back. She remembered something else from Bella's and looked up at

Keith. "They're hiring now, and I thought maybe I'd apply for a job there."

Nick and Keith stared at her.

"Why?" Nick asked.

"So I could get into their office and maybe learn more about Bella and her business."

"And I was hoping you might put in for a P.I.'s license," Nick said.

"I don't know as I'm cut out for it." She chuckled.

"Aw, you're doing pretty good. But I'm not sure you working at Bella's would help us any."

Keith leaned toward her and said firmly, "I agree with Nick. That could do you more harm than good. Think about the note you received right outside the store. I advise you to stay away from there until we've resolved your father's case."

She looked at him bleakly. That could take a long time. It was horribly possible she might never know what had happened. She cleared her throat. "I realized it would be foolish to commit to something full time, even for a week or two, when Dad is still missing. I need to use my time searching for him."

"Tell me everyone you've talked to about the Shepherd case." Keith flipped the page of his notebook.

"Well, I just found out about it yesterday. I didn't know about the murder when I talked to Clark Timmons or Nell Calhoun."

"How about Dr. Exter?"

"Nope. Just her parents and the store clerk."

Keith jotted a note.

"You think her parents put that warning on my car?" Campbell asked. "They were headed for the lake and had the boat trailer and all. I doubt they followed me downtown to leave an anonymous threat for me."

"It could be someone you talked to but didn't mention Alana's name," Keith said. "For instance, if Brock Wilson was guilty—and I don't think he was, but just for example—and he heard you asking all these questions and put two and two together that Darrin was talking about this case, then he might have done it in a clumsy attempt to scare you off."

"Okay, I guess that makes sense." She thought of all the people she'd questioned that week. The list was pretty long. "So, someone I talked to about Dad being missing is upset with me."

"I'd say so."

They sat in silence for a moment.

"We should eat lunch," Nick said.

"You two haven't eaten?" Keith looked at his watch. "It's almost two o'clock."

"I guess I forgot," Campbell said. "I was going to talk to you about some of the old crimes I learned about, though. Nick and I thought maybe Paul Exter assumed Darrin was talking about a different case at the Barn Owl. You know, like you just said. I was looking for old cases he could have been involved in."

Nick shoved back his chair. "I'll go get something while you talk. What do you want, Campbell? Pizza?"

"A sandwich is fine. Whatever you want, Nick."

"Okey-doke." Nick snatched up his keys.

Keith watched him hurry out the door. "You two getting along okay?"

"Yeah, fine." She shrugged. "We have our moments, but it's mostly because we have different styles of working."

"Well, I know your father's proud of the way Nick's turned his life around. He hasn't been arrested once in the three years he's worked for Bill."

Campbell chuckled. "He's all right, I guess. But back to Bella Chase, I hoped to meet her face-to-face. She wasn't there today. They said she was off to St. Louis on a buying trip, but she'll be back Monday. And now I'm really curious about her husband and J.J."

He smiled. "Tell me about this theory of yours concerning Dr. Exter."

"Right." Campbell quickly switched gears in her head. "So, I got to thinking, when Dr. Exter followed Darrin out of the diner, I've assumed it was because he thought Darrin was talking about him, and we know Darrin saw Clark Timmons. Did Dr. Exter have something to do with Alana Shepherd's murder?"

"Hmm," Keith said. "I don't know of any connection, but I'll go over the case file again."

"Good. But that may have been a faulty assumption on our part."

"What do you mean?"

"Maybe he thought Darrin was talking about another crime." She opened the drawer and took out the folder she'd prepared and slid it across the table. "Here's what I've found so far on local cold cases involving deaths. But it could be anything, really. Grand theft, extortion, fraud. Malpractice, even, since Exter's a medical professional."

Fuller nodded slowly. "I've tried to keep an open mind while I'm investigating Beresford's murder. What you're saying is a possibility. If Exter did go to Darrin's house that night, it might not have had anything to do with the crime Clark Timmons was suspected of committing."

"Exactly. I mean, Exter probably didn't realize Darrin had seen Clark."

Keith studied the sheets for several seconds, and she waited, hoping he'd see her logic.

"I remember the hit-and-run," he said. "A jogger was hit and left dead beside the road. That wasn't so long ago."

"About a year. I was thinking it might be too recent."

"Or not."

"Yeah. This one—" Campbell pulled out the next article. "I think they decided that was accidental."

Fuller nodded. "The drowning at LBL." Land Between the Lakes was a national recreation area, and very popular with locals and summer tourists. The articles Campbell had read described the drowning of a man who was out fishing with a friend. Doubts were cast when it came to light that the friends had argued over a business deal gone bad.

"I'll do some more reading," Campbell said, "but add that to the Alana Shepherd case, and you've got at least three suspicious deaths in the last five years. I pretty much ruled out the murder at the Campus Apartments last fall."

"Yes, that one's solved," Fuller said.

"Do you think we need to go back further?"

"Maybe." He wrote in his notebook. "I'll put some time in on this. There may be other cases we haven't thought of."

"I only looked back as far as the year Alana died. Maybe there's something older than that."

"It's possible. If there's a connection to one of these cases, we need to find it."

He'd said *we*. Campbell smiled. "Thank you, Detective."

"It's Keith." He shrugged as if slightly embarrassed. "I mean, I know we've only met on business, but..."

She nodded. "I really appreciate you not thinking I'm bonkers about this."

"Not at all." He gazed at her, a smile playing at his lips. "And I think Nick's right. You might be suited to a career in investigation."

"Thanks. After he said that, I looked up the requirements for a license, but really, I'm an English professor."

"That's important to you? Staying in your field of study?"

"To be honest, I'm not sure anymore. I haven't really had time to think what it would mean to do something totally different."

"And yet you've been doing it all week."

She made a wry face. "And yet I've made no progress in

finding Dad, I've kept Nick away from his work, and I've made things harder for you."

"You're being harsh on yourself. You've turned up a few good leads for me, but I have to admit I'm concerned about you."

They looked at each other for a long moment.

"Our lack of success is really dragging you down, isn't it?" he asked.

Campbell's throat tightened, and she nodded.

"I'm sorry," Keith said softly. "If I had the chance to solve one case by magic, it would be finding your father."

She sighed. "You've got a lot of other things to tend to."

"Actually, I've finished or delegated most of them." He held up his notebook. "You've given me some new things to check on. I'll spend what's left of my workday on Bill's case."

"Thank you."

He stood, and Campbell rose and walked with him to the door.

"One more thing," Keith said, turning to face her.

They stood close together, and Campbell held her breath.

"Keep safe. It might be wise to back off on this for a while. I *will* be looking into this note and the other things we talked about."

She looked up into his steady brown eyes and knew he'd do what he promised.

"Okay. I'll stick to computer research for now."

He hesitated, as if he thought even that might be too much, but then he nodded. "I know you have to do something for Bill."

"But be discreet?" she asked.

"And be careful." He touched her shoulder lightly. "Please."

9

Nick had emailed Campbell links to several news stories he thought might interest her, including one about Jared Chase, naming him chairman of the local Chamber of Commerce. She poked around on the internet for the rest of the afternoon while Nick set up a file for the new case for the law firm. Around four o'clock, he looked over at her apologetically.

"Mr. Lyman would really like a quick turnaround on this case."

"Anything I can do to help you?" she asked.

"I don't think so, but I need to run to the courthouse for some records."

"Go."

Campbell was starting to feel useless, but she kept Keith's admonition in mind. She answered a call from a woman asking if True Blue handled divorce cases. Campbell wasn't sure. It sounded a bit sordid—the woman wanted them to follow her husband around and see where he spent evenings when he said he was working late. She said she'd have one of the detectives call back and wrote a message for Nick.

At five, Nick called and told her he'd finished his task downtown. "I'll just go home, if that's okay with you."

Without some new break in her father's case, they wouldn't do much good hanging around the office together. She gave him the phone message about the divorce case.

"Bill doesn't like to do those unless we're really hard up for work," he said.

"That's about what I figured. But you need to tell her that, not me," Campbell replied. "And not in those exact words."

"Right. We have a standard line—the contrite letdown."

She laughed. "Okay, I'll see you tomorrow." She picked up her scattered printouts and stuck them in her case folder then turned off the lights and locked the door. She wasn't really hungry yet, but didn't feel like cooking, so she drove to one of the many eateries on Twelfth Street, near the university. The parking lot held a lot of pickups and SUVs. She hoped service wouldn't be too slow.

The waitress brought her order of a sandwich and drink quicker than she'd expected. Campbell smiled up at her. "Thanks. Can I ask you a question?"

"Sure," the redhead replied.

"Do you live here in Murray?"

"Yes, all my life."

"Do you remember any unsolved murders in town? Maybe back a few years?"

"Hmm." The waitress frowned. "There was that jogger who got killed last year."

Campbell nodded. "Any others? Suspicious deaths?"

"Oh, that woman whose fiancé killed her, but it was a while ago."

"Alana Shepherd," Campbell said, not mentioning the fact that the fiancé was innocent until proven guilty.

"That was her name. I didn't know her, but it was big. I can't think of any others. Oh, wait, there was a kid who died on the campus, I think."

"I know about that one," Campbell said. "That is, if you mean the one at the frat house."

"Oh, I'd forgotten that. But I don't think that was a murder. More like accidental overdose. No, I meant the ballplayer who died of a heart attack."

Campbell arched her eyebrows. "Surely that was natural causes."

"I suppose so. But do they know for sure it was a heart attack?"

"I think they do." It was another case Campbell had noted and mentally ruled out. She hadn't even considered that one as a possible connection for Exter.

The waitress seemed unwilling to let it go. "He was real young."

"Yes, he was."

"Well, you said suspicious deaths."

"Yes, I did." Campbell smiled. "Thanks." The waitress left, and she took a bite of her pulled pork sandwich. She'd read about the college deaths, along with a drowning, and decided they weren't murders. But was there something she'd overlooked?

The ballplayer's heart attack and the fraternity house death didn't seem like the type of incident that would bother a local dentist's guilty conscience. Regrets for the other young people who knew them, yes, but she didn't believe those were homicides. Still, it might be worth looking for a connection to Exter. If he'd been related to one of the young people who died, he might blame someone else for what happened.

No one who'd been at the Barn Owl on the fateful night remembered Darrin naming the person he was talking about on the phone. That seemed to be the crux of the matter. If Exter had heard Clark Timmons's name, he must have known the conversation had to do with the Shepherd woman. But if he didn't hear a name, what did he think Darrin meant? Exter's perception seemed crucial to solving the riddle.

"Who am I kidding?" she said aloud and took another bite of the juicy sandwich. There was no way she could know what Dr. Exter heard, or what he was thinking that night, or even that he left because of what Darrin had said to the person on the other end of his phone conversation.

She had nearly finished her meal when the waitress came back to the table.

"Everything okay?"

"It's great," Campbell said. "I'll take the check, if you've got it ready."

The redhead laid the bill facedown beside her plate. "Oh, I thought of another mysterious instance," she said.

"Yeah?" Campbell cocked an eyebrow at her.

"Not a death exactly. There was a girl who went missing. It was quite a while ago. Maybe six or eight years ago."

"And they never found her?" Campbell asked.

"Not that I recall, but I suppose I might have missed it. She was in my cousin's class at the high school. Calloway County, that is. An exchange student."

"Really?" Campbell pulled a pen from her purse. "Do you remember her name?"

"No. My cousin might."

"What country was she from?" Campbell asked.

"Let's see ... Germany? Austria? Some European country. It was after I graduated. I never met her personally, but I know all the students were upset about it. They called in extra counselors and all that."

"Would you share your cousin's name with me?"

"Karen Wells. That's her married name. She lives in Draffenville now."

"Phone number?"

The waitress hesitated. "I could ask her if she'd mind talking to you. I hate to—"

"I understand." Campbell wrote her name and phone number on a napkin. Maybe she should have some business cards made with only her name, cell phone, and email on them. She handed it to the woman. "Ask her to call me if she doesn't mind chatting for a minute about the exchange student. And would you call me if you think of anything else about that girl— or any other cold cases in this area?"

"Sure." She tucked it in the pocket of her apron.

"Thanks a lot. You've been very helpful." Campbell took out her wallet and handed her a credit card with the bill. When she brought back a sales slip for her to sign, Campbell added a five-dollar tip. She figured the waitress wouldn't forget her request if she left a generous tip, and she wouldn't hesitate to answer questions if Campbell came back again.

When she walked into her father's empty house, a wave of uncertainty swept over her. For a short time, she'd pushed down the terrible fear for her father and let herself feel she was accomplishing something in her research. But she hadn't really gotten anywhere, had she? Every item she turned up seemed to lead her further from her goal. How could she tell what were clues and what were red herrings?

Nick was on her side, and he was good at locating information on the computer, but had it really helped? Then there was Keith Fuller. He truly wanted to find her father. It was his job, but Bill was also his friend. Campbell had no doubt he'd do everything he could to find Bill.

But was it enough? At any other time, she'd be excited to embark on a new friendship with an intelligent, compassionate man. But how could she feel those things when her life had been ripped wide open?

While she'd checked her father's email, she hadn't checked the mailbox for a couple of days, so she plunked her purse and tote bag on the kitchen table and walked to the end of the driveway. Several advertising flyers curled around three envelopes. She took it all into the kitchen and threw the circulars in the trash. Two bills for Dad. She wondered uneasily if she should open them and perhaps consider paying them. They could probably wait a week or two.

The last envelope was addressed to her. Startled, she tore it open and pulled out a letter on Murray State University's letterhead. They didn't have any openings for literature professors, but they needed a part-time associate to teach freshman composition and study habits in the fall. If she was interested, she could call and arrange an appointment for next week.

Am I interested? Those sounded like the most boring classes ever, but still, she had to earn a living. And it could lead to something better.

She let out a sigh. She'd known she'd have to start over at the bottom. Setting the letter aside with her father's electric and internet bills, she told herself this could wait, too. She'd think about it, at least overnight. Maybe once they'd found Dad, she could make that kind of decision. Now that she'd had a chance to prove her maturity and independence, it might be nice to live with Dad again, or find a place of her own nearby.

And if they didn't find him? Did she want to stay here?

Going into the den, she wearily eyed the cartons of books she'd set aside. What was the point of unpacking them? Still, she opened the one marked Grammar & Comp. These were the texts she'd be teaching from in the fall if she took the job at MSU. She lifted one and gazed at the cover without a speck of joy. With a sigh, she slid it back into the box and closed the flaps.

She puttered around the kitchen for a while, loading the dishwasher and making a shopping list, trying to come up with a way to ferret out the truth of her father's situation and not overstep Detective Fuller's plea.

Maybe she could find something about that missing exchange student. Her initial search turned up a brief, two-year-old article in the *Paducah Sun's* archives reporting nothing new on the case. It did name the year of the incident. Campbell realized she was exhausted. This find should send her racing to learn more, but instead she felt sluggish and depressed. How could this possibly be pertinent?

She gave up in favor of a shower and going to bed early. Maybe after a good night's sleep she'd regain her passion for exploring all these tangents. Right now, it just seemed like one more pointless distraction.

Once settled in bed, she thrashed about fretfully, unable to stop thinking about her father in Darrin Beresford's house, holding a cup of coffee and discussing—what?—with him. Clark Timmons. The man had to be the topic of their conversation. Nothing else made sense. But her father hadn't killed Darrin. She wouldn't believe that. Keith and Nick didn't believe it either.

But where had he disappeared to? Did he confront Darrin's killer? Or did he blithely go his way without knowing Darrin was attacked?

CAMPBELL WOKE IN THE DARK. It took her a moment to orient herself. Dad's house. The lumpy hide-a-bed in his den. She fumbled for her phone on the nightstand and tapped the screen on. Quarter past one. A faint sound in the far reaches of the house caught her attention. She held her breath, listening. For a moment, she teetered on the brink of euphoria. Had Dad come home?

At once she knew it wasn't him. Her car was in the yard. If

her father had come in, he would have noticed her things in the kitchen. She'd left her laptop on the table, her sweater over the back of the chair where she'd sat browsing the Web. And most obvious of all, he'd have turned on some lights, but none shone through the cracks around the edges of her door.

She swung her feet over the side of the bed and stood, groping for her flannel robe. After pulling it on, she padded to the door with her phone in her hand, opened it quietly, and peered down the hallway.

The living room and the kitchen beyond were dark, but after standing unmoving for several seconds, she thought she saw a faint bit of light in the kitchen, and an indistinct shadow flitted across the wall. Was someone out there with a small flashlight? The sound of a drawer being opened gently confirmed her suspicion. She held her breath.

A bluish glow told her that her laptop had come to life. Then it went away, accompanied by a click as the case was closed. Her throat tightened.

A darker bulk crossed the darkness at the end of the hallway, and she ducked back in the doorway, her heart pounding. She almost slammed the bedroom door shut, but she caught another sound. Within seconds she was sure: whoever was out there was rummaging around the bookshelves and entertainment center in the living room. Would they come down here to the den and search her father's desk?

She tried to breathe silently while she considered several options. Sneak down the hall, turn on the living room light, and confront the person? She could try to slip past him—or her, though she found it hard to imagine a woman breaking into the home—and dash out the front door.

Neither of those seemed wise. In her head she could imagine Keith saying, "No, no, no!" His last words to her had been, "Be careful."

She knew her father kept a handgun, but she'd been all

through his desk and closets in her first days here, looking for a clue to his whereabouts, and she hadn't seen the pistol. That narrowed her options to her phone.

Lord help me! Make me wise, not foolish. The only sensible action seemed to be calling 911. Not ideal, since the burglar might very well hear her.

Wavering, she drew a deep breath. Every second she delayed put her in more danger. She stepped cautiously backward and swung the door to, praying the intruder didn't hear the soft *click* the latch made when she closed it and turned the button lock on the knob. She put her ear to the panel, listening, but heard nothing, then swiped her phone and punched in the numbers.

The ringing in her ear sounded deafening. She stepped quickly to her bed and picked up a pillow. Smashing it against the side of her face to muffle the sound, she turned away from the door, and when the dispatcher answered, she spoke in a low voice.

"There's someone in my house."

As she gave the minimal information the woman asked for, she wondered if retreating to the closet would help. Not much, she decided, and the hide-a-bed was too low to crawl under.

"A patrol car is on the way," the dispatcher said. "Do you think they're still in the house?"

"I don't know. Wait." Campbell went to the door and listened. At first she heard nothing, then a distant thud. "They may have just gone out. I heard what sounded like a door, but I'm not certain. They haven't tried to come into the room I'm in."

"All right, shelter where you are until the squad car arrives."

As the woman spoke to her, a chill ran down Campbell's spine. The den door rattled slightly and then someone shook the knob.

10

Campbell caught her breath. Should she call out? She could tell them she'd called the police.

"Are you still there?" The dispatcher asked.

"Yes. I—" Something heavy crashed against the door. "He's trying to break the door to my room!"

"Is there a way out?"

"The windows are pretty high off the ground." She moved to the nearest one and peered out into the darkness. Oak leaves ruffled a few yards away. Outside it was lighter than in the room. The streetlight half a block away was probably helping, and maybe the moon. The drop to the ground would be two or three yards.

Silence surprised her, and she heard the wind sough around the eaves.

"He stopped," she breathed into the phone.

In the next instant she caught the faint wail of a siren. Heavy footsteps retreated toward the front of the house. She sank onto the edge of the bed and breathed slowly and deeply.

"Hello?"

She whipped the phone to her ear. "I'm here. I think the police are outside, and he ran."

"I can stay on with you until you're sure."

She tiptoed to the door and put her ear to it for a moment, then cautiously opened it. Down the hallway, blue lights flashed across the living room walls.

"They're here. Thank you." She closed the connection and hurried to the front door, flipping on lights as she went. She recognized one of the uniformed patrolmen standing on the porch and checked his nametag to be sure.

"Officer Ferris."

"Ms. McBride. Everything all right?"

"Someone was in my house. He tried to break down the door of my bedroom, but I think your siren scared him off at the last minute."

"We'll take a look around to make sure he's gone."

"I'd appreciate that." Campbell stepped aside to let him in. While his partner radioed in and looked around outside, they went from room to room, with Campbell switching on more lights.

A few cupboard doors and drawers were open in the kitchen, but the living room was much messier. Books were tossed on the floor near the bookcase, and CD cases were strewn on the carpet near the television. Her laptop had been moved from the kitchen and now sat askew on the coffee table.

"He must have planned to take my computer." She sent up a quick prayer of thanks that he'd left it in his hurried exit.

In her father's bedroom, the dresser and nightstand drawers had been dumped out.

"This is my dad's room," she told Ferris.

"He's still missing?"

"Yes." She gulped. "The burglar tried to come in my room, but I'd locked the door." She took the officer along the hall to the den. "My dad's desk is in here. Maybe they were looking for something he'd been working on."

"But he didn't get in here?"

"No. I think he'd have broken the door, or at least the lock, within seconds if you hadn't had your siren on. He scared me pretty bad. Badly."

Ferris shot her a curious glance then stooped to examine the outer side of the door. "Yeah, there are some marks here. Good thing you called when you did."

"Campbell?" A strong voice traveled down the hallway, and she turned toward it.

"I'm in here, Keith, with Officer Ferris."

He strode toward her, his hair tousled and his eyes gleaming. "I heard the call. Are you all right?"

"Yes, I'm fine. A little shook up. Shaken up." She shrugged and gave a nervous laugh. Of all the times to worry about grammar.

"Do you need to sit down?" He touched her arm.

"No, no, I'll be fine." She had a fleeting mental image of him sweeping her into his arms, but she quickly squelched that. He asked her a few questions, and she gave him the details. He prodded when she told him she hadn't really seen the burglar, just his bulk, or maybe his silhouette.

He looked deep into her eyes. "Campbell, think. Are you a hundred percent certain that wasn't your father in the house?"

"What? You're kidding, right?"

"No, I'm not. If he's been hiding out for some reason, he might have come back here to get something important—evidence, maybe? A weapon?"

She stared at him in disbelief and waved a hand. "Keith, he tried to break this door down. Does that sound like something my father would do in his own house? My car is outside in the driveway. He would know it was me in here. He would speak to me."

"Okay, okay. Sorry." He pulled back a little. "You're right." He bent to examine the lockset.

"It sounded like he was kicking the door. Maybe shoving it with his shoulder. I was seriously considering diving out that window, which I'm glad I didn't have to do, because it's at least eight feet off the ground."

He straightened, his gaze sweeping the window she indicated and ran a hand through his hair. Campbell had never seen him this agitated.

"I'm sorry," he said. "I over-reacted. It sounds like it couldn't have been Bill."

"It wasn't," she said firmly.

The second patrolman appeared in the hallway. "Looks like he jimmied the kitchen door. I couldn't find any footprints, but a neighbor down the street said a car pulled away from the curb down there just before we got here."

"Where's your father's car now?" Keith asked.

"In the garage." Campbell had left it there and gone back to driving her own vehicle. She walked to the kitchen and opened the door between it and the garage. The detective came to her side and peered out at Bill's blue Toyota.

"Okay. What do you think they were after?"

"I don't know. If this break-in is connected to Dad's meeting with Darrin, he wouldn't have been back here to leave any evidence or reports before he disappeared. If he had, he'd have put the hamburger in the fridge and the wet clothes in the dryer."

"Right."

"He moved my laptop. I think he wanted that, or at least planned to snatch it. And if he'd gotten in here, he'd have had Dad's laptop, too."

"Do you know of anyone else who might come in here and search the place?" Keith's eyes flitted around the room, and his gaze rested on the small computer on the desk.

Campbell shook her head. "You'd have to ask Nick about past cases, I guess. Other than that, I've talked to some people this week about Dad."

"Okay. I don't think there's a lot we can do right now. I'll get my kit and see if I can get any prints off the things that were obviously handled." He looked down at her for a long moment. "Do you feel safe here, or do you want to go to a motel or something? A friend's, maybe."

She didn't really have friends in town yet. Her father's pastor might know someone who would take her in, but she hadn't seen him since her arrival, and she didn't want to deal with strangers at two in the morning. As a last resort, she could call Nick. But she didn't feel that desperate.

"I'll be all right."

"Okay." Keith sighed. "I'll have a patrol car drive by every hour or so. Don't hesitate to call again. In the morning we'll see if we can find anyone else who remembers the car driving away." He held her gaze again. "Do you have any weapons, Campbell?"

"No. Dad has a handgun, but he must have taken it with him. I've been over the house pretty thoroughly this week, and I didn't find it here or at the office, and it wasn't in his car."

"Any hunting guns?"

"No. Dad isn't much for hunting. Animals, that is. Just people."

Keith frowned. "Are you sure you—"

She cut him off by pushing him gently toward the front door. "I'm sure. Get whatever you need for the fingerprints."

"I gave you my personal number." His mouth set in a grim line. "You can call me on it, any time."

"Okay." It came out almost a whisper.

Keith spent another half hour dusting drawers, cabinet doors, and items strewn about the floors. Campbell went to her room and changed into pants and a T-shirt. She knew she wouldn't sleep anymore tonight. He was nearly finished when she returned to the kitchen, and he paused in packing up his equipment.

"Are you sure you want to stay here?"

"You asked me that. I said yes."

His face twitched, and she wondered if he was holding back disapproval, annoyance, or even anger. She didn't want to upset him, but she didn't want to be treated like a helpless child.

"All right then. I'll see you tomorrow."

"Good night." She held the door for him. As soon as he was gone, she closed it and threw the deadbolt then engaged the button on the doorknob. She turned slowly toward the house's silent interior. It did feel a little scarier with Keith gone. Had she just shoved her best chance for a friendship here out the door?

She'd been frightened on the nights she spent alone here, especially the first night, but she'd told herself there was no reason to worry. Every time she felt frightened, she calmed herself with deep breathing and relaxation techniques she'd learned in a psych class, and she'd managed to get enough sleep, though in pieces.

But it turned out there really was danger. Those nighttime noises weren't always harmless after all. Mental exercises weren't enough to hold the shadows at bay.

Her skin was cold, and she hugged herself, shivering. Reluctantly, she went back to the den, closing and locking that door as well. She had to force herself to turn off the lamp. Lying there in the dark, she listened. Nothing. But still, her heart raced.

"I need you, Dad," she whispered.

She couldn't depend on him now, though. And she couldn't keep herself safe. The police couldn't either, when it came right down to it. She prayed in short, erratic bursts for her safety and for her father's life. Finally, her heartbeat slowed and she could inhale without a catch in her breath.

AT SEVEN, Campbell rose stiffly from the desk chair in the den. After about three hours of fitful sleep, she'd given up and come to her father's computer. She'd killed the time until daybreak by going over the printed articles in her file and searching the internet for more information on the people who'd come to her attention.

There really weren't many murders in Calloway County. She'd found two in the past ten years where the killer was immediately arrested and confessed. As to unsolved cases, Alana Shepherd's and that of the exchange student seemed most promising for her purposes.

After refining her searches, she'd found a local news story and one brief follow-up on the Austrian girl's disappearance. She noted the scanty information given about the family in town who had hosted her. Had Nick known the girl? He hadn't mentioned it, but then, she was pretty sure he went to Murray High School, not Calloway County.

In the kitchen, she made coffee and forced herself to eat a slice of toast and a banana. Next, she wandered into the living room and wearily began straightening the mess left behind by the intruder and the police. With a rag, she tried to wipe away fingerprint dust from her laptop case, then the woodwork and drawer pulls. It was more stubborn than she'd realized.

By the time she'd finished, she had just enough time to shower and change before going to the office. It was Saturday, but she and Nick had agreed to open up at the usual time. He didn't work weekends unless a case required it, but they both felt they shouldn't take time off while Bill was still missing.

She arrived at five minutes to nine. Nick pulled in right behind her. While he unlocked the door, she stood back and then followed him in. She almost dropped her laptop case when she ran into his back.

"Sorry, I—" She stopped and stared past him. The file cabinet drawers were open, and several folders lay helter-skelter on her father's desk. The cover to the printer was raised, leaning back against the wall, and a pen and a few papers were scattered on the floor.

"Oh, man." Nick gritted his teeth and looked around.

"Someone's been in here," Campbell said. "I was going to tell you this after you had a cup of coffee in your hand, but someone broke into my house last night. Dad's house, that is."

"What?" Nick whirled, his eyebrows reaching for the sky.

"Yeah. I called the cops, and they scared him off with their siren. Didn't catch him, but it looks like this was his next stop— or he'd been here first."

"Bill kept saying we should have a burglar alarm, but he didn't want to spend the money. I mean, it's not like we keep anything valuable in here."

"Just your records." Campbell strode to the back door, pulled her sleeve over her hand, and tried the knob. It was locked.

"They didn't come in that way?" Nick asked.

"Probably not."

Nick grimaced and checked the windows one by one. "Aha." He stopped by the back one. "This one's unlocked."

"I hope I didn't leave it that way." Campbell's heart sank. "I don't remember opening it." But she hadn't checked it when she left the office either, just the doors.

Nick was halfway out the back entrance, and she followed him. Under the window in question, a five-gallon plastic bucket was upended. Nick took out his phone and clicked a photo.

"I'm calling Detective Fuller." Campbell fished out her cell phone.

KEITH WAS JUST LEAVING the Barn Owl when his cell phone rang. A glance showed him Campbell was calling, and his pulse picked up. Every time she rang him, it was because something was happening, either to her or in connection with his case. His inquiries at the restaurant, on the other hand, hadn't turned up anything new.

"Campbell," he said.

"Hey, Keith. The True Blue office has been burglarized. We think they came in a window."

His chest tightened. His intuition was right on the money where this woman was concerned. A call from Campbell meant trouble. "I'll be right over. Don't touch anything."

"I was trying to figure out if anything's missing, but we can wait." She clicked off, and he pulled in a deep breath. Being around Campbell McBride might be hazardous to his health. Or his heart.

He asked for another officer to go with him and drew Patrol Officer Denise Mills. When they got to True Blue, Campbell and Nick stood just inside the front door, bleakly surveying the mess left behind by the intruder.

Campbell greeted him with a nod. "It was almost certainly the same person who came to the house last night." She looked worried, but not completely frazzled. She was handling all of this better than many people would.

Papers were strewn across the floor and file drawers hung partway open.

"This is just how we found it," Nick said. "Both doors were locked, but that window was unlocked." He pointed. "We went out and looked, and there's a bucket under it they could have stood on to climb in. And then they went out the back door and locked it with the button lock."

"Do you know yet if they took anything?" he asked.

"I think they took the external hard drive from Dad's

desktop," she said. "I wish Dad was here. He could tell us for certain if anything else is gone."

"If your dad was there, they probably wouldn't have broken in," Nick said.

Campbell acknowledged his logic with a wry face.

Nick added, "But he had that computer set up to back up to the external drive every night."

"So they have all his computer files now?" Keith asked.

"Probably." Nick made a face.

"That's not good."

"No, it's not," Campbell said, "but if this is related to Darrin and the Shepherd case, there wouldn't be anything on there about it, right?"

"They might be able to see the searches you've made on the Shepherd case and those other cold cases," Nick said.

Campbell's face paled, and she leaned on the edge of the desk. "So whoever ransacked this place and my house knows exactly what we're looking at."

"Maybe," Nick said.

Keith walked to the back door and stooped to examine it, then checked the window latches. He stepped out the back door and looked over the upended bucket, then went back inside. "Okay, we'll take some prints." He nodded to Officer Mills then focused on Campbell and Nick. "Anything stand out to you?"

"The printer's open, and so are two of the file drawers," Campbell said.

"So, again, records?"

"Yeah. He may have made some copies. There's nothing in the printer now, but…" She let it trail off.

Keith could tell she felt violated. Again. That was natural, considering what she'd been through.

"Did you learn anything about the person who came to the house last night?" she asked.

"Not yet."

She frowned. "Do you think they went to the house first? I mean, the company computer is here, the desktop. Why go after my laptop and Dad's at home once he had a copy of the hard drive from here?"

"I suppose they might have gone to the house first, but you're right, it makes more sense to come here." Keith sighed. "But they probably weren't sure yet what's on that external drive. Or maybe they wanted your laptop, too."

"Yeah, you're the one who's been going around grilling people," Nick said.

Campbell sent him an acid glance.

"And your father's laptop was in your bedroom last night, right?"

"Yeah. That's Dad's home office." Her eyes widened. "They could be over there right now, still looking for it."

"I'll ask for a patrol car to swing by and check the house." He stepped outside for a minute and made the call.

When he reentered the office, Nick was opening his desk drawers with the aid of a pen so he wouldn't mess up any fingerprints. Campbell stood forlornly surveying the mess.

"After Officer Mills takes prints off the computer, file cabinet, and desk, we'll look at the loose papers," he told her. "I take it those weren't left that way last night?"

"No way," Nick said. "But I was out of the office at closing time. I called Campbell at five, so she'd know."

She nodded. "I left a few minutes after we talked. Everything was fine then."

"Okay. The stuff that's been tossed around may give us a more specific idea of what the burglar was looking at. Nick, how's your desk look?"

"I think they rummaged through it, but I don't see that anything's missing. I took my laptop with me when I left yesterday."

"Okay, then it looks like the files were the main interest

other than Bill's computer." Keith bent to examine the scattered papers.

Half an hour later, they hadn't reached any conclusions. Officer Mills got a few good prints off the windowsill and the file cabinet, and a partial off one of the reports lying on the desk.

"I didn't know you could get fingerprints off paper," Campbell said.

"Lots of times you can," Keith told her. "Smooth surfaces are better, like the metal file cabinet, or glass. We'll run this through the system and see what we come up with, but it may take a while."

"Don't you think it's odd that the copier lid was open?" she asked. "I mean, why stop to make copies when you can just steal the originals?"

Keith glanced at the machine and shrugged. "Maybe he didn't make copies. Maybe he just opened it to see if a document was left inside."

"Like...the last thing we copied, so maybe the most important?"

"I'm just speculating."

"Well, he could have put the contents of Bill's computer files on a flash drive, instead of stealing the external," Nick said bitterly. "When we get Bill back, I'm going to suggest he go to cloud storage only."

"You know Dad," Campbell said. "He likes multiple backups. He probably does cloud storage, too, along with his computer files and paper folders."

"Yeah, you're right." Nick sank into his chair.

Campbell turned to Keith. "What about the bucket outside?"

"Do you know where it came from?"

She shook her head.

"I don't recognize it," Nick said. "Maybe he brought it with him."

"Mills, dust that bucket, too, will ya?" Keith said.

The patrol officer nodded and went out the back.

"What do you folks plan to do today?" Keith picked up the evidence bags they'd prepared.

"I was planning to work on the new case, unless Campbell has something I can help with." Nick eyed her in question.

"I'm still looking for Dad," Campbell said. "I have a list of people I want to talk to."

Keith studied her for a moment. "What sort of people, Campbell? You're not going to poke around the Beresford case, are you?"

"Not directly."

"Okay, so, who are you indirectly going to talk to, if I may ask?"

Campbell's cheeks reddened. He'd expected her to bristle if he told her to stay out of it, but he knew she wouldn't give up as long as her father was missing. She didn't seem to have gotten the message yet that he was an ally.

"I thought I'd try to learn more about Alana Shepherd," she said. "It's a cold case, right? So that's okay?"

Keith pursed his lips and considered what to say. He settled a warning gaze on her. "I can't stop you, but you tell me if you find anything connecting that case with Beresford's, or with Bill's disappearance, you hear me?"

"Of course."

He swept his arm around to indicate the entire office. "I don't know if this is a result of your investigations, but it seems logical. I don't want you bringing more trouble on yourself."

"I understand," she said stiffly.

"Hmm. Oh, by the way, I got the full autopsy report on Darrin this morning. Nothing unexpected. As near as we can tell, he was hit with something that was removed from the scene."

"What kind of something?" Nick asked.

Keith hesitated. "It seems to have been something with a square edge."

"A square edge?" Nick frowned. "You mean, like ... a box?"

"No," Campbell said, suddenly sounding confident. "He means like a piece of wood, don't you, Detective?"

"Well, yes."

"There was a chair with a leg missing in that room at Darrin's."

"That's a distinct possibility," Keith said. "If the broken chair leg was lying on it or nearby, the killer may have picked it up as a weapon of opportunity. We're going back to Darrin's house today to see if we find it."

"Good luck," Nick said with a dollop of sarcasm. "I'm sure glad I don't have to sift through all Darrin's junk."

Campbell stepped closer to Keith. "What about the note on my car?"

"No usable fingerprints. Sorry. I really wanted to find out who left that. Oh, and nothing on that cigarette butt either."

"Well, thanks for trying."

"Thanks, Keith." Nick moved toward the door. "I should get going if you don't have anything else for me, Campbell."

"Not right now."

"Right." Nick stepped out.

Keith watched him go with mixed feelings. Was he trying to avoid getting caught up in whatever Campbell decided to do? Nick might not be the best protector for her, but at least when he was with her, she wouldn't be poking around on her own. Her vulnerability did crazy things to Keith's brain. He wanted to stay and make sure no one else threatened her. But that wasn't his job. The best thing he could do to protect Campbell was to find Bill McBride.

11

Alone in the office, Campbell sank into her father's comfortable chair and rested her elbows on the desk, her chin in her hands. Her face still felt warm. Had Keith noticed the slight flush she'd felt creep into her cheeks? She was too old for a crush, but she was starting to focus in on Keith Fuller.

It was crazy. She knew nothing about him, except that he was good at his job and seemed to have a quick mind. And he was stubborn. Persistence was a good thing, but did he have to keep telling her to stay out of it? No way, when Dad was out there somewhere and might need help.

She pushed Keith firmly out of her thoughts and straightened up the few things they hadn't already put away. Knowing she was no closer to finding her father disheartened her, and the break-ins had cost her what might be valuable time. She looked around.

The room was presentable for any clients who might walk in, although that seemed unlikely since she hadn't seen a client face-to-face all week. She pulled out her notebook and skimmed the list of people she'd noted as worth interviewing.

People who knew the exchange student seemed like an extremely long shot.

She grabbed her purse and file folder and hurried to her car. Thinking she might glean more information about Clark Timmons, she drove to the Realtor's office, but the office was closed. That seemed counterproductive to her. Most people were off on Saturday, so she thought it would be a big day for showing houses. But then, maybe Nell Calhoun was out showing houses that very minute.

She pulled into a grocery store's parking lot and got out to purchase a newspaper from a vending machine near the entrance. Combing the ads, she looked for an open house sponsored by Pride & Calhoun today. She felt vindicated when she spotted the boxed ad. The house was on Todd Road. Maybe she had the makings of a private eye, after all.

Plugging in the address on her GPS told her the house was a few miles outside of town. Maybe she should wait on that one. Nell would be busy with the open house, and Campbell wasn't sure she could get any more relevant information from her. She looked at her list of untapped resources. Rachel Shepherd was still on it. Did she live with her parents? Phone books weren't much use in the cell phone era.

Another person she hoped to interview was Parker Stilwell, Alana's boyfriend at the time of her death, along with Alana's former boss.

Campbell leaned back against the upholstered seat. She hated confronting people cold and fishing for information, but this was her dad. She could do this. Her mind raced with questions for the people on the list. If she could find something helpful, it might make all the difference. Dad would be proud if he knew about her efforts, she told herself. Her phone rang, and she reached for it. Nick.

"Hey, what's up?" she asked.

"I got lucky on that new case."

"How lucky?" Campbell asked.

"So lucky I think I can take the rest of the day off and help you."

"You'd do that?"

"I would. You know, I'm worried about Bill, too."

"Okay. What should we do? Do you want me to come back to the office?"

"You don't need to," Nick said. "I made a dental appointment with Dr. Exter."

"You're joking. He's not your regular dentist, is he?"

"No, but they do weekend hours, and they have a cancellation this afternoon. He'll squeeze me in at three-thirty. You can go on with whatever you had planned, and I'll call you when I'm done."

"Terrific. But we don't want to make him mad. What do you hope to accomplish, other than annoying him?"

Nick chuckled. "You never know, do you?"

AT A QUARTER to five Campbell arrived back at the office. Nick had made a fresh pot of coffee, and she poured herself a mugful.

"How did it go? Did you get your teeth cleaned?" she asked.

"It wasn't bad. He got a little tense when I casually mentioned Darrin Beresford's death, so I let it go."

Campbell eyed him soberly. "He wasn't happy when I talked about it, either, and the police have probably been around there since with questions."

"That's what I figured, so after the hygienist cleaned my teeth, I just let him look at them and told him my molar was a little sensitive."

"What'd he say? He's not going to give you a root canal, is he?"

"Nah. Told me to use special toothpaste."

"Okay." There had to be more. Campbell waited expectantly.

"By then, he'd had his hands in my mouth," Nick said.

"So?"

"So, before he left the exam room, he peeled off his gloves and tossed them in the trashcan."

"And you fished them out."

"Very quickly and discreetly."

"What good will those do you?" she asked.

"You can get fingerprints from the inside."

That surprised her. Nick knew some tricks she didn't. She would definitely have to do some reading about fingerprinting. "But…you can't give them to Keith, can you? Isn't that illegal?"

"No. He threw them away. Besides, I'm not going to tell him where I got them."

"Oh, like there are a dozen professionals who wear latex gloves all the time involved in this case."

Nick shrugged.

"Don't you think that if Dr. Exter broke in here or at my house, he'd have worn gloves then, seeing as how he's used to wearing them every day and would have a handy supply of them?"

"Maybe." Nick clicked a couple of buttons on the office phone. "Got the police station on speed dial," he said with a wink at Campbell. He sobered and said into the receiver, "Is Detective Fuller in?" He frowned. "Okay, thanks." He ended the call. "He's gone home for the day."

"Everybody needs some time off."

"Yeah, you're right."

"On the other hand…" Campbell fished in her purse and took out her wallet. Yep, there it was. She pulled out Keith's card and handed it to him. "He gave me his personal number in case I needed anything. He said I could call him day or night."

Nick spread his hands, palms up. "Look at you."

"You call him," she said.

"You sure?"

"It's your big clue."

He took the card and entered the number. "He'll come by your house in an hour," he told Campbell a moment later. "Come on, let's go eat."

She hesitated. Her available cash was dwindling, and she didn't want to dive into what she'd saved, in case she needed it.

"If you don't mind my cooking, I've got food at home."

"Sure." Nick sounded surprised.

Campbell stood before she could change her mind. "Let's go."

He followed her to the house. Although she looked around carefully when she entered, it felt good to be home. Campbell set down her laptop and files on the coffee table.

"Make yourself at home. I'm just going to take a quick look and make sure nobody's paid another unannounced visit."

Everything seemed to be in order, as she'd left it that morning. She peeked into her father's room, under his bed, and in the closet, and repeated the process in the den. After checking the bathroom, she went back out to the kitchen and smiled at Nick. "All clear. Stir fry okay?"

"Whatever you want."

She wasn't the cook her mother had been, but she could get by. A pang for her dad struck her. She had a feeling he hadn't been eating right. It was too much trouble to prepare a meal for himself, so he didn't keep the staples needed to do that on hand.

If and when he came home, she'd pamper him a bit. She'd picked up a few things at the grocery, and she had plans to do some advance meal preparations, so she'd have a few things ready to thaw and serve when he was here. They shouldn't have to come home every evening to scrounge.

If he came home.

Her father owned the house outright, but would it become hers if he didn't come back? She didn't like to think about it. But he had a will; he'd told her that after her mother died, and she'd seen an envelope in his desk in the room where she slept, but she hadn't taken it out to examine. The very thought made her feel lightheaded. When would people make the assumption that he was dead? Not yet!

She grimly turned her attention to the meal she'd promised. Rice and veggies and strips of beef were much easier to deal with than the looming idea that her father might never be found.

The stir fry went together quickly and easily. They were just dishing it up when Keith arrived.

"Want some?" Campbell asked.

"No, thanks. I ate, but I'd take some coffee." He looked at Nick. "What have you got for me?"

Nick disappeared into the living room and came back with the gloves, encased in a plastic bag. "Feel like running some prints on these?"

Keith took the bag and eyed it for a moment. "I can't."

"He threw them away," Nick said.

"Okay. But I have no chain of custody on this evidence."

"That's true." Nick sighed. "I guess you could just ask him to let you take his prints."

"I'm not going to ask you who." Keith set down the bag.

"You don't need to. You know whose they are."

"I have a pretty good idea. But I can't ask Frankfort to run them through the system. Not without some documentation, and we both know I can't give them that."

Nick's mouth twisted. "Okay, can you just run them against the prints you lifted from our office break-in?"

"What, you think a forty-year-old medical professional climbed through that back window in your office?"

"I don't know, but I'd like to." Nick stared at Keith until he looked away.

Campbell's chest tightened. She'd thought she and Nick had

been getting along pretty well with Keith, but this might sever the friendship.

"Okay, listen." Nick sagged into his chair. "What if you just visually compare them?"

"To the break-in prints?" Keith frowned and lifted the bag again.

"And the ones from Darrin Beresford's house." Campbell's heartbeat quickened.

Keith's eyes locked on hers. Campbell held her breath.

"Yeah." Nick gave a little shrug. "And if they look similar, you might be able to get a warrant and take the guy's prints. At least it would tell you we might be on the right track."

Keith sat there a long time without speaking. Campbell made herself take a few bites.

"If you need something stronger, I'm sure I could get him to punch me in the nose or something," Nick said, and Keith scowled at him.

Nick ate half his stir-fry before the detective opened his mouth again.

"Okay," Keith said. "I'll compare them to the ones from your office and Darrin's kitchen." He lifted his coffee mug to his lips.

"And the Alana Shepherd case," Campbell said.

"*What?* You can't seriously—" Keith stared at her over the rim of the mug.

"It may all be connected," she said.

Keith exhaled deeply, shaking his head. He took a gulp of coffee and set down the mug.

"There must be a print record in the file." Campbell reached for her water glass and emptied it, not looking at him.

"Look, Campbell." He got to his feet. "If I lift the prints off these gloves, I may or may not get anything usable. But even if I get good ones, then the lab isn't going to be able to use them, and I'll have ruined what's there."

"So only use one hand," Nick said.

Keith made a noise halfway between a snort and a groan and headed for the door, but he took the bag with him. Campbell wanted to rush after him, but what could she say? She let him go.

When the door closed, she sat down beside Nick.

"Are you asking him to do something illegal?"

"No," Nick said, "but I can see his point of view. Without good, hard evidence, he can't get a warrant on Exter. But if he uses *this* evidence, it's something he didn't get in the proper way."

"So what you did *is* illegal."

"No. But it's inadmissible."

She frowned. "Then why did you ask him to even look at them?"

"Like I told him, if Keith thinks they look similar to ones he got from a crime scene, he'll know Exter's in this deep, and that will keep him digging until he gets something that *is* admissible. Good thinking, by the way, on having him compare them to the prints from Darrin's house and Alana's file."

Campbell picked up her fork and put it down. "I don't know."

"Anyhow, if Exter's prints don't match up with any of those files, maybe somebody else's will."

"Whose?"

"That's what we have to find out, right?" Nick said.

She nodded slowly.

"Got any more coffee?" He looked around.

"Yeah. I'll get it." She picked up his mug and took it to the counter for a refill.

Nick sat back in his chair. "Good eats."

"Thanks."

"You know how my afternoon went," he said. "I collected all the evidence Lyman needs for his court case. Unbelievable how fast it came together this time. That's money in the bank."

"Good job." She handed him the coffee. "Dad will be pleased."

"Yeah." He blew on the surface of the liquid and took a sip. "Then I had my teeth cleaned, wasted the dentist's time, and lifted a pair of his gloves. How did you make out?"

Campbell sat down and pushed her plate aside. "Well, I did talk to Alana's sister. She lives with her boyfriend in Aurora, which was only a twenty-minute drive. But she didn't seem to know much about what's been going on down here. I couldn't get anything helpful out of her except that she thinks Clark Timmons killed Alana. Oh, and I did ask if Dr. Exter was her dentist."

"Yeah?"

"She said she and Alana both went to the same dentist her parents had used for years—not Paul Exter."

"Okay."

"Maybe I should have told Keith that." She frowned. "Anyway, I still don't know if she's in some kind of trouble. Keith was going to find out, but I forgot to ask if he'd checked to see if she has a record."

"Probably not the best time to ask him for another favor," Nick said.

"Right."

"So, what next?"

Campbell hesitated. "I'm thinking Parker Stillwell."

"Who's he again?"

"Alana Shepherd's boyfriend at the time of her death."

"Oh, yeah. I thought he had an alibi."

"He did, but I'd like to get his input. He wasn't considered a suspect in her murder, but you know, maybe it's time someone took another look at his alibi."

"You think the police might have missed something?"

"Stranger things have happened. I'd also like to go back to where Dad's car was found."

"There's nothing there," Nick said.

"I know, but...it was the last place we know Dad was alive."

"No, we don't." Nick shook his head slowly. "Darrin's house is the last place. His car could have been moved."

She ducked her head for a moment then looked up at him. "Listen, I don't even like to think about this, but it's been five days. If someone did ... kill my dad"—She swallowed the painful lump in her throat—"and then moved his car ... Well, don't you think they'd have put him in the car and moved him that way? I mean, why put potential evidence into your own vehicle when you're going to be taking the victim's car somewhere else anyway?"

"I think Bill left the car there." Nick eyed her steadily. "Maybe he parked it and walked over to Clark Timmons's house."

"Then where is he? Nell Calhoun went through that house the next morning, and she didn't see anything. The police have thoroughly searched it since."

Nick drank from his mug, and she felt as if he was ignoring her. Her phone rang inside her purse, and she jumped up to get it from the counter.

"Hello," said a hesitant female voice. "This is Karen Wells. My cousin said a Ms. McBride wanted to talk to me about the exchange student who disappeared in Murray when I was in high school."

"Oh, right." Campbell mentally shifted gears. "Thank you so much for calling. I'm Campbell McBride, and I'm the one who talked to your cousin at the restaurant."

Nick looked at her and raised his eyebrows.

"Just a minute, Karen," Campbell said. "I need to speak to someone. Can you hold on?" With Karen's assent, she muted her phone. "It's the woman who knew the exchange student."

"Okay," Nick said. "I'll shove off." He was already halfway to the door.

"Can you lock the door on your way out?" Campbell called after him.

Glad to be free of the distraction, she returned her attention to the phone call. "Okay, Karen, sorry about that. I'm all set."

"What did you want to know?" Karen asked.

From her online searches, Campbell had learned the student, Marni Schliemann, was a native of Austria and had attended the local high school for most of a school year about six years previously. The sixteen-year-old girl had disappeared in March. Her parents had flown over from Europe and stayed more than a month while authorities searched for Marni, but she'd never been found.

"Just tell me what you remember about Marni, if you don't mind," Campbell said.

"It was a long time ago, but I'll try. She was in my homeroom, and we had a couple of classes together. Biology, I think, and history."

"What did you think of her? Did you like her?"

Karen hesitated. "Sure. I mean, she was cute—not beautiful, but the boys seemed to like her. The accent, you know? She was bubbly, and she was going to try out for a spring play. I remember that because I was trying out, too, and she asked me to help her with some of the lines and American idioms. But then ... then she vanished before the auditions."

"Tell me about that," Campbell said. "When she left."

"Well, I didn't think she ran away. I mean, who cuts out the day before a big thing like that? And in a foreign country. If she just wanted to see America, she'd have waited until the school year ended, right? And she would have told her friends. I doubt she'd have gone off alone."

"Would she have gone off with someone else?"

"You mean a guy?" Karen asked. "No one else was missing from our school, and so far as I know, she didn't have any attachments outside school."

"Did she go out with boys?"

"She was at all the school events: dances, sports events, parties. But, like I said, if she dated anyone outside of school, I wouldn't know. Although …"

"Yes?" Campbell prompted.

"I almost think she went out with someone from another school. Met him at a ballgame or something. But it couldn't have been a big deal, right? She'd have brought him to our dances and stuff. I don't think it lasted long."

"Okay. Did you know the family who hosted her?" Campbell scrolled through her notes. "The Brownes."

"A little. They'd signed up with an exchange program. They wanted their daughter to be able to go to Austria the next year and have the same experience. Only after Marni disappeared, they wouldn't let her go."

"That's too bad," Campbell said. "What was her name?"

"Nikki Browne."

"Does she still live around here?"

"No, she got married, I think. I'm not sure where she is now, but her parents are still in town. They're at the same house they had then—on the Poor Farm Road. They had a boy, too. He was younger than me."

Campbell took down as much information as she could about the family who'd hosted the exchange student.

"It was so sad," Karen said. "Her parents came over here after she disappeared. They didn't speak English very well, and they were all torn up, of course. They finally had to go home without her. I think they ran out of money and couldn't stay any longer. Our school had a fundraiser to help pay their expenses during the search. I remember that. But everything has a limit, you know?"

"Yeah. So tragic. Do you remember who some of her teachers were?"

"We were in Mrs. Henner's homeroom, and she was in my

biology class with Mr. Shaw. History ... hmm, I think I had Ms. Turner that year."

"That's a big help. Listen, would you mind giving me your phone number in case I think of other things to ask?"

"Sure." Karen also gave her home address and email, though she probably couldn't add much more to Campbell's understanding of the case. No one knew if a crime had been committed, though most people seemed to suspect the girl had been abducted.

"Do you know if the police are still looking into it?" Karen asked.

"I'm not sure."

"Why are you?"

Campbell chose her words carefully. "It came up as I was looking into another case. I just thought I'd find out all I could about other past crimes in the area."

"If anything can be done to find out what happened to her, I know there are a ton of people who'd like to hear it."

"Well, we don't have anything definitive at this point," Campbell said. "But if we do learn anything solid, you can be sure it will be on the local news."

"I'll be watching."

After a moment's hesitation, Campbell added, "And if someone you know wants to talk to us, you can steer them to us here at True Blue Investigations."

12

K eith was supposed to have Sunday off, but the case
tugged at him. He caught the early service at his church
and went back to the evidence, a restlessness pulling him to the
police station. The way Nick and Campbell had ambushed him
with the latex gloves last night still stung. He had a hard time
believing a respected dentist who'd treated him for years was
guilty of murder. But it was worth a look—on his own time.
Probably it would come to nothing.

With extreme care, he worked on one of the gloves. He
checked the little finger first and determined which side the
prints would be on. Systematically he processed the others and
lifted each fingerprint. Only two were clear enough to compare
to anything else, but he set to work. Nothing was conclusive, so
what little he had was useless. After some hesitation, he tackled
the second glove.

An hour later he headed out to have another chat with one
of his prime suspects. He wasn't sure if it would pan out, but he
had a good feeling about this one. He'd managed to get his
superior on board. When the detective sergeant wavered and

reminded him that it was Sunday, Keith had stressed the urgency of the Beresford case, citing Bill McBride's potential danger.

"McBride's dead," the sergeant had said.

"We don't know that. And I can't give up until we do."

The sergeant thought for a moment. "You think he could have left voluntarily?"

"No way. I know Bill, and he's a straight shooter. He wouldn't do that to his daughter."

"All right, go bring Exter in. But you can't arrest him on what you've got."

"I know, but I can make him talk to me," Keith said.

"No, you can *try* to make him talk to you."

Keith knew he was right, but he needed to solve this case. Since he'd met Campbell and seen her press on in spite of the threats she'd encountered, it had become imperative.

Late that afternoon, he left the station tired but still keyed up. He drove by the office at True Blue and saw Campbell's and Nick's vehicles parked out front. Good. He could update them both. Maybe Campbell would feel he was making progress after all.

He wished True Blue wasn't so closely involved in his case, but he couldn't stop them, and they *had* uncovered a few pertinent leads. He figured the best way to keep a tight rein on those two was to keep them close to the investigation.

Campbell was just hanging up the phone on Bill's desk when he walked in, and she jumped to her feet.

"Keith! How can I help you?" She seemed shocked to see him again.

He smiled and gave Nick a nod. "Just wanted to touch base on those gloves." He pulled a chair over and sat across the desk from Campbell, angled so he could see Nick as well. "I took a hard look at them."

Campbell drew in a quick breath. "Did you find anything?"

"I did get a couple of usable prints from them. I can't tell if they match any of the prints from your break-ins, but one of them seems to match one we found over at Beresford's."

"Paul Exter was at Darrin's that night," Campbell said.

Nick's jaw dropped. "Wow. Do you really think he could be the one who whacked Darrin?"

"Well, I can't be a hundred percent sure. And I ended up using both gloves, but it's okay. Because if we find probable cause, we'll fingerprint Exter at the station. We won't need the gloves for the lab, and we know he wasn't committing a crime while he was wearing those particular gloves."

Campbell laughed. "Unless he stole Nick's gold teeth."

"Very funny," Nick said.

"Anyway, I took my dentist in for questioning." Keith grimaced. "It was almost as painful as a root canal."

"Is he talking?" Campbell asked.

"He lawyered up first thing, which is why I'm not over at the station interviewing him." Keith sighed. "I'm not through with him, but I need to do some more research. Eventually I hope we'll find solid proof that he killed Darrin. I'm pretty sure the fingerprint on Darrin's doorknob is a match for one from Exter's gloves."

"But if you have to wait, his family and staff are probably getting rid of evidence," Nick said.

Keith suppressed a shudder. "Look, we're working on it. Stay away from this thing for a day or two, okay?" He eyed Campbell closely.

"I guess I should tell you, I went to see Parker Stillwell this afternoon." She watched him guiltily from beneath lowered lashes.

Keith's gut tightened. She was at it again, and a jump ahead of him. "At the campground he runs over near the lake?"

"Yeah."

"What on earth does he have to do with this?"

"By this, you mean Darrin Beresford's death? Nothing that I know of." Campbell got up and walked over to the coffeemaker. "Would you like some?"

"No, thanks."

She poured herself a mugful. "Parker was polite but not helpful. He assured me everything in the police file concerning his whereabouts at the time Alana was killed is the solid truth. He also said he's glad someone's looking at the case again. He'd heard Clark Timmons was in town, and he wondered if that was why you were digging into it."

Keith opened his mouth to object.

"I didn't give him anything, though," she said quickly. "Just told him someone had raised a question or two, and you were giving it a second look."

"You're trying to connect Beresford's death to the Shepherd murder, aren't you?" Keith said.

"Aren't you?" she asked.

"Well, the prints from the gloves and Beresford's house didn't match anything in that file."

"So you did check." She came back to the desk with her mug of black coffee and sat down.

"Once we officially establish a link between Exter and the Beresford case, I'll have more freedom in that direction. Give it a rest, Campbell," Keith said gently. "You'll have the whole town mad at you and your dad's agency."

She raised her chin. "Some people are glad we're looking into it."

"Oh yeah?" Keith tried to pin her with his gaze, but she calmly sipped her coffee. "Like who? Not Alana Shepherd's parents, because they called me yesterday to complain about you snooping around and digging up painful memories."

"Don't they want you to find her killer?" Campbell asked.

"That's right, me. The police. Roger Shepherd seemed to think you'd muck things up. Case in point, I tried to contact

Clark Timmons, the prime suspect in that murder, today and couldn't get hold of him. He hasn't shown up again at the farmhouse, and he may have left the area again."

"That's not our fault," Campbell said. "And Roger was very nice when he talked to me."

"Well, I wanted you to know we're looking hard at Dr. Exter for Darrin's murder."

"But not our break-in or Bill's disappearance," Nick put in.

"We didn't find any prints from the break-ins here and at Bill's house other than his own and you two's."

"Okay." Nick's voice was tight.

Keith assumed he was taking the office intrusion personally. He was in charge while Bill was out of sight—though you wouldn't know it from a look at Campbell's activity.

"Well, I guess if you can only solve one of those crimes, I'd rather it was Dad's whereabouts." She gazed at him over the rim of her mug with those big green eyes. "And then the homicide. That's more important than the break-ins."

Keith bit back the harsh reply. If she would just stay out of the way, he might be able to solve them all. But if he said that, she'd point to the results she'd come up with and the fact that he didn't have a single clue on Bill's disappearance.

"Look, we don't want to cause you any trouble or make your job harder." Nick shot Campbell a glance that may have been a plea or a warning.

"I know," Keith said. "You're good at what you do, Nick, and Campbell's showing some aptitude for investigation, too. I'm sorry. It's just getting a little tense at the station. The chief's wife and Wanda Shepherd are cousins, and they're close."

"I'm sorry." Campbell's placid expression morphed to regretful concern. "We'll wait until we hear from you about Exter and all that."

"Couldn't you get his prints some other way that's admissible?" Nick asked.

"Not without arresting him," Keith said.

"What about getting him to touch something in the police station and taking them off that?"

"His lawyer told him while I stood right there not to touch anything."

Nick sighed. "I guess you tried."

"Well, Nick and I have some new things we're working on anyway, don't we, Nick?" Campbell gave him a brisk smile.

"Yeah, we do," Nick said.

Keith frowned. "Like Parker Stilwell."

"I did talk to him, but like I said, he wasn't much help." She shrugged. "Said he was in New York when Alana was murdered."

"That's true. Our department checked up on his alibi, and it's solid."

Campbell sighed and leaned back in her chair.

Keith checked his watch. He'd planned one more thing for tomorrow, when he was officially on duty, but he could do it on his own time. It might be smarter to do it tonight, rather than wait. In fact, if he did it as a casual drive-by, he might be able to keep an eye on Campbell at the same time. He probably shouldn't, but something told him the investigation was more secure if he knew where she was.

"Look," he said, searching her face. "I thought I'd make a run out to the lake."

Her eyes widened. "Are you going to see Parker Stilwell?"

"No." He hesitated, then took the plunge. "When Clark Timmons was engaged to Alana Shepherd, they bought a cottage together on this side of the lake, but north of the Kenlake resort. He still owns it. When she died, it went into his name only. They'd signed some kind of agreement to that effect."

"Wait a sec," Nick said. "Didn't they break up quite a while before she was killed?"

"Yeah. Over two years earlier."

"So, why didn't they change that?" Campbell asked. "I mean, if I broke up with my fiancé, I wouldn't want to go on owning property with him."

Keith said, "From what I gather, it seems they both loved the spot, and neither wanted to give it up. So they had a lawyer draw up a document saying that if either of them decided to sell, they would offer the other first refusal, and if one of them died, the other would own the property outright."

Campbell frowned. "That's kind of weird."

"It's unusual. And, by the way, I've spoken to the lawyer about it. He said when he drafted the document, they seemed civil with each other, but they were tired of discussing it and wanted to settle things. They made it so Alana could use the cottage every year from February through July, and Clark used it August through January. That way they both got some hot weather and some balmy weather."

"Huh." Campbell drew a notepad closer and jotted something down.

"So, anyway, I'm going to drive by the cottage just in case Timmons is out there. I don't suppose you'd like to go along, Campbell?"

She looked up, her lips parted slightly and her eyes huge. "Sure. You mean it?"

At once, Keith knew he was getting too deeply involved. His slamming pulse told him that. Still, she wasn't a suspect in any of the crimes he was investigating.

"Do you want me to take my own car?" she asked.

"Uh, that might be good." It wasn't the way he'd pictured it, but her suggestion was probably wise. If he ended up being delayed for whatever reason, or if he found cause to go on to another spot afterward, she could just go home. "Yeah, follow me."

CAMPBELL PULLED her Fusion up behind Keith's vehicle in the parking lot of a country store and bait shop beside Route 68. Keith got out and walked over to her driver's side window.

"It's only another mile or so," he said. "Do you want to ride with me from here?"

She put the window up and turned off the ignition. Grabbing her phone, she slid it in one pocket, her keys in another. She hadn't expected this, but it made sense. They'd be going off on a gravel camp road, and it would no doubt be easier and draw less attention if they went in one vehicle.

As soon as she had her seatbelt buckled, he pulled out. She took a quick look over her shoulder. The back seat held a lightweight jacket, a clipboard, and a Bible. It was Sunday. She'd meant to visit her dad's church, but when Nick called suggesting they meet to go over all their notes, she'd gone to the office instead. She watched Keith's sober profile for a few seconds but said nothing.

A few hundred yards past the store, he nodded toward a dirt road they were passing. "My folks have a cottage down there."

"Really? That's so cool." She immediately felt like a teenager, except that her slang was definitely out of date.

"Yeah, it's a nice location on a point. They've had it winterized. When I was a kid it was for summers only."

"So they live there all the time now?"

"Yeah. Sold me the old house in town at a rock-bottom price. It's nothing fancy, but it gives me a base."

Campbell nodded, thinking of her father's own modest two-bedroom ranch. Keith turned off the pavement, and they plunged into a wooded lane. Oaks and hickories hovered over the narrow road. A couple of branches wended off the main drive, and soon she could see the sparkle of water beyond the foliage.

The Tennessee River had been widened here a half century or more ago. The Tennessee Valley Authority had built dams at the top of the new Kentucky Lake, in the town called Grand River. The same was true of the Cumberland River, a few miles away. Both elongated lakes enclosed the Land Between the Lakes.

Campbell was always sad when she thought about the people —and entire towns—who'd been moved out of the area when the project was begun. But overall, she supposed it was good for Kentucky and the surrounding states. It not only increased the production of electric power, but it eased barge transportation and brought many tourists to the area for camping, boating, fishing, and hiking.

"His cottage is right up there." Keith nodded ahead, and she leaned forward to see between the trees. "I touched base with the Realtor. She says he's not staying at the farmhouse anymore, and he's cleared everything out that he wants to keep. If he's not out here, he's probably gone back to Tennessee."

"Is that where he lives now?"

"Yes, over near Knoxville."

Soon he stopped in front of a rustic, board-sided building with a no-frills back entry. She supposed it had a screened porch facing the lake. A dusty, green pickup sat in the short driveway, and her pulse accelerated.

"That looks like the truck that was at his house the last time I went there," she said.

Keith squinted at the rear license plate. "It's Clark's. So he didn't leave the area after all."

He smiled at her, and she returned it. They both climbed out.

"Stay behind me, okay?" he said.

"No problem." After her last encounter with Timmons, Campbell had no desire to confront him. She would gladly let the detective handle that.

As they approached the cottage Keith looked all around.

Instead of knocking on the back door, he took a path that led around the building. He stood at the corner for a moment, looking down toward the shore, where a wooden dock stuck out into the lake. Campbell peered around him, but she didn't see anyone down there. Off shore several hundred yards, a motorboat floated peacefully while two fishermen plied their lines.

Keith glanced at her and jerked his head, indicating that she should follow him. They went back to the rear door, and he positioned her behind him and to the side before he knocked firmly. After waiting a few seconds, he knocked again.

"Clark Timmons, open the door. Police."

A dull thud came from inside. Keith held his ground, and a few seconds later the door opened a few inches. Clark glared out at them.

"Hello, Clark. I'm Detective Fuller," Keith said. "We met the other day. I'd like to ask you a few more questions."

Clark looked past him, and his gaze locked on Campbell. "What's *she* doing here?"

"She's hoping to learn something about her father." Keith didn't even glance at her but kept his attention on Clark.

"She told me he was missing," Clark said grudgingly.

"Yes. His car was found near your farm. Do you mind if I take a look around here?"

"I didn't have anything to do with that."

"Okay. So, can I rule you out?"

Clark hesitated, and Campbell feared he'd demand Keith get a warrant. The two men kept staring at each other, but after a few tense seconds, Clark relaxed his posture and stepped aside.

"All right. Not her, though." He shot a glare at Campbell.

In that moment, she believed he was capable of killing Alana Shepherd. She pulled in a breath that didn't seem to reach her lungs.

Keith turned and arched his eyebrows at her. "You wait here, Ms. McBride."

Although it rankled, she nodded, and Keith crossed the threshold. She felt unwanted and abandoned, but at least there would be walls between her and the suspected murderer. Clark closed the door in her face.

13

The kitchen, dining, and living areas were sparsely furnished with old pieces, probably castoffs from the elder Timmonses' home. A stone fireplace nestled in one side wall. Cardboard cartons were stacked against one wall and all but obscured the dining table.

"Stuff from the farmhouse?" Keith asked.

Clark nodded. "The agent said to clear it out so I don't have to come back if it sells. I stored some things. I brought this stuff out here so I could sort through it. A lot of it will probably end up in the trash." As he spoke, he fingered the handle of an old aluminum saucepan, and Keith wondered if he was remembering his mother cooking with it in the old house.

A cursory round of the downstairs showed Keith one bedroom where the bed was made up but rumpled. The small bathroom held fixtures at least fifty years old. With Clark's permission, he mounted the stairs and checked the loft sleeping area. When he came down, Clark opened the door to the screened porch facing the lake without being asked, and Keith stepped out onto it.

"Nice view." He gazed at the grayish water below. Today the

lake was mostly flat, but a slight breeze caused ripples. Off to the south he could see a snag sticking up about ten yards offshore. They were too far above the Eggner's Ferry Bridge for him to see it, since wooded undulations of the shore obscured the view.

"Anything under the house?" he asked.

"No cellar. It's open under the porch. You can take a look if you want." Clark was calm now, and his voice held only a slight edge of resentment.

"I will," Keith said. "And I saw a shed."

Clark nodded. "It's for tools, and I've got some firewood stacked. I'll show you." He pulled a keyring from his pocket.

They went out through the porch door and down some steps. Keith ducked in under the opening at the end of the porch and looked around. Besides a couple of old inner tubes, nothing was stored there.

When they walked up the path toward the driveway and the shed, Campbell was standing at the corner of the house watching them, her forehead wrinkled like a washboard. Keith flicked a quick smile, and she fell in behind him as he followed Clark to the door of the shed. Had he made a huge mistake in bringing her along? Still, Clark was cooperating. When he'd removed the padlock, Keith did a quick but thorough inspection of the small building.

Nothing suspicious there, but he hadn't expected anything.

"So, are we done?" Clark asked as he emerged.

"I'd like to have some officers go over the farmhouse, too," Keith said.

"You already looked at it."

"I know, but we want to be thorough and not ever have to go back there. I know you've listed the place for sale, so I don't think we'll find anything pertinent to this case. But it would let us tick off another box, and you could rest assured that we weren't wondering."

Clark frowned at him for a long moment. "I'll bet a judge wouldn't give you a warrant," he said at last. "You've got nothing to make you think you should look there."

"I could simply make an appointment with Ms. Calhoun and ask her to show me around the house."

Clark sighed and shook his head. "When will you people leave me alone?"

"We have left you alone, for the last three years."

"Only because I left Kentucky."

Keith considered how to get to the next place he wanted to be with Clark. He looked over at Campbell, who had stationed herself a couple of yards down the path.

"Ms. McBride's house was broken into Friday night, and her father's office was ransacked."

"So?" Clark blinked. "Oh, wait, I get it. You think I did that."

"I'm not saying that, but I wouldn't mind if you told me where you were around one a.m. Saturday."

"I was here, of course."

"Alone, I suppose."

"No, all my friends were here with me." Clark's lips twisted. "Of course I was alone. And there's no way you can say otherwise."

Keith inhaled slowly and looked around. To his relief, Campbell kept still. He turned back to Clark. "Listen, you're right. At this point, we have nothing pointing to you so far as those break-ins go, or Bill McBride's disappearance. But can we talk about Alana for a few minutes? I'd like your take on things."

"Oh, we're back to that."

"You're not under any obligation," Keith said. "I wasn't on the original investigation, but I'd like to hear it from you how things were at that time. And before she died. For instance, how it was when you bought this cottage together."

Clark snapped the padlock into place on the shed door and shoved his keys in his pocket. "We wanted a place together. Her family loved the lake, but they didn't have a camp out here. We figured after we got married, both our families would visit us here. It came up for sale at a good price, and it seemed like a good investment."

"Did you spend a lot of time here together?" Keith asked.

"Not as much as I'd have liked."

"How long did you own it before you broke up?"

"It was about eight months after we signed the deed. But we were still making payments. I thought maybe Alana would sell to me, but she wanted to keep making half the payments. She had a decent job."

"She was Bella Chase's personal assistant," Campbell said.

Clark shot her a dark glance. "Yeah. We both wanted to keep the place, and we'd chipped in halves on the down payment, so we worked out a way that we could both use it and enjoy it."

"I've seen the contract," Keith said quickly, hoping Campbell wouldn't jump in. Clark still seemed hostile toward her, but so far he was cooperating. Keith didn't want to ruin that.

"Look, I didn't do anything to Alana. I loved her." Clark looked at Campbell and raised his chin half an inch. "I didn't do anything to your father, either. I don't know him. As far as I know, I've never even seen him."

"I didn't mean to imply that you did," Campbell said stiffly.

"Then why are you snooping around here and at the farm?"

"I'm desperate to find my dad." Tears glistened in her eyes. "We found out Darrin Beresford saw you out the window of the Barn Owl Diner, and he called my father. We wondered if he and my dad were talking about you."

"How should I know?"

"You're right." Campbell held up both hands, palm out. "I was grasping at straws, hoping. Just hoping."

"Well, I don't know anything about it." Clark turned back to Keith. "If Darrin thought he knew something about me, I don't have a clue what it was."

Keith nodded. "I told you earlier that he'd called the police station. All he said was that he'd seen you in Murray. But the police didn't do anything that night. They didn't have a reason to come looking for you. You have a right to be here, Clark."

"Can you just leave me alone?" He sighed.

"The best way for that to happen is to tell me anything that might shed light on Alana's death. If Bill McBride thought you were still a suspect, that might help us find out what happened to him."

Clark said nothing.

"I mean," Keith went on, "if you truly weren't involved in Alana's death…"

"There's nothing." Clark ran a hand through his hair and looked up at the sky for a moment. The sun was setting and shadows stretched out beneath the oak trees. "I haven't been back here much. Hannah and I came a couple of times after we got married. But it was hard after Alana died. It was all mine then, but honestly, the memories kept me away."

"What happened when you heard Alana had died?"

"You mean about the cottage? Alana … was killed … during her half of the year to use this place. The lawyer gave me the papers, and I signed them, but it was months before I could make myself come out here. I let her folks come and take her clothes and personal stuff, but there were still a few things."

"What kind of things?" Keith asked.

"Books, a few pictures. A lamp she bought for the bedroom." Clark exhaled heavily. "I hadn't been out here since right after I was arrested and held for a while. Hannah had left me, and then we got divorced. I never came back here again until the day before yesterday."

"You're staying here now?" Keith had seen a duffel and a few clothes in the downstairs bedroom, but he wanted to hear it from Clark.

"Yeah, the Realtor said it would be easier to show the old house if I wasn't living there."

"Are you going to sell this place, too?" Campbell asked.

"I haven't decided. The value's gone up."

She nodded. "Lake property must go higher every year."

"It does. But I'm not sure I'm ready to part with it yet."

Keith said softly, "Would it be too painful to let me take another look inside? I know I was in there before, but that was mostly to confirm that nobody else was here. I didn't look closely at any of the things inside."

"I suppose." Clark bit his lower lip. "I can tell you what was hers." He looked at Campbell, and his eyes narrowed. "You might as well come in, too, but it's got nothing to do with your father. And I didn't break into your house."

"Okay," she said. "Thank you for telling me."

They followed him in through the back door, and he opened the kitchen cupboard doors.

"She'd gotten a set of dishes, and her mother took them, but some of those mugs were hers." He waved toward a shelf. "And some of the pans and things."

Keith quickly but thoroughly examined the dishes and cookware, and Clark led them into the living room. He pointed to the mantelpiece.

"That clock was hers, and the elephant statue. I remember she got that at a yard sale. She just liked it. I'm not sure why Wanda didn't take it. Maybe she didn't know Alana had bought it." He walked over and picked up the six-inch-tall wooden elephant and turned it over in his hands. After a moment, he replaced it and turned toward the built-in bookcase. "Most of these books were hers. She read a lot."

While Keith examined the clock and knickknacks, Campbell scanned the spines of the books, apparently trying to stay out of Clark's way. Keith appreciated that. He stepped over beside her and saw that a lot were mass-market paperbacks—fat romances. Beach reads. Some were older hardcovers. One book had no writing on the spine, and Campbell reached out a finger to touch it, shooting a glance toward Clark.

"May I?"

Clark nodded curtly.

Campbell pulled out the volume and opened the cover. Inside were handwritten pages. The script filled two-thirds of the book. The latest entries were dated the year Alana died.

"This looks like a journal, Keith," she said softly.

"Alana's diary? I didn't know it was there." Clark strode toward her.

Reluctantly, Campbell placed it in his hands. Keith knew Clark might not give them another chance to look at it. He wished Campbell had read the last entry or two before announcing its existence.

"I know this is a lot to ask," Keith said quietly. "But would you allow me to borrow that journal?"

Clark jerked his face toward him in alarm.

"It might have evidence," Keith said. "From what little I saw, it was written after you two split up, or at least some of it was. The police didn't have this when they investigated. It could tell us something about her relationships with other people back then."

"I'd like to know what's in it." Clark's lower lip trembled.

"Of course," Keith said. "But if it sheds light on the events leading up to her murder, it could be invaluable to the investigation. If she was having problems with someone else, it might weigh in your favor."

"Could you return it to him after you read it?" Campbell asked.

"I guess that would depend on what we found," Keith said. "But, Clark, I would tell you if we did find something significant. And eventually it would be returned to you."

Clark looked down at the volume he held tenuously in his hands. "It should probably go to her folks."

"If you want, but she left this cottage to you, and I assume that included the contents."

"I guess," Clark said.

Keith nodded. "But you graciously allowed her parents to come and take away some of her personal things."

Tears misted Clark's eyes. "I couldn't deal with it. Seeing her clothes, her makeup. It was just too hard." His voice cracked.

Campbell reached toward him as if she wanted to offer comfort, but she let her hand drop and kept her distance.

"I understand," Keith said. "And they probably just missed the journal. If there's nothing pertinent to the case, we'll bring it back quickly."

"What if there is?"

"Then I would enter it into evidence, and it would be marked to be returned to you when it's no longer needed."

He could tell from the way Campbell's eyes flicked back and forth that her mind was racing. She was always thinking, that one.

ON THE SHORT ride back to where they'd left her car, Campbell skimmed the diary entries from the back. She had no doubt this was Alana's last journal, as the final entry was made less than a week before she was killed, and a dozen blank pages were left in at the end of the book.

"Hmm, she wasn't happy at work, that's for sure," she murmured.

"Anything specific?" Keith asked.

"She thought Bella had it in for her, for some reason, but Alana insists it wasn't her fault and it wasn't fair."

"Hmm. Maybe some of her coworkers could shed some light

on that. It's possible something happened at the store that upset the boss."

Campbell's mind raced. She wondered if Keith could make a photocopy of the pages for evidence, or give Clark copies if they needed to keep the original. She flipped back a few pages to an entry a month earlier. Alana had moved out to the cottage temporarily and was driving into town from there each morning for work, but there didn't seem to be anything relevant there.

They were nearly to the country store. She turned back a clump of pages. The entries were short, and Alana seemed to have skipped weeks at a time. Some mental calculations told Campbell they were written halfheartedly during the time after the breakup. She delved farther toward the front of the book as Keith turned into the parking lot and pulled up next to her car.

"I don't suppose you'd let me take this?" she asked. "I could type it up for you."

"It's tempting, but no." Keith turned off the motor and shifted to face her. "As I said, it could be evidence."

"I know." She scanned one last page and stopped cold. "Hey, what does this mean? 'We went to the movies. Clark stopped on the way to leave something at the shelter.'" She arched her eyebrows at Keith.

"Shelter? Let me see." He took the book from her and scowled over the place where she pointed. "Hmm. What do you make of it?"

"Maybe he volunteered at the Humane Society," she said. "Or is there a homeless shelter in town, or a battered women's shelter?"

"Yeah, there is now, but it's fairly new. I'm not sure it was up and running then."

"What else could it mean?"

Keith's brow furrowed, but before he could respond his cell

phone rang, and he fished it out of a pocket. "It's the station. I've got to get back."

"Are you sure you won't let me take the diary?"

"Campbell, I can't." He truly looked regretful.

"Can I just take a picture of that page, so I can puzzle over it tonight?"

He hesitated then said, "Okay, but just that one."

"Thanks." She quickly focused her phone's camera and snapped the picture. "And you'll call me if you come up with anything pertinent to Dad's case?"

"I will. And just so you know, you've really gotten me thinking about past crimes. Darrin's death was not accidental. If Exter killed him, he had to have a motive. I'll take a hard look at what he was doing at the time of those cold cases you turned up. There could be something there."

Campbell tried to picture the dentist looming over Darrin's body. Not entirely unrealistic. But still … "You know, when Clark shut the door in my face, I sort of felt like maybe he did kill Alana. But after talking to him, I'm not so sure. And if he didn't do it, he sure got the short end of the stick. He talks like everyone here hates him."

"I'd say his life was pretty much ruined by her death and his arrest."

"And with no resolution." She held out the diary. "Well, thanks for taking me along, and for letting me have a peek at that."

She got into her car. Keith was out of the parking lot and off down Route 68 before she had her seatbelt fastened. With a sigh, she turned on her headlights and set off for Murray.

At home, she wearily let herself in and walked through the house, doing the security check that was becoming habit. When she checked her father's room, her gaze fell on his nightstand, and she walked over to it. His Bible sat on top, where it had ever since she'd arrived.

Tears welled in her eyes. She sat down on the bed and touched the leather cover with her fingertips. Somewhere she had a Bible, too, but she hadn't bothered to unpack it. She hadn't attended a church service since she'd been here at Christmas and gone with her dad to a special program. How had she slipped so far from the heritage her parents had taught her?

On a lower shelf of the stand were two albums she recognized. Family photos. She picked them up and carried them to the kitchen. While she waited for her frozen dinner to heat, she flipped open the first one and smiled. The pictures started with her parents' wedding and chronicled her arrival and first five years.

The tears flowed freely as she perused the photos of her mom and dad—so young! Her own likeness greeted her on nearly every page. She paused at the one of her father in his police uniform, carrying her in his arms. He was a handsome man, and she had to admit she was a photogenic child. Her mother had captioned each picture with the subject and date taken.

One view showed her father and his brother Richard, in his navy uniform, with their arms around each other. She'd reached out to Uncle Rick and other family members during those first few days to see if Bill had contacted any of them. They were widely dispersed, none of them in western Kentucky, but she'd had phone messages and texts almost daily from extended family, and she usually responded briefly.

She should call her uncle again and update him on her fruitless attempts to find her father. Campbell's stomach clenched. Was she slowly coming to believe she'd never see her dad again? She dreaded telling his family. And she should tell his friend Mart Brady she'd made no progress all week.

The microwave oven's bell rang, and she got her meal, silverware, and a glass of water. She settled in at the table and opened the second album. It picked up where the first one left off. The photos weren't quite as numerous, but every one of her birthdays was represented, and several camping trips and other family times. Her high school graduation merited several pictures, and then they stopped. She swallowed hard.

There were a few blank pages at the end of the album, but Dad hadn't added to it since her mother died.

Campbell supposed that was partly her fault. Sending him photos of herself was something she did rarely, and then it was a quick snap on her cell phone. She couldn't blame him for not printing them out. The pictures she kept herself weren't in a physical album, only online collections. She always tried to add a few new shots when she visited him, but it wasn't enough.

A sound caught her attention, and she froze for a moment, listening. It was only rain pattering on the roof. She relaxed and listened as the volume increased. Thunder rumbled in the distance, and a deluge released, pounding down on the roof.

The hum of the electric heater's fan switching on automatically signaled a drop in temperature. She closed her eyes for a moment. She was physically comfortable, here in Dad's house where he ought to be. *Wherever he is, Lord, keep him warm and dry!*

14

Campbell spent another night tossing and turning and wondering where her father was. She prayed intermittently, mostly from a hollowness deep within her that said she could do nothing to help him. Her hopes of finding him alive ebbed with each hour.

When she rose, she had no appetite for breakfast but carefully typed into her laptop her recollections of the interview with Clark Timmons the day before and the bits she'd gleaned from Alana Shepherd's journal. Then she headed to the office.

On the spur of the moment, she detoured a couple of blocks and drove slowly past Dr. Exter's dental practice. Two cars sat in the main parking lot, and a shiny red Jaguar was parked in a solitary slot at the side of the building.

That must be his ride, she thought. *He parks away from the other cars so it won't get dinged.*

She arrived at True Blue just as Nick was unlocking the door. She greeted him, and he asked soberly, "How are you doing?"

"Not too well." *He really does care. He's worried about Dad, too.*

It's not just a job to Nick, and I haven't treated him fairly. "How about you?" she asked.

He shrugged and swung the door open. Neither said anything about the fact that the office looked untouched today, but Campbell was sure his mind was also on the break-in. Determined to make an effort with Nick, she went straight to the coffee maker and set up a fresh pot. She really knew very little about him.

"Where do you live?" she asked. "Are you still with your folks?"

"Nah, they moved to Florida a couple years ago. I've got an apartment on the west side of town."

"Oh. Siblings?"

"Scattered."

He set up his laptop and some paperwork, and she figured he didn't want to make small talk this morning. Okay. As she poured out coffee for both of them and sat down in her dad's chair, her mind went back to the convoluted case.

"How'd your chat with Clark Timmons go yesterday?" Nick asked.

"Up and down. He was tense at first, but Fuller talked him down and he mellowed out a little."

"So? Did he tell you anything useful?"

Campbell gave him a streamlined account. "So this morning I typed up everything, and I can send you the file if you have time. I mean, I know you're busy..."

Her father's weeklong absence hung between them, unspoken.

"I can take a look," Nick said.

"Thanks." She opened her laptop and booted up. As soon as she could, she went to her email program and sent him her file.

"So, I got a look at Dr. Exter's car this morning."

"Yeah, I saw it Friday," Nick said. "Doctors get a lot of perks."

"Must be nice." Campbell smiled tightly. "It looked brand new."

"Nah, it's a couple years old."

Her mind ticked through some items she'd noted in her file. Keith had said he'd look into Exter's activities at the times of the cold cases. "I wonder when he bought it." She gazed across the room at Nick. "Can we find out?"

"Is it important?"

"Could be."

"Well, there are ways. One, we could ask him or one of his family members or coworkers. Two, we could ask Keith if he's looking into Dr. Exter's financials. Maybe he could spot it there. Three, we could nose around the nearest dealership and chat the salespeople up to see how many new Jags they've sold in the past couple of years."

"I was hoping for something quick and simple." She took a sip of her coffee.

"Okay, I'll bite. What do you think this has to do with anything?"

Campbell picked up the file folder that held the printouts she'd made of news articles concerning past crimes. She laid it on Nick's desk and leafed through them to the one she wanted. After a look at the date, she turned the folder to face him.

"The jogger?" Nick asked.

"Yeah. Just wondering what car Paul Exter was driving when that accident happened."

Nick stared down at the article. "It's a long shot."

"I know." She watched him, almost able to see the cogs whirling in his head.

"There's a car dealer on Twelfth Street who handles a few Jags. If Exter bought it new ..."

"Let's do it."

He shook his head. "You stay here."

"Why?"

"I think you should keep your head down today."

First Keith and now Nick. She hated the stark rejection that slammed her.

"Seriously," he said. "Word's gotten around town that you're digging. I know you just want to find Bill, but someone's afraid you'll find something else. Something they want to keep hidden."

She sighed. "Okay. I'll stay here and see if I can find out anything more about Alana's boss or the exchange student."

"Good. If I get anything, you'll be the first to know."

"Is there anything I can do for True Blue? I know we're neglecting the business—"

"Fill out the app for a license." Nick grinned.

He hurried out and she sat staring at the closed door. He was kidding, of course. But she hadn't replied to the letter that arrived Friday from Murray State. If she didn't act quickly, that job would disappear. Even the thought of it depressed her. She wanted to teach, didn't she? But not freshman basics.

Was it only wishful thinking to imagine she could step into another job teaching literature classes? And how could she commit to anything until she knew what had happened to her dad?

She opened her laptop. Bella Chase. She'd planned to go to the store and try to talk to her today. Would Keith put the kibosh on that? She pulled up a sketchy background on Bella. Graduated with a business degree from Murray State and had gone to Vanderbilt for a year. Pursuing an MBA?

Campbell couldn't find anything indicating she'd finished the program. Bella had worked at a large clothing store in Nashville, learning the ropes, then come back to Murray. For several years, she'd been assistant manager of an independent clothing store here and eventually bought out the owner. How had she afforded that?

Campbell tried another search. Bella had served on the

Chamber of Commerce for a couple of years. Wasn't her husband on it now? Yep, Jared.

The desk phone rang, and she grabbed it. "Campbell?"

"Yeah, Nick." She glanced at the clock and was surprised that forty-five minutes had passed since he left. "What's up?"

"You're gonna love it. Exter bought that car used from the dealer I mentioned."

"Used? I thought you said it was last year's model."

"The year before. But it was repossessed, so he got a good deal on a nearly-new Jag. Wanna know when he bought it?"

"Uh, yeah. That was the whole point, right?"

"May 26, last year."

She grabbed the file and pulled out the article on the hit-and-run. "Nick! That was, like, four days after the jogger was killed."

"Bingo."

She pulled in a deep breath. "We have to tell Keith."

"You want to call him?"

"No. He's not happy with me right now."

"Oh, come on, he likes you."

"I'm not so sure about that." She scrunched up her face. "He keeps telling me to stay out of his investigation. You heard him."

"And yet he took you on a ride-along yesterday."

There was that.

"Okay, I'll call him. But tell me you didn't get anyone's radar running overtime."

"I'm not sure that's a thing, but no, I was very tactful. Buddied up to one of the salesmen and let on that I was interested in a Jag but couldn't afford a new one. He said they get used ones now and then, and he could put me on a list to call. As a matter of fact, they got one that was repoed last year. It was a beaut, so he says."

"I'll bet it was shiny red."

"Yup, and a local professional is driving it."

"Okay, I'll alert Keith. Maybe he can check into Exter's finances last spring. I wonder if he sold the old car?"

"Mention that to Keith. He should be able to check out the doc's old vehicle and see if the registration and title changed hands."

"Good thinking." She gave herself a minute to calm down before she made the call.

"Hello, Campbell." Just his tone made her regret calling.

"Hi, Keith. Sorry to bother you, but Nick turned up something that could be important."

"What is it?" Keith asked.

"We noticed that Dr. Exter drives a fairly new car, a Jaguar."

"I'm sure he can afford it."

"Yeah, well, the thing is, he bought that car four days after that hit-and-run we talked about, where a jogger was killed." The detective didn't say anything, so after a moment Campbell said, "We, uh, wondered if he got rid of the old car right away. Is that something you could look into? Nick thought you could check out his old car's title and see if it was transferred or if—"

"I'll do it," Keith said. "I'm swamped, but I'll make sure we take a hard look."

She smiled. "Thanks. I hope it's a connection for you, not just—"

"I've got to go," Keith said.

"Right. 'Bye."

He'd already ended the call.

Nick walked in the door a few minutes later. "Did you talk to Keith?"

"Yes."

"Did he sound interested?"

"Yes, but harried."

"That means annoyed?"

Campbell frowned. "Busy. He's busy."

"Okay."

"Look, I was thinking I'd go to Bella Chase's store and see if I could talk to her."

Nick gritted his teeth.

"What?" she asked.

"I dunno. After what Keith said ..."

"What harm could a little dress shopping do?"

The office phone rang, and Nick picked it up. He listened for half a minute then responded. Campbell gathered from what she heard that an insurance company wanted to hire True Blue to investigate a client's claim.

When Nick clicked a button and laid down the receiver, he gave Campbell a wry smile. "Well, it's more work, but that case may be a dud. The subject is claiming a work injury, and he's wearing an orthopedic boot, but the company has doubts. The fellow has been out socializing, and they want to be sure his injury is genuine."

"Don't they ask for medical records to back up his claim?"

"Sure. But he might be saying it's worse than it is. So far he's been out of work a week and has asked for the rest of this week, too."

"What kind of work does he do?"

"He's a delivery truck driver."

"So, the insurance company will have to pay for everything? That sounds like you'd have to prove a negative—he's not really injured as badly as he says."

"We get that all the time. I'll watch him a few days and see if we get anything. I'll check out when he's due for another doctor's appointment, and we'll see how that turns out."

"How do you get that information?" she asked.

He wiggled his eyebrows at her. "Trade secret."

"Hmm. Well, if he really was injured as badly as he claims, then the insurance *should* pay for his treatment."

"Of course. And sometimes it works out that way. But they don't usually put us on a case unless there's some doubt. This guy had another—very large—claim three years ago. With a different company."

Campbell frowned. "If the company paid, why did he switch his insurance?"

"He also changed jobs, which probably had nothing to do with the previous injury, but you never know."

"Has anyone talked to his former employer?"

"I knew you had a detective's mind." He smiled. "That will be one of my first acts. But they can be pretty tight-lipped. Privacy laws and all that."

She nodded and clicked a few strokes on her keyboard. "Well, as far as Alana Shepherd's case goes, I haven't found a lot of new information. It's been four years since she died. I found some of her sister Rachel's social media accounts, but it won't let me look back that far."

"There's a memorial post on one, though, marking the anniversary of the murder." She scrolled down on her screen. "Meanwhile, I found out who a couple of her high school teachers were. I may be able to ask for some general info on Alana's situation. How she was as a student, that sort of thing. But that's going back even further. I think I'd find out more at Bella's, where she was employed right up to the end."

"True, but since she stayed in the same town with her former teachers and a lot of her classmates, she probably kept up some contacts," Nick said.

"Okay." Campbell browsed through the comments on Rachel Shepherd's memorial post. "Several people who commented say they miss Alana, and it sounds as though a few of them were close to her. Here's one who worked with her at the time she was killed."

"Let me see."

She turned her laptop around, and he studied the screen. "Get their names. Any who still live in Murray, we can contact.

And maybe you could see if Rachel will friend you. Meanwhile, I'll set up a file on the insurance case."

Half an hour later, she had a list of nearly twenty people with connections to Alana Shepherd. Campbell put asterisks beside the names of those who seemed most likely to have been close to the young woman at the time of her death. It was hard to muster much enthusiasm, though. Surely the police had contacted most of these people four years ago. She wasn't sure she could uncover anything helpful now.

She closed her notebook and stood. "Hey, Nick, I'm going over to Bella's. I can't stop thinking that she's important in this."

"I can't stop you." He eyed her cautiously. "But don't say I didn't warn you."

"Okay. I won't say it."

"I think I'll go drive by this injury guy's home address." He smiled. "Who knows? Maybe he's chucked his boot and is out gardening."

"Good luck with that."

She headed for the door.

"Hey, we're going to get to the bottom of this," he called after her.

"I think we will. For Dad."

Nick nodded. "And for Alana Shepherd."

The rabbits flashed into Campbell's mind, along with the unlikable man who'd owned them. She felt sorry for anyone who'd been rejected so often. She opened the door and looked back at Nick. "I hope we can help get some justice for Darrin Beresford, too."

15

Bella's had a sophisticated feel about it, one Campbell was sure Bella Chase cultivated carefully. That woman considered herself high above most of the local people, and she wouldn't want to own a clothing shop that was less than the finest in Murray. It was perhaps even a little too chic for the college town in a rural county, but Bella apparently made it work. The website where one could order its high-end fashions probably helped carry it into the black each month.

As she entered the store, Campbell saw the owner engaged in conversation with the clerk she'd befriended on her last visit. She recognized Bella from a photo on the website. The two women stood near the closest checkout station, apparently discussing a business matter. Bella did not look happy.

Campbell turned to the nearest rack of summer tops and slid the hangers along the rail as she waited for the conversation to end. It sounded as though Bella was scolding the clerk for not doing something exactly right. When she finished, she turned away from the checkout and walked past Campbell.

"Oh, Ms. Chase?" Campbell tried to put a bright note in her voice. "I wondered if I could speak to you for a minute."

Bella looked her over, and Campbell wished she'd worn something a little more stylish.

"If you're here about the job, applications are at the service desk in the back."

"Uh, no, actually." Campbell stepped closer and lowered her voice. "I hoped I could ask you a few questions about Alana Shepherd."

Bella's face hardened. "What about her?"

"I understand she was employed here at the time of her death."

"Yes. What of it?"

"What can you tell me about her?"

"I'm sorry. What is your interest in all this?"

Campbell had a feeling she was about to be dismissed. She decided to target Bella's sympathy, if she had any. "Well, you see, my father, Bill McBride, is missing. The police are searching for him, but I'm very worried. The investigation is complex, but—"

"I don't have time for this." Bella shook her head.

A large man in blue work clothes strode into the store and made straight for them.

"Bella! What's this about Tom Hazelton? He just told me you fired him and are going with another firm."

Chin quivering, Bella strove to keep a calm demeanor. "Really, Jared, we can discuss this later."

"No, I want to know now." He towered over her threateningly.

Bella clucked her tongue. "For heaven's sake! I simply made a business decision. You can keep using Tom for your own accountant if you want, but I'm making a change as far as the store goes. That's all. Now, I have work to do."

"Wait!" Jared grabbed his wife's arm. She pulled away and fixed him with a frosty stare.

"Not here, not now," she whispered fiercely.

Jared let his arm fall to his side.

"Now, if you want something to make a fuss about," Bella said, "this woman was just asking questions about Alana Shepherd."

His eyes narrowed and he focused on Campbell as Bella made a beeline for her office.

"What about the Shepherd girl?" Jared asked sharply, but keeping his voice low.

"It's complicated," Campbell said.

"Try me."

She hesitated. Why would Jared care so much about her line of questioning? And why did his wife know he'd be interested, enough so that she used Campbell's visit as a distraction for the angry man. Best tread carefully.

"Have you ever heard of Bill McBride?" she asked.

He frowned.

"True Blue Investigations?" she added.

"I've heard of it."

"Well, Bill McBride is the owner of the agency, and he's my father." He said nothing, so she went on. "Mr. Chase, my father is missing, and I'm trying to find him."

"And you think that has some connection to a girl who's been dead for years?"

Customers were brushing past them, giving them quizzical glances.

"Why are you here? What exactly do you think my wife has to do with that?"

"Nothing," Campbell said quickly. "I only hoped to learn more about Alana, since she held a prestigious job here."

He barked out a laugh. "Oh, she loved her job. Not. She was going to leave Bella high and dry. She'd applied for some fancy position in Atlanta. My wife was quite upset about that."

"I'm sorry." He was becoming agitated again, and Campbell couldn't see any point in getting him riled. "I'd better get going," she said. "I have another meeting." If telling Nick about this scary guy could be called a meeting. She chalked up another thing Nick was good for.

"Hold on." He reached toward her, but Campbell stepped back. "Are you saying your old man is investigating Alana's death?"

"I'm not saying that at all."

"Then what's the connection?"

"I can't give you that information. It has to do with a client who hired my father." She was stretching it a little, but Darrin had either hired her dad or wished he could.

"So, your client wants to know about Alana. Your father's reopened the investigation? But he's not a cop."

"No, he's a private investigator. But I didn't say he's looking at the Shepherd case."

Jared leaned in closer. "Then what is he looking at? You can tell me."

His breath smelled like beer, and his glittery dark eyes sent a zing of fear through Campbell.

"Excuse me. I really have to go." She turned and walked out of the store without looking back. As she approached her car, she remembered the note she found on the windshield after her previous visit. She checked but was thankful to see no new messages had been left for her.

Her hands shook as she started the car. She drove around the corner onto Chestnut Street and pulled in at the post office, though she had no reason to go there. As she eased the gearshift into park, her phone rang. Seeing Keith's name on the screen made her feel a little steadier.

"Hello?" she said tentatively.

"Campbell, I wanted to thank you and Nick for the tip. I found out Paul Exter sold his Cadillac a couple of months after the hit-and-run accident. I followed up with the new owner, and he said it needed a little body work when he bought it. The front fender on the passenger side was dented, and the headlight was cracked."

"So, he hadn't gotten it repaired," Campbell said slowly.

"Right. I think he bought the Jaguar right away and kept the Caddy out of sight for several weeks. He was probably afraid someone would see it, or the mechanic would ask him what happened. Anyway, he sold it after a bit to a couple up in Calvert City. Probably figured they wouldn't come to Murray too often, so people who would recognize his car wouldn't see it and make the connection."

"That sounds about right," Campbell said. "How can you be sure he was involved in the accident?"

"We brought him in again, and based on that, combined with my unofficial knowledge about the fingerprint at Darrin's house, we've charged him. We fingerprinted him at the station as part of the booking, and it's a match. We've got nothing on your break-ins, but this is solid."

"That's fantastic."

"I was able to put together other events surrounding the hit-and-run that were just too coincidental. His lawyer apparently advised him to cop to that, swear it was an accident and he didn't realize he'd done it at first, and keep mum about anything else."

"So, he doesn't admit he killed Darrin Beresford?" she asked.

"Not yet. His lawyer pointed out that the fingerprint on the front doorknob could have gotten there quite innocently at another time."

"Can you tell if it's fresh?"

"Not really," Keith said. "Darrin himself didn't use that door much. Seems he always went in the back way."

Campbell exhaled, glad neither she nor Nick had touched the front doorknob the night they found Darrin's body. "Wow. Well, that's something. I guess if he won't admit to being at

Darrin's last Monday, he didn't say anything about seeing my dad."

"No, and I asked him, but he still claims to have nothing to do with any of that."

Campbell bit her lip, wondering if she should tell him about her encounter with Bella and Jared Chase. Before she could choose her approach, Keith spoke again.

"So, I thought we should celebrate. Can I take you to dinner tonight?"

"R-really?"

"Well, yeah. If you want. I mean, I know your father's still out there and all, but we did some good today."

You did some good, she thought. All I did was upset people.

"What about Nick?" she asked. "He's the one who found out when Exter bought his new car."

"Hmm. Well, I suppose we could ask Nick to join us." His tone said that was far from what he'd envisioned. "I could give him a call, or you could ask him. Are you at the office?"

"No, I ... Look, I have something else to talk to you about. Maybe tonight?"

"Okay." He named a restaurant, and she agreed to meet him there. "But if it's important to the case, tell me now, please," Keith said.

"I'm not sure how important it is, but it's about Bella Chase."

"You went back to the store."

"How did you know?"

"I didn't," he said. "I'm just getting to know how you operate."

Campbell wasn't sure that was meant in a good way. "Well, yeah, I did. As soon as I mentioned Alana, Bella got snippy. And then her husband walked in, and he was even worse. I felt intimidated. He demanded to know why I was interested in Alana."

"Did you tell him?"

"No, not really. But I did tell him who my father is, which was probably a copout, but I was a little scared. Now he sort of thinks someone hired True Blue to investigate Alana's death."

"And he didn't like that?"

"No. So I remembered how her parents had said Alana didn't get on very well with the Chase family."

"Did you ask her sister about that when you talked to her?"

"No. I probably should have, but she was in a hurry, and I didn't want to say too much on our first contact. Did you check on Rachel's record?"

"She was arrested for drugs once when she was enrolled at the college. That and speeding tickets were all I found. Look, I should probably get back to work, but I suggest—with all the best intentions—that you stay away from the Chase family and the Shepherds for today. We'll talk about this more tonight, all right?"

"Sure," Campbell said.

WHEN CAMPBELL WALKED into the restaurant, the hostess showed her to Keith's table near the back. He stood and smiled, and she was glad she'd taken time to change into something nice. She was mildly surprised he was alone—Nick wasn't one to turn down a free meal.

Keith stood and pulled out her chair. "Nick said he was on surveillance and couldn't make it."

"Oh, that's too bad," but she smiled as she said it. Although Nick was growing on her as a colleague, she was much happier to have dinner with only Keith. "How did the rest of your day go?"

"Pretty good, actually. We're holding Dr. Exter, at least overnight. He'll have a bail hearing tomorrow, but I'm hoping I can put together enough evidence that the D.A. will also charge him with Darrin's murder."

"That's great. I just wish he'd tell you something about my dad."

"Maybe he will. That's something we might be able to use as a bargaining chip. But the more of a case we can make against him, the more likely he'll tell us something relevant in exchange for a better deal. Oh, and another thing ..."

"What?"

"The note on your car," Keith said. "I found out who left it, and it's not Exter."

"Who, then?"

"Clark Timmons."

"Wow. I'd almost, but not quite, decided he was innocent of everything."

"He may be—except that. It wasn't very smart on his part. I talked to him late this afternoon, and he admitted it. Said he was scared after you went to the farm. He was afraid the whole murder case would blow open and we'd lock him up again."

"I'm sorry I put that kind of stress on him."

"Well, he's remorseful, and he's being cooperative now."

The waiter came to their table and took their beverage orders. Campbell and Keith turned their attention to the menus. When their food arrived, Campbell looked down at her grilled salmon. It looked and smelled wonderful, but guilt ate at her. How could she even enjoy a meal while her father might be in dire straits?

"I usually ask a blessing," Keith said.

"Certainly." She bowed her head. She shouldn't have been surprised, but it had been ages since she'd prayed over her food in a restaurant.

"I was pretty sure you prayed," she said when he finished.

"I do. And I've prayed for Bill since you first told me he's missing."

"Thank you." She picked up her fork and took a few bites. "You think he's dead, don't you?" She'd asked him before, but that was several days ago. Things looked grimmer now.

"I won't stop hoping until we have proof," he said.

Tears spilled over and ran down Campbell's cheeks. "What if we never find it?"

Compassion radiated from him, and she had to drop her gaze.

"That would be very hard for you," he said. "You'd have to build a new life without him. I hope you don't have to do that, but it's not morbid to start thinking about it. It's practical."

"Tell me about it. His bills are starting to stack up. I don't even know how often Nick is paid. I should ask him, I guess. And maybe I should go to the bank and have a heart-to-heart with the manager."

"Does he have a will?"

"Yes. There's a copy at home in his desk, but I haven't opened it. I don't know if it's cowardice on my part, or just stubbornness."

"It's hope," Keith said. "You don't want to use it unless you absolutely have to."

She nodded.

"Why don't we think about something else?" Keith pushed his plate aside and set a small paper bag on the table. "I brought Alana's journal along. There are some interesting things in it, and I thought maybe we could brainstorm a little."

Thankful not only for the change of topic but for this sign of trust, she managed a smile. Keith had marked several pages with sticky paper flags, and she opened to the first of those.

"Take a look at the first entry on that page." Keith pointed to the place where the flag was stuck next to an entry date.

"Went to LBL with JJ," she read. She glanced up to find Keith's eyes riveted on her. "J.J. Chase?"

He lifted his shoulders. "That's my guess. Keep reading."

"Made me think he knew something about M, or at least he wanted me to think so." She frowned. "Who or what is M?"

"Look at the date."

She thought for a moment then turned wide eyes on Keith. "I see. This entry is about four months after Marni Schliemann disappeared."

"I asked Rachel Shepherd to come in this afternoon," Keith said. "I asked her about her sister's relationship with J.J. Chase. She said they never dated so far as she knew. J.J. was several years younger than Alana. But there was something odd between them back in high school. J.J. would tag along after Alana like he worshipped her."

"Really." Campbell tried to make that fit what she knew of Alana.

"Yeah. Rachel said Alana couldn't stand him, but then later, when her sister went to work for Bella, Alana seemed to tolerate J.J. better. She said they'd hang out and talk, almost like he was a little brother. After J.J. went away to school, he would always visit Alana when he came home on his breaks."

The waiter came to remove their plates and asked if they wanted dessert.

"None for me, thanks," Campbell said.

Keith asked for more coffee.

"I wonder if she told the police about that when her sister died—about her connection to J.J., I mean."

Keith shook his head. "She said not. Didn't think it was important."

"So, J.J.'s parents sent him away." Campbell turned the page in the diary. "It says they suddenly packed him off to a private school in Vermont. I wonder why."

"I understand J.J. was quite the cut-up," Keith said.

"Yeah, so Nick told us. Maybe they felt he needed some overdue discipline. Military school, maybe?"

"No, I checked it out online. The school wasn't overly strict, but it had a good reputation for getting grads into prestigious colleges."

"Where did J.J. go?"

Keith smiled. "A not very prestigious, small private college in Wisconsin."

"Which tells us what?" Campbell asked.

"His parents didn't want him too close to Murray. That, and he didn't get very good grades at the prep school for which they paid dearly. Look at the next flag."

She turned to it. The entry was written several months later. Campbell read a few sentences and looked up in surprise. "'J was upset with her.' Jared, the dad?"

"I think so. J.J. was off in Vermont, at the prep school. I haven't found that they kept up any correspondence at the time. Alana's computer was taken after she was killed, and the police copied her hard drive. I went through all that, but I didn't find anything to do with J.J. She was seeing Parker by then. There's a lot of back-and-forth between the two of them."

"And Jared?"

"Not on her computer."

"Where then?"

"Nowhere until now—in the diary. I think Alana was careful. But look at the next place I marked."

"Hmm, Christmas vacation. 'J.J. is home on break. He was at Lisa's party last night, and he told me some interesting things.' What's that about?"

"Go on," Keith said.

The next entry was made early in January. She read aloud, "'J is angry, but he'll put up.'" She looked up at Keith. "What does that mean?"

"That's where I hope you can help me. I have a theory, but it's a little wild."

Campbell studied the dates and read a few more sentences, but there was no further reference to 'J' on that page.

"J is angry. Does she mean J.J.?"

"I think he'd gone back to school by then."

"His father then?"

Keith lifted one shoulder. "It's a possibility."

"He'll put up," she mused. "What does that mean? You—you don't think she was blackmailing Jared Chase?" She looked around quickly to make sure no one else was listening to their conversation. She didn't want to make the same mistake Darrin had made at the diner.

Keith grinned. "I didn't want to be the one to say it, but that's my latest theory, yeah."

"You have his financial records," Campbell said.

"Yes, and I couldn't find any large, unexplained payments from his and Bella's joint accounts."

Campbell's pulse picked up. "But ...?"

"But I found a few in Jared's business account. One was shortly after J.J. went back to school that New Year's. There were two more between then and Alana's death. On the books, they're listed as promotional expenses for the business. But I couldn't find any place that specified what for."

"So, he deducted his blackmail payments," she whispered. The image of Jared's angry face at their encounter in the store made her shudder.

"The last unexplained withdrawal was two days before Alana wrote her last journal entry. But get this: The day after she died, the money was redeposited to the account."

She stared into Keith's deep brown eyes. "He didn't have to make the payment after all."

"That's how I see it."

Campbell sucked in a painful breath.

16

"So, what now?" Campbell asked, gazing at Keith across the table.

"Well, J.J. has an ironclad alibi for the time of Alana's death. The police didn't look at him at all when she died, but I have. He was at the college in Wisconsin."

"Are you certain he didn't come home?"

"Yes. He got into trouble that week. Doing a little partying with some buddies. He was arrested for drugs."

"And his father?"

"Jared and Bella got a lawyer up there to bail out their son. Jared drove up a month later, when J.J. had his court appearance. But Alana was dead by then."

"Where's J.J. now?" she asked.

"Not in Murray. I checked, and he never came back for more than brief visits. I didn't want to make his parents suspicious, so I didn't ask them directly, but some of his former classmates said they'd heard he was in California. I did some online searches, and I found a social media account that sure looks like him, but he's going by his middle name, Harrison."

Campbell made a mental note to search online for Harrison

Chase. "How can you connect everything to Marni Schliemann? Will you question Jared and Bella about her?"

"Jared certainly, but I'd like to have something a little more concrete before I bring him in. I don't want to alert him and then lose him."

Concrete. Campbell caught her breath. "You should find out what project his construction company was working on at that time."

Keith was silent for several seconds then stirred, reaching for the journal. "That's good thinking, Sherlock. Come on. I'll take you home. Something tells me I'm going to be up late tonight."

"I've got my car, remember? I'll be fine."

His smile had a wistful air. "This was a productive evening, but it's not quite the way I imagined things. Can we have a do-over sometime soon?"

"I'd like that."

NICK WAS at the office when she arrived Tuesday morning, and he'd already made fresh coffee.

"Thanks." She poured herself a cup and raised it in salute. "This hits the spot."

He grinned. "How was your big date?"

"It wasn't a date."

"Wasn't it? Shoot. He called me, but I figured I'd be a fifth wheel."

"I thought you were on surveillance."

"Sort of."

"You lied to Keith?" She scowled at him.

"Don't get all tied up in knots, girl. I did some work."

She sighed. "Speaking of which, you must be short a paycheck by now."

Nick shrugged. "It can wait a few more days."

"All right, but if—" She swallowed hard. "If nothing's changed by Friday, we'll figure out how to pay you, okay?"

"Yeah." His tone had softened, and his eyes looked moist. Her father's absence was sinking in.

Campbell pulled her chair closer to his desk and gave him a rundown on everything she and Keith had discussed.

"So all we can do is wait?" Nick said.

"I hate this." She took a big swig of coffee then faced him squarely. "Look, I'm glad we've helped Keith crack a couple of cold cases, but even if he nails someone for Darrin Beresford's death, we still have no idea what happened to Dad."

"Yeah." Nick studied the contents of his mug.

"I mean, all this stuff is peripheral. Exter admitted he hit the jogger, so a manslaughter charge for him. And maybe Keith will pin the exchange student on Jared Chase, but—"

"But where's Bill?"

"Yeah. Where's Bill?" Overwhelming grief washed over her. She tried to hold back a sob, but it hiccuped out.

Nick reached out with his index finger and pushed a box of tissues across the desk toward her. "Okay, what have we got, really? Bill's car was near the Timmons farm. Clark says he knows nothing about it. The guy who owns the land, ditto. What else is there?"

She racked her brain and felt her brow furrow. "That thing Alana wrote about a shelter still bothers me."

"You mentioned that to me yesterday, I think."

"Alana and Clark were on their way somewhere—movies, I think—and he stopped to leave something at a shelter. I thought maybe it was a charity thing, but Keith wasn't sure." She ran a hand through her hair.

"How about the animal shelter?"

"I thought of that. We could ask if any of the Timmons family had a connection there."

Nick started clicking on his computer. Campbell reached for the phone book.

At the same time she said, "Found it," Nick called out, "Got it!"

They both laughed.

"Do you want to call, or should I?" Nick asked. "Flip a coin?"

"Oh, I'll just do it." Campbell punched in the number on the desk phone, and a woman answered. "Hi, my name is Campbell McBride with True Blue Investigations. We wondered if you have, or had in the past, a volunteer named Timmons."

"Timmons?" the woman asked. "I don't think so. Let me put the director on."

A moment later, another woman came on the line. She sounded older than the first one, and more confident. "Why do you want to know this?" she asked.

Campbell swallowed hard. "We came across a reference to a Mr. Timmons leaving something at the shelter. We wondered if you know anything about that."

"No, not recently."

"This would have been several years ago," Campbell said.

"Oh. Well, if they left an animal here, I'm not sure our records would have that. Not more than five years ago, anyway."

Campbell checked the date. The incident happened before Alana and Clark broke up, so it was more than six years ago.

"Well, thanks," she said. "I'm not sure it was an animal. I thought maybe a donation or something."

"I've been here since 2009, and I don't recall what you're talking about."

"Thank you for your time." Campbell hung up. "I guess it was a long shot."

"Yeah. Any more bright ideas?"

She told herself he wasn't being sarcastic. That was just the way Nick talked. "There was another house we could see from the spot where they found Dad's car. We never got to talk to them. I went once, but they weren't home." Campbell pulled out her car keys. "I think I'll go out there. How about you?"

"I can come if you don't want to go alone, but it might be more efficient for me to do some more work on that case I started."

"Okay, that makes sense. If Keith Fuller calls..."

"What?"

"Tell him where I've gone, I guess. He won't like it, but I can't sit here and do nothing."

THE TWO-STORY white house looked lived in and loved, unlike the Timmons house. A pickup and a sedan were parked in the dooryard, and on the lawn lay a bicycle and several toys, waiting for their owners to swoop out the front door and grab them up. A tractor sat in front of the open barn door, where Campbell had seen it before.

As she approached the covered porch, a young man in jeans and a T-shirt came out.

"Hi," Campbell said.

He nodded. "Can I help you?"

"I'm Campbell McBride. Have you lived here long?"

"All my life." He stuck out a tanned hand. "Gordy Martin."

"Nice to meet you, Gordy. I wondered if you know the Timmons family." She waved vaguely toward the rundown farmhouse just down the road, on the other side.

"I knew them when I was a kid, but you should talk to my father." He turned toward the barn and whistled. A white-haired man leaning over a hay mower jerked his head up and waved then ambled toward them.

"This was my folks' place," Gordy said. "Dad's lived here over forty years."

"Hi, Mr. Martin." Campbell smiled at the older man. "Campbell McBride."

"Howdy."

"This lady was asking about the Timmons family," Gordy told him.

Mr. Martin's white eyebrows shot up. "What do you want to know? They've been gone some time."

Campbell tried to choose her words carefully. She didn't want this nice old man to think she was a nut case. "Would you say the Timmonses were—well, an average farm family?"

"Not sure what you mean by that. I always considered Melville to be sort of a lazy farmer. I think he could've done better with the acreage he had. But they only had one boy, Clark. I'm not sure they could afford to hire much help. Now, Clark had a lot of troubles." He eyed her keenly.

"Yes, I'm aware of his situation in the Shepherd case," she said. "Actually, my father runs True Blue Investigations. Maybe you've heard of it?"

"I've seen the sign and wondered about it." Mr. Martin said, "So you're investigating the Timmons clan."

She decided to lay it out for him, since he seemed like a nice person and may have known the Timmons family better than just about anyone else left in Murray. She told him about her father's disappearance and that she and the police had been led in a roundabout way to take a look at the Shepherd murder case and Clark Timmons.

"I'm not saying he did it," she said quickly, "but the police are looking into it again, and if he is in any way connected to my dad going missing, I want to know. It's been—" She choked up suddenly and gave a little cough.

"You aren't related to Clark, are you?"

"No, just curious. As I told you, my dad's been missing eight days now, and I admit I'm grasping at straws. But if you can tell me anything about them—anything!"

He smiled and looked up at the bright sky. "Well, so long as you're not a reporter or anything like that."

"No, I assure you my interest is only in a possible connection to my father."

"Okay. Well, off the record, as they say, Melville Timmons was nutty as a fruitcake." His smile slipped.

"How do you mean?"

"My wife used to have tea with his wife, Olive, and she said she thought maybe Melville got violent sometimes. I know he had a temper. A cow kicked him once, and he got his rifle and went out and shot the cow on the spot."

"Yikes." Campbell grimaced.

"Yeah, well, I'm not saying he ever struck his wife or the kid, but my wife suspected it. Clark didn't mix much with our young'uns, but he was odd, too. A loner. We were all surprised when he got engaged to the Shepherd girl. But that didn't last long."

Campbell nodded, wondering how much to reveal. "When she was engaged to Clark, Alana Shepherd kept a diary. She mentioned once that she was with Clark, and he went to leave something at a shelter."

Mr. Martin laughed.

"We thought it might be a charity thing," she said, watching his face. "Maybe a homeless shelter or—"

"No, no," he said, shaking his head and grinning. "It was a place to survive in, just in case we had an asteroid strike or a solar flare or something. You know, what they call a bunker?"

Campbell's heart pounded. "Were they preppers?"

"Hmm. Well, I don't think so, not at first. Back in the sixties, I think it was, Melville's father—that would be Clark's grandfather—was afraid of a nuclear meltdown. I believe that's when he built a fallout shelter."

"Really?" Campbell's hope flared up, but she made herself take a slow breath. "Where was it?"

"Not sure. He was kind of secretive about it. But I'm pretty sure it's on their property."

"Do you remember anything else about it?" Campbell asked. "Anything more recent?"

The old man scratched his head. "Well, more recently, maybe in the eighties or nineties, seemed every time I saw him, Melville would mention what he'd do if we had a disaster. Talked about stockpiling firewood and drinking water, stuff like that. Melville and Olive passed a long time ago, though. Melville went in a farm accident, and I believe Olive had cancer. But you could ask Clark. I hear he's in town, and I saw a for sale sign by the driveway."

"Thanks, I'll check in with him." Campbell nodded at the father and son and turned toward her car.

She drove slowly past the Timmons farm, but Clark's truck wasn't there. An urge to head up Route 68 and try to see Clark again at his cottage struck her. But she didn't want to do that on her own. Probably she should tell Nick what she'd learned, and maybe Keith as well. Of course, Keith would tell her to stay away from Clark. Reluctantly, she drove back to the office but found it empty.

"Okay, Campbell, think." She made herself a cup of coffee and sat down with it at her father's desk. When the mug was empty, she sighed and leaned back in the chair. Thinking didn't seem to do any good.

Lord, please help me, because I'm getting nowhere. I just can't believe you want me to go the rest of my life not knowing what happened to Dad.

She speed-dialed Nick's cell phone, and he picked up almost at once.

"Hey, I may have solved the shelter mystery. The neighbor says Mr. Timmons was kind of over the edge on survival. And his father had built a bomb shelter."

"You're kidding me."

"No, I'm not. And later he thinks it became more of a prepper thing for Clark's parents."

"You mean, like in case of a big disaster? The End of the World as We Know It?"

"Yeah. You know, store food and water, hand tools, that kind of stuff. Clark's a little off-the-wall. Maybe his parents were, too."

Nick didn't answer for several seconds. "It makes sense with what Alana wrote, I guess. So, what do you want to do?"

"Where are you?" Campbell asked.

"At the judicial building. I'm picking up some documents for the other case."

"When you're done, what do you say we go up to Clark's cottage and ask him about it?"

"Eh, I don't know. Wouldn't that ruffle Fuller's feathers?"

"Maybe." She scowled. "Probably."

"Well, when you looked at the property maps last week, did you see anything that could be a shelter?"

"Not that I recognized. But maybe the city didn't know. The point of those shelters is to keep them secret, right? So that if there's a huge disaster, you can hide and other people won't know you're there. It's not like they'd tell the assessors and pay taxes on an extra building."

"But people could see an extra building," Nick said. "Maybe it was in that barn that's no longer there."

"That's been gone longer than Clark's parents." Campbell was certain of that. She remembered the overgrown foundation blocks behind the Timmons house. She froze for an instant. "But."

"But what?"

"There was a smaller building, an old cabin, out in the field. It's gone now, too, for a long time. Remember? Nell Calhoun mentioned it."

"I remember. You said the guy who bought the land where Bill's car was left thought it fell down a decade or so ago."

"Or more than that. Keith said Clark was a kid when it came down." She sighed. "So, before Alana wrote that, for sure."

"Unless…"

She waited, wondering what was tumbling around in Nick's head.

"Sometimes people build them underground," he said.

"Yeah. But if that's the case, it could be anywhere on their farm."

"True."

"Okay, how about we talk to Nell Calhoun again?" Campbell asked. "Wouldn't Clark tell the real estate agent about something like that?"

"He should have," Nick said pensively, "But she sounded as if she didn't know a thing about it. Nell thought he was holding something back."

"She did."

"Which makes me think he didn't tell her about it, so talking to her again wouldn't do any good." After a moment he said, "Okay, you talked me into it. We'll go see ol' Clark. But I need to stop by my place first. I should be back there in, say, half an hour?"

Campbell smiled. "I'll get us some burgers."

She knew Nick well enough now to pick up a lunch that would please him. She was just returning to the office with a fragrant bag of bacon hamburgers on the passenger seat when her phone rang. She took a quick look then slid into a parking spot.

"Yeah, Nick? Are you on the way?"

"No. I'm at my place, but there's somebody in there." His voice was low and intense.

"What? Call 911!"

"I'm going in and see what's going on."

"No," she all but screamed into the phone. "Get away from there and call—

"Hey!" She heard what sounded like a scuffle, then a moan and muffled footsteps.

"Nick? Nick!" Campbell's hands shook as she dashed to the office door and fumbled to unlock it.

17

"Nick, are you there?" she called out as she ran in and grabbed his desk phone. He didn't answer, so she tried to call 911 on the landline. She missed the button for 9 and had to hang up and start over, but she finally got through to the dispatcher.

"What is your emergency?"

"It's not me, it's my friend. He went to his apartment, and he said someone was in there, and then I heard shouting, and it sounded like fighting."

"Slow down, ma'am. Where is the location?"

Campbell sank into Nick's chair and hauled in a deep breath. She tried to keep her voice level and calm as she gave Nick's home address and explained more coherently what had happened.

"Officers are on the way," the dispatcher assured her.

"Thank you. I want to go over there."

"How far away are you from the scene, ma'am?"

"Uh, five or ten minutes, I think. I've never actually been to his place."

"I can't tell you not to go, but when you get there just be sure to stay out of the way and let the officers do their job."

"I will." She hung up and put her cell phone to her ear again. "Nick? Nick, answer me."

But only silence greeted her.

TWO PATROL CARS and an ambulance were outside the apartment building when Keith arrived. He nodded to a patrolman keeping spectators out and strode toward the ambulance. Campbell McBride hovered anxiously as the EMTs loaded a gurney into the back. He touched her arm, and she swung around to face him.

"How is he?" Keith asked.

"Not good." Tears smeared on her face, and her eyes were red and puffy. "Someone attacked him while we were on the phone."

"I heard. I'm so sorry."

"Head injury." She looked like she would crumple on the asphalt.

Keith reached for her. She leaned against him for a moment, shivering but at the same time warm to his touch.

She eased away and straightened. "Thanks. I'm okay."

"These are his keys." Patrolman Jerry Stine came over and held out a key ring to Campbell. "I locked the car, and we'll secure the apartment when we're done." He glanced at Keith. "Detective Fuller. I thought Detective Jackson was handling this."

"I came as a friend," Keith said. "I'm afraid I'm up to my neck in other things at the station, but I'll be looking closely at this. It may be related to one of the matters I'm handling."

Stine nodded. "Well, Jackson's inside if you want to talk to him."

"Thanks." Stine walked toward the building as the ambulance driver shut the doors.

"Is he going to Murray Medical?" Keith asked.

"Paducah," the driver said. "Baptist Health."

If they were bypassing the local hospital, it must be pretty bad.

"I'll be right behind you," Campbell said.

Keith hesitated. "I wish I could go with you."

"It's okay," she said. "I don't know who to call, though. His parents, I guess, but they moved out of state a while ago. I know he has siblings."

"Detective Jackson will find them."

"Thanks."

There was so much he wanted to tell her, but now wasn't the time. Paducah was a good hour away. He couldn't leave now, not with so much pending in his cases.

"Look, I'll come up there as soon as I can. Probably after five. Phone me if you're leaving Paducah?"

"All right, thanks." She blinked back fresh tears. "Keith, someone who wants us to quit investigating did this. And we think we have a breakthrough."

"Something urgent, or can it wait until later?"

The ambulance was pulling away.

"We'll talk later. I have to go with Nick."

"Call me when you get an update. Are you sure you're all right to drive?"

"Yes."

"I'll see you later then."

CAMPBELL SIPPED the coffee she'd gotten from a machine. Her stomach growled, but she didn't want to leave the waiting room long enough to find the cafeteria. She'd waited more than four hours, with only two unsatisfactory briefings from a nurse. Campbell wasn't family and so wasn't privy to Nick's personal information. But they couldn't make her leave. She remembered the bag of fast food she'd left in the car. It seemed like eons ago when she'd bought it.

Other people came and went in the large waiting room, families of other patients. Some cried, some spoke in whispers, others were loud and cheerful, buoying each other's spirits. She wished she had one friend to console her.

Keith would come soon. He'd promised.

She reached for the box of tissues on the end table by her chair. She'd already half-filled the plastic wastebasket beside it.

"Campbell." Keith entered from the hallway and she jerked to her feet.

"Thank you so much for coming. They won't tell me anything. Nothing important, I mean."

"Jackson located Nick's parents in Florida. They're booking a flight. Nick's father promised to call the hospital and give the medical staff permission to give you medical updates." He handed her a folded memo sheet. "This is Mrs. Emerson's cell phone number. They said you could call if you want."

"When does their plane land?"

"I'm not sure yet, but Jackson said they'll probably have to route through Nashville. It'll be late tonight or early tomorrow."

She nodded and sat down. Keith took the vinyl-covered chair next to hers.

"Did they find out who did this to Nick?" she asked.

"I can't give you details, but they've got some promising leads."

"Good." On impulse, she reached for his hand, and Keith gave hers a reassuring squeeze.

"How are you, really?" he asked.

"Overwhelmed. I called Dad's best friend, Mart Brady. He's

in Bowling Green, where we used to live. I told him I don't know what to do with Dad still gone and Nick injured. He said he'd come over tomorrow and try to help me sort things out at the office."

"That's good, I guess," Keith said.

"He's a retired cop, too. He and Dad worked together a long time."

"Even better."

"Yeah. I just—I don't know if I should try to keep the office open or not. I'm not licensed. Mart said he could stay a while if I need him." She looked anxiously up at Keith's calm, solid face. "Nick was in the middle of a case for an insurance company. If nothing else, Mart may be able to help me wrap that up for them or find someone else to do it for them. I'm just lost."

"That's good of Mr. Brady."

She chuckled and swiped at a tear. "He said he could use something to do. But I could tell he's really worried about Dad. And it will be good to have an old friend nearby."

"Yes."

Keith hadn't let go of her hand. Should she pull it away? She didn't want to.

"So, what *can* you tell me?" Her voice cracked a little.

"Somebody was inside the apartment when Nick arrived."

"I know. He said that over the phone, and I told him not to go in. Then I heard—I don't know, I guess you might say a scuffle. Then nothing. I kept the connection open for a bit, but I called 911 on the landline in the office."

"That's good. You did exactly right."

"Cops were there when I got there, and the ambulance came right after me. They wouldn't let me inside, but an officer told me my friend had been hurt. I couldn't see Nick until they brought him out, and he was unconscious." She shivered. "He looked awful. And blood!"

"Head wounds tend to bleed a lot." Keith patted their clasped hands. "It looks as though Nick fought back. And when he wakes up, he may be able to tell us who it was."

"Ms. Campbell?" a man said from the doorway.

She shot to her feet. "McBride. My name is Campbell McBride."

The man in blue scrubs walked toward them. Only one other person was still in the room with them, and he slumped in a chair at the far end, flipping through a magazine.

"I'm Dr. Winthrop. Nick Emerson's family has designated you as someone who can receive medical updates and relay them."

"Thank you," Campbell said. "This is Detective Fuller."

The doctor nodded, seeming to accept Keith as part of the investigation into the violent attack. "Nick has a lot of bruising and a broken ulna, but the head wound is the main thing. We've done some scans, and there was some swelling caused by bleeding in the brain. We've relieved the pressure, but he won't be out of the woods until the swelling is down. Maybe by morning. Then we'll see how he does."

Campbell felt sick. She didn't want to know what they'd done to relieve the pressure on Nick's brain. "Will he wake up soon?" she asked.

"Doubtful. Probably tomorrow."

"Okay. Can we see him?"

"Well, since you're not family, it might be best to just let him rest. I believe his parents are on the way?"

She nodded.

"All right then. The staff can keep you informed." He told her how to contact the nurses' station in the recovery area where Nick was sequestered.

When he'd gone, she turned to Keith in hopes he had more comfort to offer than the surgeon. "That .didn't sound very reassuring."

"I'm sure things will look and sound better after he's had a night's rest," Keith said. "I should call Jackson and tell him not to bother coming up tonight."

"And I'll try Mrs. Emerson. If they're already on a plane, I won't be able to get them."

Keith went out in the hallway to make his call, and Campbell entered the phone number he'd given her.

A woman answered on the second ring. Campbell started to explain who she was.

"I know—Bill's daughter. How is Nick?"

"He's out of surgery, but not conscious yet. They think he may wake up in the morning, but they aren't sure. I guess the head injury was fairly bad. I'm sorry. Oh, and his arm is broken."

Mrs. Emerson gave a little sob. "I understand there's some trouble with Bill, too. Nick told us a few days ago he was missing."

"He still is. We're looking for him."

"Did this attack on Nick have something to do with that?"

"I'm not sure. He was working on an insurance case earlier today. Maybe he'll be able to tell us more tomorrow."

"Of course. Thank you for being there. We're on our way to the airport. We won't land until after eleven, I'm afraid."

"Do you have a hotel?" Campbell asked. "I'm not sure the police have finished at his apartment."

"I made a reservation at one near the hospital. We'll go there first."

"If he's still asleep, you might do better to get some rest and go over in the morning."

"We need to see him," his mother replied.

Campbell could understand that. "They won't let me in where he is because I'm not related, so I'll probably go home for the night."

"Of course, dear. You do that. We can talk in the morning.

And I hope you find your father. We've been praying for you and Bill."

Campbell's heart lurched. Maybe she wasn't friendless after all. She had Keith and Mart, and now the Emersons.

As she gathered up her things and grabbed one last tissue just in case, Keith returned.

"Jackson says a neighbor saw a truck parked around the corner. The timing is right, but he didn't see the driver. Another resident in the complex did see it leaving."

"What about in the apartment?" she asked. "Did they find any evidence there?"

"They're working on it."

She knew he wasn't telling her everything.

"Look, we should get some dinner," he said. "Are you planning to go back to Murray tonight?"

"There doesn't seem to be much point in staying here."

"Then let's eat. You must be hungry."

"A little."

"There's a quiet place between here and Route 24. Do you want to follow me? I'd like to hear what you were working on earlier."

Twenty minutes later, Campbell was seated across from Keith at a small table in a family restaurant. On the way in, she'd tossed the lunch bag from her car into a trash can. Her hunger had returned, and she ordered the day's special, meatloaf with mashed potatoes and two vegetables. Keith ordered barbecued chicken.

"Okay," he said when the waitress had left them with tall glasses of iced tea, "You said you had something. A possible breakthrough."

Campbell took a deep breath. "Wow, yeah. It seemed so important then, but I don't know."

"Try me."

"I went out to see Clark Timmons's nearest neighbors this morning."

"The Martins?"

"Yeah. Have you already talked to them?"

"Last week. They didn't know anything about your father or his car."

"Right. But I asked them about Alana's journal. The shelter thing." She shrugged. "See, Nick and I had checked with the animal shelter, and they said the Timmons family had no connection there."

"And what did the Martins tell you?"

"It's some kind of prepper shelter that started out fifty or sixty years ago as a bomb shelter. Clark's grandfather built it. We don't know where it is, but old Mr. Martin seemed pretty sure it was on the Timmons farm. He thought Clark's father was—well, 'nutty as a fruitcake' was the way he put it."

Keith gave her a half smile. "Melville Timmons did have a reputation for being a bit eccentric."

"Hmm. If that's what you call it." She returned his smile.

"He wasn't crazy," Keith said. "He did go kind of overboard on the survival kick, from what I'm told."

"But you didn't know he had this shelter?"

"No, but I can't say it surprises me."

"Nick was going to meet me back at the office, and we were going to go up to Clark's cottage and ask him about it."

Keith frowned.

"I know, I know," she said before he could object. "Clark doesn't trust me, but we figured if we could impress him with the urgency of my dad's situation, he'd at least tell us if it's still there."

Keith's brown eyes had a sorrowful cast.

"What are you not telling me?" she asked.

"Nothing, I was just wondering how urgent it is. I'm sorry. But I don't think you should approach Clark on your own."

"That's why I was waiting for Nick."

Their plates arrived, and after the waitress left, Campbell automatically bowed her head. Keith said a brief prayer in quiet tones, thanking God for the food and asking for healing for Nick and wisdom in looking for Bill.

She opened her eyes. "Don't take away my hope for my father, Keith."

"I'm trying to hang on to it myself."

She nodded. "It's getting harder. Every morning I wake up and I have to convince myself my dad's still alive and I need to keep looking. When do I stop?"

"Not yet," he said decisively. "Keep looking and keep praying, Campbell."

"I haven't prayed as much as I should." She looked away.

He stroked her hand. "God doesn't give us what we want based on how many times we pray."

"I hope you're right."

When they'd eaten in silence for a few minutes, he cleared his throat. "Listen, I spent time with Paul Exter and his lawyer this morning. I couldn't tell you earlier, but I can now, and I hope you'll find it encouraging. I think we're making progress with him. He's worried about his career and his reputation."

"You've got him for the hit-and-run death."

"Yes, that's rock solid," Keith said. "This afternoon I did some research and prepared documents for the district attorney's office. Exter will be arraigned, and he'll probably be out on bail tomorrow. Of course he wants to keep it quiet, but there's no way."

"It will be in the paper?"

"For sure, and on the local news." His voice dropped. "Please don't let this out yet. We'll be telling the press tomorrow, but we don't want any interference until we do."

"Sure. But he'll be walking around free until it goes to trial?"

"I don't think the judge will deny bail. Unless I can pin

Darrin's murder on him, too. He won't discuss that, and his lawyer's pretty in-your-face about the whole thing."

"So, they hope you'll take what you can get and forget about the rest?"

Keith shrugged. "I won't."

Campbell's phone rang and she pulled it out of her purse. She frowned at the screen. "It's a Murray number, but I don't recognize it."

"Take it," Keith said.

She pushed a button. "Hello, Campbell McBride."

"You're the one who was asking about Darrin Beresford at the diner?"

"Yes." She looked sharply at Keith. "Who's calling, please?"

"This is Brock Wilson. You came to my store last week to talk about it."

"That's right, Mr. Wilson. Do you have some information for me?" She wished they weren't in the restaurant, so she could put the phone on speaker and Keith could hear him, too.

"I might. Can you come see me?"

"Well, I'm not in Murray right now. Maybe in the morning?"

"Oh." He sounded let down.

"Can't you tell me over the phone?" she asked.

"I'd … rather not."

She frowned. "What's your address, Mr. Wilson?"

When he gave it to her, she repeated it distinctly out loud. Keith yanked a small notebook from his shirt pocket and began writing. Campbell raised her eyebrows and lifted her shoulders. He nodded vigorously.

"All right, Mr. Wilson. I'll be there, but it will take me at least an hour."

"Thank you." He hung up.

"He says he has information for me."

"Why didn't he tell the police?" Keith asked.

"I don't know." She quickly shoveled in the last few bites of her meal.

"I'll follow you," Keith said, taking out his wallet.

"Why don't you lead the way? I'm not as familiar with the roads as you are."

He paid for their dinner, and they went out to the parking lot.

18

For the next hour, Campbell tried to concentrate on following the SUV ahead of her. She felt like they were driving away from her father, not toward him. They'd planned to go directly to Clark's cottage, but now they had to go all the way back to Murray. She clenched her hands on the steering wheel and prayed in desperation.

"Lord, you keep throwing things my way that keep me from finding Dad. Please don't let this distraction make things worse."

Darkness fell as they made their way southeast. They drove into an upscale housing development, and Keith parked at the curb outside Wilson's house. Campbell pulled into the driveway and waited for him to join her before approaching the door.

Wilson opened the door within seconds after she rang and stared at Keith over her shoulder.

"Who's this?"

"Detective Fuller," Campbell said.

"I—" Wilson gave a sigh and stepped back, allowing them to enter.

"You didn't want the police," Campbell said. "I was with Detective Fuller when you called me. One of True Blue Investigations' employees was attacked earlier today, and we had been to the hospital in Paducah."

Wilson stared at them. "I'm sorry. Is he okay?"

"No. He's seriously injured."

He swallowed hard. "Come sit down." He led them into a comfortably furnished living room.

Quiet noises came from the kitchen, and what Campbell thought were sound effects from a video game filtered in from another room.

"I should have contacted you earlier, I guess." Wilson's expression was almost a plea. "I thought about it for a few days, but I couldn't make sense of it. I should have just called the police." He looked Keith in the eye. "I'm sorry. I didn't know someone else could be hurt."

"What is it you know, Mr. Wilson?" Keith asked.

He turned his attention back to Campbell. "You said your father was missing. I've watched the paper, but I didn't see anything about it. Is he back?"

"No," Campbell said. "We're still looking for him."

Wilson nodded. "Okay, I didn't see how this fit in, but—" He broke off and looked at Keith. "Have you found anything in the Beresford murder?"

"I can't really discuss an open case," Keith said.

Campbell squared her shoulders. "Well, I can. If you're saying my father's disappearance is connected to Darrin Beresford's murder, you need to speak up, and I mean now."

Wilson glanced toward the kitchen and swallowed hard. "Please. My family. I told my wife about this, but we don't want the kids to know."

"Okay." Campbell lowered her voice. "Just say it, Mr. Wilson. It was important enough for you to call me."

He licked his lips and shot Keith another glance then refocused on Campbell. "I think I told you that Paul and I had a golf date for Saturday."

"You did mention that," Campbell said.

"Yeah, well, we didn't play."

She waited, resisting the urge to lead him with more questions.

"Paul called me along about Thursday and said the weekend looked great and did I want to go fishing instead. I suggested we go out on Kentucky Lake, but he said he was thinking Barkley. Well, it was his boat, so I said sure."

Lake Barkley was on the eastern side of Land Between the Lakes, and Campbell wondered what the difference was, so far as fishing was concerned. Maybe different species? Better luck in the past for Exter? Or maybe he wouldn't run into as many people he knew over there as he would on the closer Kentucky Lake.

"Anyway, long story short," Wilson said, "I met Paul at his house early, around seven-thirty. He'd already packed his gear, and I put mine in the back of the vehicle for the ride over. Once we'd put the boat in at the landing, I climbed aboard with my stuff. At one point I was going to shift some things, but when I touched a duffel bag of Paul's, he said, 'No, leave that there.' I thought it was a bit odd, like he didn't want me hefting that bag."

This wasn't going anywhere, Campbell thought. She wanted to scream, *Just spit it out!*

"And he was acting kind of off all day."

"How do you mean?" she asked.

"Well, he drank more than usual, for one thing. We'd brought our lunch and a six-pack, but Paul was really guzzling it, to the point where I started getting nervous about him driving home, or even landing the boat okay. So, when it got down to one beer left, I grabbed it, thinking at least I could keep him from drinking it. But, no. Paul says, 'Oh, there's more in the cabin,' and off he goes to get another six-pack."

"Where's this going, Mr. Wilson?" Campbell asked softly.

He stared at her for a moment, then blurted, "I opened the bag and took a look while he was in the cabin. I didn't know what it was at first, but then I saw what looked like blood on it."

"Did Exter know you saw it?"

"Pretty sure he didn't. I acted all innocent and kept away from it after that. Later, when we decided we'd enough, I went aft to make sure the fish were all on ice in the cooler. When I came back, I noticed it was gone. I'm pretty sure he'd dumped it in the lake."

"The whole bag?" Campbell asked.

"Yeah."

"Did you ask him about it?"

"Yeah, not right away. I was thinking about it and wondering if I should mention it. When we got to the landing and were getting ready to trailer the boat, I said, 'Hey, where's your duffel?' He looked at me kinda funny and said, 'Oh, I stashed it in the cabin.' And that was all."

"So, you didn't do anything," Campbell said.

"I thought about it all weekend, but then yesterday when I got home from the store, my wife tells me Paul's being questioned by the police. Apparently his wife stopped by and told her, and Julie said she was very upset. She didn't know why they had him down at the police station."

"And you think it's related to the duffel bag?" Campbell said.

Wilson's lips twitched. "I couldn't sleep last night. All day today, I'm thinking about it and wondering if I should do something. Finally, I told Julie what happened on the fishing trip. She said I had to tell someone. But I didn't want to go to the police."

Campbell eyed him closely. "Why not?"

"I guess I was scared. I mean, Paul is my friend. I didn't want something bad to happen because I'd misread the situation. But Julie said the police might think I was some accomplice to something if I didn't tell anyone. So, then I remembered you and your father and the private agency. I thought maybe I could tell you, and then you could tell the police, and..." He trailed off with an apologetic look at Keith.

"And you're telling us both at once," Keith said. "What you haven't told us is what was in the bag."

"Yeah. Did I mention that I took a picture while Paul was in the cabin?" He reached for a smartphone on the end table, tapped it a few times and handed it to Campbell.

She studied the photo on the screen. An open canvas bag displayed a square-cut piece of wood, slightly tapered, walnut stained and broken on one end. A chair leg, smeared with what could be blood. It was nestled in the canvas bag with three rocks about the size of misshapen grapefruit. With a trembling hand, she passed the phone to Keith.

"Please send me a copy of that and any other pictures you took on the boat." Keith took a card from his pocket. "Here's the number."

"Sure." Wilson started in on the task.

A woman of about forty with short-cropped brown hair came to the kitchen doorway and smiled nervously. "Coffee, anyone?"

"No, thank you," Campbell said.

She nodded and disappeared.

"I have to go back to the station and deal with this," Keith said to Campbell.

"But we're going to—"

"If I don't get right on it, he'll be released in the morning."

Campbell felt a huge weight, once more crushing her hopes. "Please, Keith. You know how important this is."

"Yes, I do, and I'm sorry. But it's vital we get this entered into evidence." He looked at Wilson.

"All done," Wilson said. "You should have four photos."

"Good. I'll need you to come to the station and give an official statement."

"Now?"

"Yes, now. Right away. You can tell your wife. I'll try not to keep you long. And tomorrow morning you'll go to Lake Barkley with a team of officers and show them as nearly as you can where this took place." Keith stood and looked apologetically at Campbell. "I'm truly sorry, but we can't let this slide."

Defeated, she rose. "Thank you, Mr. Wilson. You did the right thing." She just wished he'd done it quicker.

Keith walked with her to the door. "Are you okay? I'll wait here for him and take him in my car. I've got to make sure he gets there in a timely manner."

That made sense, since Brock seemed slow to move on anything.

"I'll call you in the morning," he said.

"You'll be busy tomorrow with court and all this other stuff. You'll try to match those pictures to Darrin's furniture, right?" She looked into his eyes and saw that her assessment hit home.

"Yes. Listen to me. Don't go out there tonight, Campbell. Don't try to see Clark Timmons."

"But my dad! I've got to follow up on this. I've waited all day."

"I know, but it could be dangerous. We don't know who went after Nick. Do *not* go to see Timmons alone. Promise me."

She tried to stare him down but had to look away. "I promise." It came out disillusioned and broken. She turned and lurched out the door without another word.

Back at her dad's place, she paced the floor for an hour, wishing she'd requested a copy of those pictures, too. She knew she'd seen a three-legged chair in Darrin's house, but the clutter had overwhelmed her at the time. But Keith and his men would find it tonight.

Even in her disappointment, the new evidence gave her hope. If Keith could pin Darrin's murder on Paul Exter, the dentist might give up some information about her father. It was another shard of a broken picture, but there was another fragment still pricking her, and she couldn't let go of it. The shelter.

Near midnight she considered making more coffee and decided that wouldn't be productive. She found herself at her father's desk. His will was in a drawer, in a thick envelope secured with an elastic closure. Campbell took it out and held it in both hands, staring at it. It was irrational, but she felt as if opening it would put an end to her father's life. It would be admission on her part that he was dead. She shoved it back into the drawer and slammed it shut.

BRIGHT JUNE SUNLIGHT slipped in around the window blind. She hadn't set the alarm. What was the point of going to the office? Nick wouldn't be there. Someone was knocking on the front door, and she realized the ringing doorbell had awoken her. She grappled with her phone and saw that it was after 7:30, then grabbed her robe and staggered barefoot down the hall.

"I'm coming!" When she got close to the door, she called, "Who is it?"

"Campbell, it's Mart. Sorry to disturb you so early."

She threw the deadbolt off, turned the button lock, then yanked open the door.

"Uncle Mart!" She fell into his embrace, surprised at the tears and sobs erupting from somewhere deep within.

"Hey, little girl." He stroked her hair. "I should have called you last night. This morning I woke up early and thought I'd just hit the road."

"I'm glad you did," she choked. His shirt was damp, and the driveway was dark with spent rain. Droplets glistened on the finish of his black SUV. "Come on in. It's wet out here."

"No word on Bill yet, I guess?" he asked as they went to the kitchen.

"No, but we have some leads. Let me start the coffee."

"I can do that," Mart said, opening the cupboard where the canister was stored. "You go get dressed, and we'll sit down and talk."

He seemed to know his way around the kitchen, so Campbell complied. Five minutes later, dressed in jeans and a striped pullover, she emerged from her room to the enticing aroma of coffee and found Mart scrambling eggs.

"That smells so good," she said.

"I didn't find any bacon. You want toast?"

She fixed the toast while he finished the eggs and poured coffee, and they sat down opposite each other at the small kitchen table. As she ate, she began to feel more normal, and Mart's obvious care and desire to help enveloped her with a warmth she'd missed.

"I'm so glad you're here."

He smiled. "I'm glad I came. If I'd had any idea what you were going through, I'd have come sooner. From what you've told me, we should go find this Timmons guy first thing."

"You'd go with me?"

"Of course I would, kiddo."

"That's such a relief. I had to promise the detective I wouldn't go by myself, and with Nick out of commission—" She glanced up at the clock. "I should phone his mother and see how he's doing. It's after eight, and they're probably at the hospital."

"You do that, and I'll clean up here. If you don't need to go to the hospital right away, we'll head for the lake."

Campbell had risen, but she paused. "Clark might not be there anymore. I think he was only staying a few days to settle things about the farm."

"We'll find out, won't we?"

His optimism had changed her whole outlook, and she grinned at him. "Yes, we will!"

A quick call to Mrs. Emerson told her that Nick had awoken briefly but was still groggy.

"He asked about you," she said. "He was worried."

"Tell him I'm fine," Campbell said. "I'll probably come up there later today and catch him up on what's happening down here. Oh, and please tell him my dad's old partner is here. He's going to help me check out a few leads this morning."

"I'm sure that will be good news for Nick."

"So, did the doctors say he'd get better?"

"They expect a complete recovery, but it may take a while," Mrs. Emerson replied.

"I'm so glad. Does he know who hurt him?"

"He says he's fuzzy on that. The doctor said he might remember better after he's rested."

"I hope so," Campbell said.

"Well, we're glad your father got him such good insurance. I have to say, Bill McBride takes good care of his employees."

She shared the good news with Mart and joined him in his Trailblazer, acting as navigator. When they passed the restaurant on Route 68, where she'd left her car on the expedition on Sunday, she wondered if she should tell Keith that Mart had arrived and they were following the shelter clue. But Keith had said he'd call her, and she imagined he was at the courthouse this morning.

"Mart," she said, "I really want the police to catch Darrin Beresford's killer—"

"He's the rabbit guy?"

"Yes, the one whose body Nick and I found. But I'm feeling a little guilty, because what I'm really hoping is that the murderer will be able to tell us where my dad is."

"We can pray to that end," Mart said, "but things don't always turn out the way we expect them to."

She nodded, knowing prayer would help calm her fears. "Thanks. I should be trusting God to keep Dad safe, I know, but all this time I've been thinking it's up to me. That's pretty silly, isn't it?"

"Not silly, but normal." He reached over and patted her hand. "We tend to think we can do something to change things. But, Campbell, you know this might not end well."

"I know," she said in a very small voice.

"I don't want to discourage you, but nine days is a long time for a missing adult. Like you, I know Bill wouldn't drop out of sight intentionally without telling someone—you, or Nick, or even me."

"Something bad has happened to him," she whispered.

"Maybe. In fact, probably. But God knows about it. You need to trust Him, no matter how this turns out."

She bit her lip, refusing to think how she'd react if her father was dead. After a moment, she turned toward Mart. "I think the worst thing is not knowing. If we never find out, I don't think I can stand it."

"I know. I'm praying for some closure. And for peace in your heart, even if it doesn't go the way we hope."

As she absorbed that, her phone rang, and she pulled it out. "Hello, Keith," she said in surprise.

"Hi. Sorry I had to bail on you last night."

"It's okay. My father's friend, Mart Brady, is here. I told you about him. He's going with me to Clark's cottage."

They were approaching the road that led to the lake, and she looked at Mart and pointed to it. He nodded and put on his turn signal.

"I'm not sure that's a good idea," Keith said.

Campbell frowned. He never thought her investigations were a good idea. "Well, we're on our way. So how is your case against Dr. Exter coming along?"

"Good. We spent some time at Beresford's house, and we've got a match on the bloody piece of wood. I hope we can find the actual piece, but that's a long shot in the Cumberland River."

"Can you convict Exter without it?"

"Yes. We've got him for Darrin's murder as well as the hit-and-run."

"That's fantastic." Campbell gave Mart a thumbs up. He nodded and maneuvered slowly along the cottage road.

"But just so you know," Keith said, "I've spent several hours talking to him, and after everything he said to me, I don't think Dr. Exter had anything to do with your father's disappearance."

"Are you sure? Did he see Dad that night?" Campbell asked.

"Sort of."

"What? Hold on, please." She touched Mart's arm. "Can you pull over? I want to hear this before we talk to Clark."

Mart complied, and she asked Keith, "Can I put you on speaker so Mart can hear?"

"I suppose so," Keith replied. "Hello, Officer Brady."

"Hello, Detective. Campbell's brought me up to speed on this very complicated case, and I appreciate all you're doing on behalf of Bill and the other victims."

"Thank you. As I was about to tell Campbell, Dr. Exter said he left the Barn Owl diner because he overheard a conversation in which he thought Darrin was implicating him in a hit-and-run, and he was involved in that crash last year. He drove from the diner to Darrin's house to confront him, but when he arrived another car was just turning in at the driveway."

"My dad," Campbell said.

"I think so, but we're not positive yet. Exter drove by and

came back about twenty minutes later. The other car was gone. That's when he confronted Darrin."

Campbell huffed out a breath. "That seems almost too easy."

"Not to me. Exter's basically a nice guy, and he was tired of lying. When he heard we had evidence he'd thrown the murder weapon into Lake Barkley, he broke down."

"Is he going to take it out on his buddy Brock now, for ratting on him?"

"I don't think so. He knows Wilson struggled with it and followed his conscience."

"Good. But why did he kill Darrin?"

"Exter was carrying a pile of guilt about the hit-and-run."

"Yeah, but …" Campbell's brain whirled. "If he killed Darrin to keep him from telling anyone, and Darrin had already told my dad, wouldn't he then go after my dad?"

"I've pushed him on that. He says he didn't know who had visited Darrin before him. He made a few quiet inquiries the next day, but he couldn't find anything. Then he heard you were asking around town about Bill."

"And I went to his dental practice to ask him about it," Campbell said, with a little moan.

"Yes. He had a possible identity on Darrin's visitor then. He called the True Blue office once and asked for Bill, but apparently Nick told him Bill was out. He stepped back for several days. Didn't want to draw attention to himself by being one of the people searching for Bill. But then he decided to take a look around the office and your house to see if Bill had collected any evidence against him."

"So, he was the one who broke into my house and the office after all?"

"Yeah, that was him. I'd never ruled him out, but he finally owned up to it."

Campbell shook her head. "I just don't see how you can be so sure he didn't do something to Dad. I mean, if he did all these other things—"

"That's exactly why, Campbell." Keith sounded tired but as though he was making an extra effort to be patient. "He's willing to admit to the other crimes. Why not that one? If it was a crime."

"Okay, Keith. Thank you." She ended the call and looked at Mart. "He didn't say we couldn't talk to Clark."

"He can't stop us."

"And I'm not going alone," she added. "Well, at least they've solved Darrin's murder and the hit-and-run now. I suppose he'll get back to Dad's case after Paul Exter's charged and he's done whatever he needs to do for paperwork and whatever else they do." She heaved a big sigh. She wasn't angry with Keith, but her frustration level had about reached its limit.

Mart gazed at her thoughtfully. "Since this guy we're calling on is not very happy with you, do you want me to do the talking?"

"No, I will, but thanks. Just be ready to back me up."

Mart nodded. "What if he killed her—his fiancée?"

Campbell raised a hand in protest. "I don't think he did."

"I know you don't think he did, but what if he did?"

She sat very still. "I guess … I guess we need to find out. But right now, I'm just worried about Dad."

"Okay, I get that, but keep in mind this may be a killer we're talking to, and he may not feel like being nice to you."

"Right." She was glad Mart was a big man and carried himself with confidence. He was trained to watch a suspect for body language that signaled trouble. But she couldn't let suspicions of Clark dominate her mind. If she thought too hard about it, she'd tell Mart to drive away. She couldn't let Clark intimidate her into not following up on this lead. If it was a lead. Maybe it was just an odd phrase in a girl's diary. She shoved that thought down, too.

"Come on."

Mart lifted a cautious eyebrow. "You ready to go ask ol' Timmons about the shelter?"

"Yeah, let's get on with it."

19

Mart put the vehicle in gear and eased it down the road. Campbell directed him to turn off on a dirt side road, and they rolled along until she saw the back of Clark's cottage. "Here we are."

Mart flipped on the turn signal and came to a stop on the edge of the narrow road. Clark's pickup sat in the driveway, backed up to the rear entrance. As they got out of the Trailblazer, he came out of the cottage carrying a cardboard carton and set it inside the tailgate. He looked up at them, and his face skewed.

"Again?"

"Hello, Clark," Campbell said.

"Who's this? Another cop?"

"No, he's my father's best friend." She didn't mention Mart's status as a retired officer.

"Did your old man come home?"

"No. We're still looking for him."

"Sorry." Clark had the grace to give her a less antagonistic look.

"This is Mart Brady," she said.

Mart nodded. "Hello, Clark. Are you heading out today?" He glanced at the full bed of the pickup.

"Planning on it."

"I'm glad we caught you," Campbell said. "We're here to ask you about something in Alana's journal."

His eyebrows lowered. "I gave that to the detective."

"Yes, and he still has it. But there was something I noticed that day, when we first found it."

He blinked but said nothing.

With a deep breath, Campbell plunged in. "Back during the time you were together, Alana wrote that you stopped one day to leave something at the shelter. Can you tell me about that?"

Clark glanced from her to Mart and back. "It doesn't matter."

"Probably not." Campbell tried to keep her voice smooth and friendly. "But we did wonder. At first, I thought maybe it meant a charity shelter or the animal shelter in Murray. But now I think it meant something else."

He stood still, staring at her, but he sucked in quick, choppy breaths.

"Would you like to talk about it inside?" Mart asked with an easy smile.

"No!" Clark lifted the tailgate and slammed it into place.

"Clark," Campbell said softly, "I heard that your grandparents built a bomb shelter on the farm back during the Cold War."

"So?"

"Is it still there?"

The silence stretched so long she didn't know if it would ever break. Would he throw them off his property? Would he hurl something at them? Or call the cops and file a harassment complaint?

Finally Mart said, "We don't mean any harm."

Clark's gaze shifted to Mart and back to Campbell.

"We just want to find my father," she said.

"Yeah. So, what do Alana's diary and my family's quirks have to do with your father?"

"I don't know. Maybe nothing." Campbell sagged a little. "We've looked everywhere else we could think of."

"We're just trying to follow up every potential clue," Mart said. "Anything that seems odd or out of place."

Grateful for his support, Campbell straightened her shoulders, wondering if Clark would take offense at his use of the word *odd*. "That's right. Look, you must have been wondering for the past four years what happened to Alana. You must want to know."

Clark swallowed hard. "Of course."

"Well, I don't want to find myself four years from now, still wondering what happened to my dad. Now, my father's last known act was to talk to someone about Alana's murder. If he was going to dig into that, then I'm going to dig into it."

Mart nodded. "True Blue Investigations will honor Bill McBride by carrying out his last wishes and try to find out who killed Alana Shepherd."

Campbell gulped. Mart was talking as if her father was dead. But he couldn't be. He just couldn't. A lump burned in her throat, and tears flooded her eyes. "Please, Mr. Timmons," she squawked out. "Clark."

"Get out."

Campbell's jaw dropped.

"Hey, we're not trying to cause trouble," Mart said.

"Go away. And don't come back."

"Come on." Mart grasped Campbell's wrist.

She wanted to protest, but Clark didn't look willing to negotiate. Her hopes evaporated, and she followed Mart toward the Trailblazer. As they passed the front of Clark's truck, her steps faltered. She wasn't ready to give this up.

Mart tugged on her hand, pulling her toward the road.

"Keep walking," he whispered. "That man is riled, and he's got a gun in his truck. I saw it when we first arrived."

"What kind of gun?" Campbell's pulse raced. "A hunting rifle?"

"No, a handgun. It's on the front seat."

She should have noticed that. Some detective she'd make! Mart gritted his teeth and got in the SUV. Campbell went around and climbed in on the passenger side.

"Well, aren't you going to say something?" she asked.

"What do you want me to say? Are you scared of him? You think he's going to shoot us and stuff our bodies in his preppie shelter?"

"Maybe that's what happened to Alana." She scowled. "And—and to Dad."

Mart sighed and fitted his key into the ignition. "If you believe that, maybe you should call Detective Fuller again."

She frowned, knowing Keith didn't want to hear from her at this moment. She scrunched up her face. "Look, if I tell Keith about this, he'll be upset and say we shouldn't be bothering this guy. He wants me to stay out of it."

"So, where to?" Mart put the Jeep in gear and backed out toward the road.

"Down 68 to 80, I guess, and then back over to Murray."

They drove in silence for about fifteen minutes, until they came even with the Timmons farm.

"That's Clark's old house," she said, and Mart slowed and took a gander.

They were about to pass Halley's property.

"Pull in here," she said.

Mart frowned but hit the brakes and turned in.

"This is where the cops found Dad's car."

Without prompting, he swung the Trailblazer around so they were headed out toward the road.

"Park under the trees," Campbell said. She didn't want anyone to notice the SUV.

Mart backed carefully between two oaks and put the transmission in park. He looked over at her. "All right, now. Spill it. What are you thinking? Because we're not doing any breaking and entering."

"I know." She felt the blood rush to her cheeks. "It did occur to me that the shelter could be connected to their cellar, but you're right. We can't go in his house. But the neighbors were sure it's on the farm property somewhere."

"And?"

"I want to watch and see if Clark comes back here. We shook him up a bit. I thought maybe he'd want to at least check on the shelter and make sure no one's been poking around there. Like us. Or like my dad."

Mart looked in the direction of the farmhouse. "We can't even see his driveway from here."

"I know. But if he sees this vehicle it will make things worse." She reached for the door.

"Tell me you're not going to sneak over to the house," he said.

"No, only as far as I need to go, so I can watch for his truck. This is land Clark sold to a man who said I could be here. As long as we're on Mr. Halley's property, we're okay. Clark can't run us off even if he spots us."

"He could shoot at us from his land."

She looked at him sharply.

"Look, the man is edgy," Mart said. "I've seen crazier things happen. He told you to stay away from him, and if you show up again, he could really lose it." He sounded uncannily like her dad.

"Fine." Campbell hauled in a breath. "You stay here."

He leaned across the seats toward her. "Campbell, think. He might not come back here ever again. He was packing stuff up and said he was heading out. Didn't you say he lives out of state now?"

"Tennessee." She straightened and stood beside the SUV's open door, gazing at the sparse trees between Halley's land and Clark's. Was she being illogical?

Mart said, "He might never come back to the house. Is it empty?"

She tried to remember what Nell Calhoun had said. "I'm not sure if all the furniture is moved out. He might just leave some of it." She hunched down and peered in at Mart. "I thought maybe he'd bring some of those boxes in his pickup out here."

"Why? Why would he put more stuff in the house he's selling?"

"You're right." Campbell slumped against the Trailblazer with her hand on the door. "I guess I'm hung up on that journal entry. He left stuff at the shelter once. Maybe he'll do it again."

"But he's selling the land. He would never be able to access it again."

She put a hand to her forehead. He was right, but she hated his conclusion. It blocked off another possible path to her dad.

The rain was long past, and the sun was beating down now. She hadn't brought a hat. "Look, I'd like to stay here a while. I'll find a good place to watch, over in those trees. I'll be able to see his driveway, so I'll know if he comes back here."

"And what am I supposed to do?"

She had no answer.

"Campbell, you wanted to go see Nick today, remember?"

"Not as much as I want to see Dad."

She stood there in silence for a long moment, and then Mart's door opened. He closed it quietly and walked around to where she stood.

"Hey, I'm on your side."

Her tears broke and she dove into his arms. "I'm sorry, Uncle

Mart. I feel like we're close. Either that, or we're so far away we'll never find him." A sob shook her.

"I know." He patted her back. "You've been under an awful strain for the last ten days. I'm here to help you, not get in your way. Tell me what you want to do."

"I guess just watch his house today. See if he does stop back here. If he doesn't, well, then, I guess the shelter's not important to him."

"It might not even be there anymore," Mart said. "Most people wouldn't sell property with a hazard on it like that and not declare it to the Realtor."

Campbell sniffed.

"Do you think it's possible the Realtor knows and just didn't tell you?" he asked.

"Not really. She said she felt as if he was keeping something back, but she didn't know what. I think she'd have told Nick and me if she knew."

"But it's been over a week since you talked to her."

Campbell straightened and dashed away a tear. "Uh, it was last Thursday, I think."

"Okay, six days. She may have learned more in that time."

"Yeah. I almost went to see her again, but something came up."

"We could go now."

"Or I could call her."

Mart nodded and shrugged at the same time. "Or I could call as a potential customer and ask to tour the house."

"And show particular interest in the cellar?" Campbell smiled for the first time in hours. "It just occurred to me that, if the shelter was in the basement or off it, Alana wouldn't have written that they stopped by the shelter, would she? She'd have said they stopped by Clark's house."

"Good thinking," Mart said.

Campbell couldn't feel glad at his praise. She'd just debunked one of her reasons for thinking their watchfulness was a good idea. "But were the cops thorough when they searched the house?" she murmured.

"I'm sure they were."

"But they didn't know about the shelter, so they wouldn't be looking for it." She huffed out a breath in frustration. "My father's been missing all week. Isn't that reason enough to think Clark's up to something fishy?"

"Well, I hate to say it, but it seems to me the connection between Bill and Clark is pretty thin."

That hurt. Campbell turned on him. "No it's not! Darrin saw Clark near the real estate agent's office and called my dad. Dad disappeared that night, and Darrin was murdered."

"Yes, but by someone else. The dentist. You said he's confessed to it."

She plowed on, ignoring his interruption. "And the next day, Clark hired the agent from Pride & Calhoun."

"Like I said, that has nothing to do with Bill."

"It could."

"Clark was already planning to sell the house before Darrin saw him. That's why he went to the real estate office."

Campbell clenched her fists. She wished desperately that Mart was wrong, but she knew he wasn't. Arguing was fruitless.

"Come on, let's go back to town." He turned toward the SUV. "You can get your car and come back if you want."

She gritted her teeth and tried to weigh her options—let him drive off and leave her without transportation, versus going to get her car and possibly missing Clark's next move. She knew she'd never forgive herself if something horrible happened to her father and she'd missed her chance to help.

"I'm not ready to leave yet."

Mart sighed. "Well, what other options are there?"

"Let's get where we can see Clark's driveway while we talk." She swiveled toward the farmhouse and frowned.

"Okay, but let me get my binoculars." He took them from the back seat of the Trailblazer.

They made their way through the trees toward Clark's fields. She stopped at the edge of the property, beneath a big sycamore. She could see a good portion of Clark's house from there, and Nell's sign at the end of the drive. Mart sidled up to her.

"Decent view for surveillance," he said.

"Yeah." She thought for a moment. "Okay, one option is that you could leave me here and go do other stuff. See the agent, check back at Dad's house and the office. Check the office phone messages, that sort of stuff."

"I'd hate to leave you here with no car, Campbell."

"Yeah." If Clark did visit the property, she'd want to be prepared to follow him. She leaned against the tree and waited.

Mart took his binoculars from the case, raised them, and peered toward the farmhouse for half a minute then handed them to her.

"Have you got a good view from here?"

She put them to her eyes and focused. "Yeah. The times I've seen his truck there, he parked up near the house." She started to lower the binoculars.

"You keep them for now," Mart said.

"One of us could sit while the other keeps watch," Campbell said.

"We'll see."

He didn't ask how long she wanted to stay, and she was grateful. She wasn't ready to set a time limit.

She swatted at a fly. Her arms grew tired, and she passed the binoculars to Mart. The minutes trickled away. Keith would be furious when he learned what they were doing. Or would he? Keith was in some ways an enigma. He wanted to find her dad, too, but he took his responsibility to find murderers very seriously. He'd found Darrin's. Would he stay immersed in that, or would he shift his concentration to Alana's killer?

Maybe she wouldn't tell him about this surveillance stint. If nothing happened, there was no reason for him to find out. Unless Clark filed a stalking complaint or something. Her throat was dry. Suddenly she was desperately thirsty. Why hadn't she grabbed a water bottle?

Mart glanced over at her and held out the binoculars. "Do you want—"

"Wait!" She stared toward the road and the tiny dot of a vehicle approaching from the west. "Is that him?"

Instead of looking, Mart thrust the binoculars into her hands. She scanned, found the truck, and focused.

"It's him."

"I see him turning in," Mart said.

"If he goes in the back door, we won't be able to see him." She watched the truck move slowly up the drive toward the house. Instead of stopping outside the house or close to the detached garage, the green pickup rolled slowly past the corner of the wrap-around porch and out of sight.

"He's driving into the backyard. I lost him." She handed over the binoculars. "He's probably going in the back door."

"Maybe." Mart panned with the field glasses.

"So, we just wait until he comes out?" Campbell asked.

"Knowing he's armed, I don't think it's wise to approach him again."

She knew he was right. "Maybe he's just picking up a few more things here, and then he'll be off to Tennessee."

"Could be." Mart stiffened. "Wait. What in the world?"

"What?" she asked.

"I think …" He glanced at her. "You're shorter than me, so maybe you can't see him. Take these and look over the roof of the house, at the field out beyond."

Campbell took the binoculars and focused once more, this time on the house's main chimney. Then she eased her view beyond the roof and caught movement. A moment later she said, "I see it. He's driving out into the field where they used to grow tobacco." The pickup was swallowed by a dip in the land. "We could lose him, especially if he gets down over a hill."

Mart hesitated. "Do you want to go after him? I've got four-wheel drive."

"You'd do that?"

"Only if you call your detective friend first."

Clark's truck was getting smaller, disappearing and reappearing as it crossed the undulating land. "Let's do it." She handed over the binoculars and turned toward where he'd parked. Her toe caught a root and she sprawled in the weeds.

"Easy." Mart put a hand on her elbow and gave her the leverage to rise. "You all right?"

"Yeah, let's go." She limped slightly as she hurried to the Trailblazer.

Mart opened her door, and she dove in. While he rounded the vehicle, she buckled her seatbelt and keyed in Keith's cell phone number.

"Yeah, Campbell? What's up?"

She tried to gauge his mood and decided he was upbeat and not angry with her.

"Mart and I talked to Clark. He was upset and wouldn't say anything about the fallout shelter, so we came back to Murray. But we decided to stop where Dad's car was found, and we just saw Clark drive into the farm lane. Keith, he didn't stop at the house. He's driving out into the fields behind it."

"Which means what?" Keith asked.

She almost pounded the dashboard with her fist. Keith wasn't stupid.

"What we said about the shelter and Dad still being missing must have set him off. I think he's going to the shelter."

"You don't know that."

"No, but we're going over there."

Mart had started the engine, and they were rolling toward the paved road.

"I wish you'd wait for me," Keith said. "It may have nothing to do with anything, and you might make him mad again."

"This is too important, Keith. We can't wait any longer."

"Okay." He sighed. "I'll be there as quick as I can. Don't do anything rash, Campbell."

He was gone. Surprised, she closed her phone. He hadn't told her if Exter had been arraigned. He hadn't given an update on Nick or asked if she'd been in contact with the Emersons.

"He's coming out here," she said.

Mart shot her a sidelong glance. "You want to wait?"

"What do you think?"

They were nearly to Clark's driveway, and he slowed and turned in.

"He may have planned to come here anyway," Mart said. "He was packing when we got there."

"But it keeps coming back to why would he leave stuff here and sell the place?"

"You reminded him of the shelter. There could be something in it he wants to retrieve."

Campbell grimaced. "Or he left my dad there and knows we'll get the police to check into it." An image of her father's body huddled in an underground concrete hovel rushed into her mind.

"You don't really think he killed his ex-fiancée. You told me that yourself." Mart shifted gears and eased from the end of the driveway into the grass, following the telltale path left by the pickup's tires. "You and the detective figured out she was blackmailing someone."

Campbell nodded. "Her boss's husband." Her foot still throbbed, and she noticed now that her knee was sore, too. She rubbed it through her jeans. "Okay, so maybe he's just going to build a bonfire out here and burn a bunch of old love letters."

Mart smiled. "Maybe we should stop here so we don't spook him."

"But what if he's taking a shortcut? He might drive on through the field and out onto some other road."

"He's going pretty slow." Mart stopped the SUV and reached for the binoculars. "What do you say we walk to the top of the next rise and see what we see?"

She patted her pocket to be sure her phone was at the ready and climbed out, closing the door quietly. The grass had dried out from the overnight rain, and they walked quickly. A faint trail led through the tall grass, and she followed the tire tracks where the bluestem stalks were bent over. She couldn't see Clark's pickup now, but its distant humming abruptly stopped.

She crested a mound in the field and stood still. Mart came up beside her. About three hundred yards ahead, Clark had parked in the grass. He was out of the truck, walking away from them, but suddenly he was out of sight. She blinked.

"Where'd he go?"

20

"There must be a dip in the field there," Mart said. She looked back toward the farmstead. The back of the house was plainly visible, but they were on a rise. She looked at Mart.

"Come on, but be quiet." He walked forward, toward the truck, and she followed.

For the first time she noticed the small bulge under his left arm and realized Mart was carrying a handgun. She wasn't sure if that made her feel safer or more wary.

They walked cautiously until they came to the pickup. Mart paused and shielded his eyes to peer through the driver's side window. He turned, and they tiptoed past the truck. Campbell didn't stop to look in. A faint trail through the grass showed where Clark had passed moments ago.

Just beyond, a ravine cut through the land, and an opening about twenty feet square lay below them. A sinkhole? If so, it had been here a long time, and its shape was too regular. A cellar hole then, about eight or ten feet deep.

The recess was lined with grass and brush, and at the far side, Clark stood with a box in one hand. With the other, he fumbled with his key ring. Campbell touched Mart's sleeve gently, and he nodded, watching Clark.

To her left, she could see the most gradual descent into the ravine, and she could tell Clark had used that path. The grass was flattened there and caught the light differently. Down below, footprints led from the base of the descent to where he stood.

Of course, she thought. This was where the old cabin stood. The depression must be its foundation. She leaned close to Mart and whispered, "Could the old cabin that used to be out here have a cellar?"

He looked doubtful, but he put his forehead to her temple. "Maybe a root cellar under it?"

She noted that the wall nearest Clark seemed to have been built or reinforced with large, rough stones that peeked through the grass and bushes on that side of the hole. Squarely before him stood what appeared to be a door built into the side of the cellar hole, though it was camouflaged by a tangle of blackberry bushes. It would lead directly into the steep side of the ravine.

Mart crouched in the grass, gesturing for Campbell to join him. She hunkered down, though her ankle protested with mild pain. If Clark looked up, he could see them, but the sun was in their favor. She looked at Mart, wondering what to do. Should they call out? Clark would be angry if they did. Mart put a finger to his lips and she nodded, prepared to just watch and see what happened.

Of course, Clark might have more things in the back of the truck to unload. She glanced back at it. The tailgate was still closed.

When she looked down again, Clark had apparently dropped his keyring. He set down the carton he was carrying and stooped to pick up the keys. At last, he selected one and inserted it in the lock.

Mart lay down on his stomach and peered through the

binoculars. Campbell inched back as far as she could get from the rim and still see the doorway. She looked around for something other than the truck that they could hide behind, but there didn't seem to be anything close—no trees or large rocks out here.

Clark hefted his box and stepped into the doorway. Campbell held her breath.

A muffled cry reached her ears, then Clark put the box down, almost tossing it out behind him. She couldn't make out his words, but he was talking loudly, urgently. She gaped at Mart.

"Stay behind me." He was on his feet.

Campbell rose and followed as quickly as she could down the steep path. When they reached the bottom, Mart paused to make sure she'd made it down safely and drew his gun from his shoulder holster.

"Quiet."

She tiptoed behind him, across the depression to the door. Mart flattened himself against the wall to one side, the way the cops did on TV. She could hear Clark talking beyond the open doorway. Mart held up a hand, signaling her to keep still.

"I didn't know," Clark said. "I'm so sorry!"

Mart stepped into the doorway, and Campbell crowded close, trying to see beneath his bent arm.

"Bill!" Mart surged forward.

Campbell shoved past him and ran into the dim room. Clark was holding the arm of a hunched man, and they both stared at Campbell and Mart.

"Dad!" Campbell felt her chest would explode.

He staggered as she launched herself at him.

"Hey, sweetie, easy does it." He managed a couple of backward steps in the small space and sank onto the edge of a bunk. "Wow, it's great to see you. How did you find me?"

She stared at him, taking in his gaunt face, scruffy beard, and hollow eyes underscored with dark smears.

"We've been hunting for you for ten days, Dad! Me and Mart and Nick."

"I didn't do much," Mart said, grinning broadly. "It was mostly Campbell and Nick."

"Where is Nick?" Her dad looked toward the doorway expectantly.

"Oh, Dad, I'm sorry. He's in the hospital up in Paducah. He was injured yesterday."

"What happened?"

"First let's get you out of here," Mart said firmly. "Are you okay? Can you walk?"

"Of course." Bill stood as if to prove it. He swayed, and Mart reached out a hand to steady him. "I may be a little wobbly, but that's just because I've been stuck in about eighty square feet of living space for the last ... What day is it, anyway?"

"It's Wednesday." Campbell laughed and hugged him again. "I arrived last Tuesday morning, and Nick told me you'd talked to him the night before. That's the last contact anyone had with you. I assume you've been in here since then?"

"Yeah, Monday." Bill shook his head. "It seems like about a year. My phone lasted for a while, but I didn't have a charger, so I lost track. There's no service down here, anyway, or I'd have called Nick right away. I didn't even have it for a clock after a couple of days."

Campbell looked around. The bunker was probably less than ten feet square, with concrete walls. The ceiling seemed to be sheet metal reinforced with beams. On a shelf at the back of the small room, a candle flickered, revealing extra blankets and a few dishes.

"Well, let's get you home," Mart said.

"Uh, listen." Clark stepped forward. "I didn't know he was in here. I still don't know how he got in, but it's not my fault."

"No, it's not," Bill said quickly. "It was an accident, Mr. Timmons. Entirely my fault. And I'm alive thanks to you for leaving a stash of freeze-dried meals and bottled water."

"Those meals are probably thirty years old." Clark winced. "I'm sorry. My folks stockpiled some food and water back then, just in case."

"Well, it didn't kill me," Bill said with a laugh. "I made good use of them and the composting toilet."

Clark nodded slowly. "My father upgraded that and the ventilation system in the nineties. I had no—" He shook his head looked away.

As they turned toward the door, Campbell noticed they were wading through about half an inch of water.

"Why is the floor all wet?" she asked.

"Oh, that's probably my fault, too," her father said with an apologetic chuckle. "I couldn't break the door down. At first, I thought I could chip away at it and eventually get out of here. But it's a very solid steel door, so I started digging away at the threshold instead. And then there was a huge, soaking rain, and it started coming in under the door."

Campbell remembered the deluge they'd had Sunday night.

"I thought for a little while I might drown in here," Bill said. "It got up to about my ankles, but finally I was able to plug up the hole enough to hold some back, and eventually it quit. But it's been wet in here ever since."

"It rained again this morning, while I was driving over from Bowling Green," Mart said.

"Yeah, it had nearly dried out until then." Bill sloshed a ruined shoe sideways through the water. "I've been chipping and prying with whatever suggestion of a tool I could find, but it's slim pickings in here."

"I'm sorry," Clark said. "I took out everything I thought would be useful. I should probably have had this place bulldozed before I put it on the market."

"Might be a good idea," Mart said. "At least tell the real estate agent. Come on, Bill, let's get you over to the hospital."

"What? I don't need a hospital."

"You need to be checked over." Mart draped an arm over Bill's shoulders. "Dehydration if nothing else. Come on, get in my truck or I'll call an ambulance."

"Good luck with that," Bill muttered. "No phone service here." Outside, he scrunched up his eyes against the glaring sun. "Ouch. Do we really live in this harsh daylight?"

"We do, Dad." Campbell took his arm. "The best way up is over here. Think you can make it? Mart and I will help you."

They'd just reached the top of the of the cellar hole when Campbell spotted Keith walking toward them through the rank grass. His SUV was parked right behind Mart's Trailblazer in the field. He surveyed her, Mart, and her father. Clark climbed up over the rim, and Keith quickened his steps.

"Bill! Great Scott, man! What happened?"

"We're taking him to the hospital," Campbell said. "You can ask him there."

"Of course. Put him in my vehicle. I'll put the blue light on."

"Don't fuss over me, Keith," Bill said. "It was an accident, my own fault, but I'm very glad to see you."

AT THE HOSPITAL, Keith took them into the emergency room and left them there while he went to take a statement from Clark. The doctor on duty immediately ordered intravenous fluids. Once that was set up, Campbell sat with her father in the exam room while Mart went to gather information wherever he could.

Bill lay back on the gurney with his eyes closed for a couple of minutes, then he stirred. "Don't know why they're doing this. I'm fine."

"Well, Dad, you didn't get enough fluids over the past ten days, even with the old water bottles you drank."

His face twisted. "I'm very thankful Clark left those in there."

"You'd be dead if he hadn't."

"So, baby girl." He let out a big sigh and reached for her hand. "Why don't you tell me why you're here? I was thrilled to see you when that door opened, but more than a little surprised. Why were you even in Murray, looking for me?"

She gulped. "The semester ended and I thought I'd come for a visit."

"Delighted, as I said, but you hadn't mentioned that. I thought you were going to teach some summer classes."

"Long story short, Dad, I'm no longer employed at Feldman."

His eyebrows shot up. "What happened?"

"Budget cuts."

"Okay. So, you're not in trouble."

"No way. Come on, Dad!"

"Just checking." He grinned and gave a half shrug. "So, what are your plans?"

"I thought I'd stay here this summer if you don't mind, while I send out resumés."

"Sounds great."

She relaxed, finally. "Thanks. I was keyed up when I got here Tuesday, dreading this conversation. And then I found out you were AWOL."

"You don't have to worry about me, honey. I'm proud of the way you turned out, whether you're teaching at some fancy college or flipping burgers."

"Thanks." She smiled. "Nick suggested I might want to apply for a P.I.'s license. I'm not sure, but he might have been joking."

"Well, I'm not laughing. Would you really consider it?"

She met his gaze, trying to gauge his mood. "I don't know, should I? Everything was so crazy when I got here. I just wanted to find you, but Nick was all over the place."

"What do you mean?"

"He wasn't sure whether to keep working, or to take any new cases, until we found out what happened to you."

"You thought I was dead?"

Campbell looked away. "It was one possibility we had to consider."

"I'm sorry, honey."

"It's not your fault." She squeezed his hand.

"Even so …" His gaze sharpened. "I thought you didn't like Nick."

"Oh, I don't know. He was … helpful while we were looking for you." She decided not to tell him how much they'd argued about following up leads versus keeping the business going.

Her father pushed the button on the side rail to elevate his head a little more. "He's getting to be a good investigator. It's taking a while to polish the rough edges, but he'll come out of this all right."

"Assuming that he recovers from his injuries, that is," Campbell said.

"Yeah. Who do you think did that to him?"

"I don't know, but I sure don't think it was random. I hope Keith can tell us something." She already knew her father would do a good job mentoring Nick, even if he wasn't the easiest person to train.

"Of course," Bill said a moment later, "Nick will never be as good as you could be. You're sharp from the get-go. I had to teach Nick to notice things. That and a million other skills. But you …" He shook his head. "Honestly, if I had to choose an apprentice from all the people in the world, you'd be the one."

Campbell was surprised, both by his words and the pleasure that washed over her. Of course, her father was prejudiced. "Thanks. I take that as a great compliment."

KEITH ENTERED the exam cubical to find Campbell sitting on a stool and Bill's friend, Brady, standing near the foot of the gurney where Bill was ensconced, carping at his restrictions.

"I'm telling you, they can't keep me in here. I'm not sick. The worst thing is, my toes look like raisins. But they already put a quart of saline in me. When are they letting me out?"

"Soon, Dad," Campbell said. "They just need the doctor to sign off on you."

"Hey, Keith." Bill lifted his chin. "Can you spring me?"

Keith smiled. "Let's just let them check you out and tell us you're okay."

"They've checked everything but my teeth." Bill scowled and folded his arms across his chest.

Campbell stood and faced him. "So, where's Clark?"

"I let him go, but I asked him not to leave the area quite yet. He's promised to stick around for another twenty-four hours. He swears he didn't know Bill had followed him out to the shelter, but I'd like to hear Bill's side of the story." He smiled at Bill. "If you're up to it."

"Sure, might as well. Got nothing better to do." Bill rubbed his chin. "Except shave first chance I get."

Keith peeked into the empty cubicle next door and commandeered another stool. He rolled it over toward Mart. "Have a seat, Mr. Brady."

The older man sank down onto it. "Thanks."

"What's the prognosis?" Keith looked at Campbell.

"He's doing pretty well. They want to keep him overnight, but Dad put up a big fuss. He wants to go home and get cleaned up, and I don't blame him. But still, I would feel easier if I knew everything was okay. He's very dehydrated—"

"I'll drink lots of water," Bill said irritably. "I'm right here, you know. You don't have to talk like I'm deaf."

Campbell smothered a laugh and shrugged at Keith.

Her father scowled at her. "Can't you get that doctor in

here?" He looked down at himself and wrinkled his nose. "I stink, and I'm about starved. I want to go home and take a shower and get something to eat and let my daughter pamper me a little."

"Of course," Keith said. "I'm sure he'll be in any minute. Now, Bill, while we're waiting, Campbell's told me what she knows. We found your prints on a coffee cup at Darrin Beresford's house. What was that all about?"

Bill sighed, and his head drooped for a moment. "Darrin. I'm so sorry to hear he's dead. I hope it's not my fault for visiting him that night."

"It had nothing to do with you," Keith said. "I've got the killer behind bars—Paul Exter."

"The dentist?" Bill eyed him in disbelief.

Campbell went over Darrin's actions at the diner and how Exter had followed him out.

"We assumed he saw Clark Timmons out the window, when Clark went to the real estate office and found it closed."

"That's right," Bill said. "Darrin called me and told me the police wouldn't talk to him. He insisted the man he saw outside was connected to the Shepherd murder case. I remembered the case—it happened not too long after I moved here, and I had nothing to do with it, but I'd read about it in the paper and online."

"So Darrin wanted to meet with you?" Keith asked.

"Yeah. I went over to his house mostly to reassure him. I knew Timmons had been arrested when his fiancée was killed, but he never went to trial for it. I told Darrin that Timmons wasn't a fugitive, but he was very agitated. In the end, I promised him I'd look into it, mostly just to calm him down. He said he had five hundred bucks and he'd pay me if I'd dig into the Shepherd case."

"That's pretty unusual for Darrin," Keith said.

"Yeah, well, he wanted to see Timmons behind bars, or

whoever was responsible. He'd taken a real interest in the case, and he was angry that the police hadn't been able to put the killer away." Bill shrugged. "Looking at his place, I figured he couldn't afford it, but I'd let him pay me a really low rate just to save face. He seemed to have an obsession about putting the killer away."

"That may have been how he could find a way to do something meaningful," Mart mused. "Somebody like that might not have many chances to make a difference in life."

Campbell hadn't thought much about Darrin's motives, other than calling attention to himself, but Mart might be on track. "So after you left him, you went out to Clark Timmons's farm," she said.

"Right."

"Did you see anyone else at Darrin's?" Keith asked.

"You mean besides the rabbits?" Bill asked.

Keith laughed. "Yeah. Exter said he saw your car there—or *a* car there, so he went on past and came back later, after you'd gone."

"Sounds reasonable. I didn't notice anything." Bill shifted on the narrow bed and grimaced.

"Dad, are you in pain?" Campbell asked.

"Nah, I'm okay." He smiled at her and reached for her hand. "So, anyway, I didn't take everything Darrin said at face value, but I thought it was worth following up on. Darrin's a kooky kind of guy, but I figure if he wants to see justice served, he should get that." His face drooped. "Man, I can't believe he was killed within hours after I left him."

"Probably within minutes," Keith said.

They were all silent for a moment before Bill picked up his tale. "I went out to the farm and parked down the road. I guess you found my car."

Keith nodded.

"It's in your garage now," Campbell said.

"Thanks. Well, I walked closer to the house, and I was surprised that Clark's truck wasn't in the driveway. And then I saw it was parked way out in the field behind, with its lights on. I walked toward it. It was several hundred yards from the house —well, you all know. I couldn't imagine what he was doing out there. And then I saw someone beyond the truck, walking real quietly. And then he disappeared." Bill clapped his hands, and Campbell jumped.

"He went down into the hole?" Mart asked.

"Yup. I crept on out there and hid in the grass near his truck. I figured Clark had to go back to it sometime. Then I heard a creak, like metal moving. I went closer, and I could see down into that old cellar hole, and there was a light in a doorway in the ground. Freaked me out. I got down close to it and hid in the bushes to one side. About ten minutes later, Clark comes out. He walked right past me in the dark. Went up to the truck and drove away."

"What did you do?" Campbell asked.

"I turned on my flashlight, and I found the entrance to the bunker. A padlock was hanging on a hasp. I was surprised the door wasn't locked, so I went in. It was a little doomsday prepper's bunker, and there were some supplies there in case of a nuclear attack or EMP or whatever. But there wasn't a lot. I wondered if they'd quit using it. I looked around, hunting for anything that would link Timmons to the crime, but I didn't find anything."

He glanced at Campbell, and she patted his arm.

"After about fifteen minutes, I heard footsteps and realized I'd stayed too long. I hadn't heard the truck, but he'd come back. I was caught! I dove under a bunkbed and pulled the edge of the blanket down. Someone comes in, sets down a box, and leaves again. I hold still and listen, and I hear the door close. And lock."

Campbell's jaw dropped.

"Can't believe you did something that dumb, Bill." Mart shook his head.

"You're telling me." Bill smiled ruefully at his friend. "By the time I figured out he'd locked it from outside and I wasn't getting out, he was long gone. I pounded on the door and hollered until I was hoarse. Tried everything I could to weaken that door, but it's solid."

"That was a big old padlock on the outside," Keith said. "He told me his father had always been afraid kids would find the shelter and get in there, so they always locked it up tight whenever they were leaving."

"Well, this is one kid they caught." Bill's expression turned glum.

Keith smiled. "I can't tell you how happy I am that you're safe."

"I'm pretty glad myself." Bill leaned over and draped an arm around Campbell. "I'm sure glad you're here, too, honey. You said you got here last Tuesday, the morning after I started my little vacation in the bunker."

"Right," Campbell said.

"But you didn't know I was missing."

"Not until later."

Bill sighed and leaned back against the pillow. "Maybe that was God's way of bringing you here to find me."

"Maybe so." Her cell phone rang, and she peered at the screen. "It's Mrs. Emerson. Excuse me."

She hurried out into the hallway.

"Tell me again what happened to Nick," Bill said. "Campbell said he's in the hospital, but not this hospital, right?"

Keith sat down on Campbell's stool and told him about the attack on Nick. Campbell was just returning when he finished.

"Nick's in and out of consciousness," she said. "They're optimistic, but he needs some rest. Detective Jackson is waiting to talk to him when he's a little more lucid. I think I'll go up later."

"Take me with you," Bill said.

"Oh, Dad, I think you should go home and rest."

"I'll stay with you, Bill," Mart said. "Let Campbell go see him. I'll cook supper and we can catch up."

Bill's brow wrinkled as he looked at Mart. "Are you staying at my place?"

"I'll get a hotel. Campbell's got your hide-a-bed."

A white-coated doctor peeked in from the doorway. "Is this a party?"

"Sort of," Campbell said with a laugh. "We're celebrating my dad's return after ten days locked in a fallout shelter."

"So I heard. Well, Mr. McBride, I'm told you don't want to stay with us. Let's take a look at you."

Campbell squeezed past Keith into the hall, and Mart followed them.

"I'm pretty sure they'll let him go home," Campbell said. "He seems okay, considering."

Mart nodded. "Looks awful, but he sounds rational. I guess it depends on what the tests show."

"I'll get back to the station and finish my report on all this," Keith said. "May I check in at the house later?"

"Sure." Campbell patted his arm. "We'd be happy to have you. Especially if you bring some ice cream."

Keith grinned. "Absolutely."

"Then everything's all right."

"Well ..." he hesitated, and she sobered. "There was one other thing I wanted to tell you."

"What? Have you arrested Jared Chase?"

He swallowed hard. "Not yet." He leaned in close. "This is just between us, but I've got a team of concrete-scanning specialists coming down from Paducah."

She caught her breath. "To look at Chase's old projects?"

"One in particular. They have new equipment that scans for voids in the concrete." His phone rang. Although he dearly wanted to, he couldn't ignore it and pulled it out. "I'm sorry, Campbell. It's an emergency. I've got to go, but we'll talk later." He hurried off down the hallway.

"What's that about?" Mart asked.

"Jared Chase, the construction company owner. Keith's determined that Alana Shepherd was blackmailing him before she was murdered, but we don't know what she was holding over him. Chase is a builder, and we discussed using a building project as a way to get rid of a body."

"I thought they found Ms. Shepherd's body."

"They did," Campbell said, "but not the exchange student who disappeared a few years earlier."

21

K eith rang the doorbell and looked around. The yard was bright, thanks to security lights that had come on when he drove in.

A stocky man of about forty opened the door.

"Thomas Crider?" Keith asked.

"Yes."

Keith showed his credentials and introduced himself. "I understand you're Jared Chase's foreman?"

"Yes."

"I'm sure you know Mr. Chase is in custody. Are you in charge while he's otherwise engaged?"

"Yeah, I am," Crider said. "Is there a problem with the strip mall?"

"No, I'm here about an older project. Were you working for Mr. Chase when the Slate Hotel was built?"

"Yeah. I wasn't the foreman then, but I was on the crew."

"Tell me about the concrete work there."

Crider frowned and ran a hand through his hair. A large Band-Aid wrapped around the side of his hand. "If I remember right, we were supposed to pour on a Monday. The forms were all set and everything was ready. Mr. Chase was already there when we got there. He'd done some last-minute things and even had set the concrete mixing. Wanted to get it done fast."

"Why?" Keith asked.

"He's always pushing. I think in that case, if we finished before our deadline, we'd get a bonus, and he wanted that. There's a lot of profit in bonuses."

Keith nodded. "Did he want a particular section done first?"

"Yeah." Crider's bushy eyebrows almost met in the middle of his forehead. "I think he did."

"Why?"

He shrugged.

"Was there anything different about that part?" Keith asked. "Had the ground been disturbed?"

"If it had, I didn't notice anything." Crider lifted his chin slightly. "It had been prepared by the best crew in Calloway County. If anyone messed with it, it had been gone over by a professional."

"Like Jared Chase."

Crider's jaw tightened. "You sayin' he tampered with something on that job?"

"I'm not saying anything, Mr. Crider, but you're giving me a vibe. What did you do to your hand?"

Crider's eyes narrowed. "I hurt it at work."

"I see. Did something bother you about that hotel job? Is this something you've wondered about over the years? Because if you know something, it would be to your advantage to tell me now. I intend to get the proper equipment and scan that concrete tonight. Anything you want to tell me first?"

Crider swallowed hard and shook his head. "Nothing. Sorry."

Keith walked briskly to his car.

CAMPBELL COULDN'T RUN off and leave her father without giving him some TLC. She and Mart took him home, and Campbell made sure Bill was comfortable in his recliner while Mart made her a shopping list. A quick run to the store assured her they'd have plenty to eat while she was gone.

As she came out of the store with her cart, a woman going in stopped in her tracks.

"You! This is your fault!"

"I beg your pardon." Campbell stared into Bella Chase's face.

"My husband is down at the police station. They're accusing him of all sorts of things, because of you poking your nose into other people's business."

"I—I'm sorry. I thought Mr. Chase was out on bail." Campbell wished she hadn't spoken. She was glad to see a man getting out of his car in the next row over. "Excuse me." She pushed on past Bella to her Fusion and grabbed her three plastic sacks from the cart. Rather than stop to open the trunk, she tossed them onto the passenger seat and climbed behind the wheel.

"You'll be sorry," Bella screeched as she shut the car door.

Campbell was shaking, but she made herself back out carefully and drive away as fast as she dared. With relief, she exhaled her pent-up breath as the car rolled out onto Twelfth Street. By the time she got home, she felt calmer. She decided not to tell her father and Mart about the encounter. They'd just worry about her. Maybe she'd let them know later.

Mart had already started preparing a salad. Campbell didn't make him work too hard to persuade her to eat supper with them and postpone her drive to Paducah until afterward.

"All right," she said, "but I'm helping. And I've got to be out of here by six if I want a decent visit with Nick. I'm not going all the way up there for a five-minute stay and then get kicked out when visiting hours end."

Mart called the Best Western to reserve a room for himself.

Bill apologized several times for not being prepared to put his friend up for the night.

"Look, Dad," Campbell finally said, "I can sleep on the couch if you want, and Mart can stay in the den."

"No, none of that." Mart's eyes bored into hers. "You belong here tonight. I'll just be a couple of miles away, and I don't mind a bit. I'll have a nice queen bed to sprawl on, and I don't need to worry if I make a mess of things."

As they ate supper, Campbell filled in a lot of details for her father, so he'd understand all the tangled threads they'd encountered in their search for him.

"And while all that was going on, Nick wrapped up two regular cases for you. He did a great job."

Bill eyed her dubiously. "I thought you and Nick didn't get along so well."

"I told you, he's growing on me." She rolled her eyes. "Not someone I'd choose for my BFF, but I've got to say he put in a lot of work over the last ten days."

"Nick is a good guy," her father said.

"I met him once or twice when I came over," Mart said. "Seems like a smart young man."

"And he's loyal," Campbell added. She hated to leave them, but she knew that if she didn't make the trip to the hospital, her father would insist on going himself. She gathered her purse, phone, and keys and went to her dad's chair to give him one last hug.

"I'll be back by nine. You be good," she said in mock sternness.

"I'll ride herd on him," Mart said.

"That only works if you be good, too." She gave Mart a quick hug and went out the door.

KEITH LEANED over the screen of the scanner while the officer loaned from Paducah's detective unit explained the display to him.

"There's something in there, all right."

"A body," Keith said.

"Not for sure, but it's probably worth investigating. It's roughly the right dimensions. Could be wrapped in something —a heavy tarp or a carpet, maybe."

"How thick is this concrete?" Keith looked around. They stood on the floor of a hotel's lower-level parking garage. The structure had been built six years ago.

"It's an industrial slab with rebar in it, but they could have dug a hole before pouring."

Keith frowned. "You're saying it could be buried under the concrete, not embedded in it.

"It's impossible to tell for sure without excavating, but it could be partly below the level of the slab."

"There's nothing more you can do with that thing?" Keith sighed and straightened.

"That's as good as it gets, Detective."

"Okay. Thank you. You'll send me the report?"

"It'll be in your email by 8 a.m."

The forensic team waited for Keith's instructions. The chief wouldn't like it if he was wrong. The city would have to pay for the repairs, and it wouldn't be cheap.

"Okay, here's what we'll do." His cell phone rang and he pulled it out, distracted, but when he saw Detective Jackson's name on the screen, he told the team, "Excuse me just a sec. This could be important." He turned away and said into the phone, "Yeah, Matt, what have you got?"

"You were on the lookout for Jared Chase, Junior?"

"Yeah."

"Something just came in," Jackson said. "He flew into Nashville today, landed about four o'clock."

Keith clenched his teeth. As far as he'd been able to find out, J.J. hadn't been home since Christmas. Why now? "Did he connect to another flight?"

"Nope. So, either somebody picked him up or he took a rental."

Those were the most likely scenarios, Keith knew. But the Nashville airport was a good two hours away. "You're sure he didn't take a puddle jumper to Paducah?"

"Well, not a scheduled flight, anyway."

"Check everything. And check the car rentals, too."

"Got it. Anything else?"

J.J.'s father, Jared Chase, was in custody at the Murray police station. And now his son had come home—the son who'd been sent away and rarely returned.

"Yeah," Keith said. "Find out where his mother is." J.J. might still have some friends in the area, but the most likely person to make the airport run was Mom. She was a busy woman, but this would qualify as a family emergency, wouldn't it? He supposed she could have sent one of her store employees. But no, if discretion was needed, she'd handle it herself or spring for a rental for her son.

"Check with the store manager," he added. "See if Bella was there this afternoon and when she left." If she'd planned to pick J.J. up in Nashville at four, she'd have to have been on the road by two.

ON THE OUTSKIRTS OF PADUCAH, Campbell noticed her gas gauge was low. She didn't want to have to fill up later, when she left the hospital and it was dark. A filling station sat beside the road ahead, so she pulled off there and into one of the self-service bays. Only one other driver was gassing up. Twilight had fallen, and a few tall streetlights illuminated the area. She looked around for an attendant, but the booth down the row seemed empty.

As the other driver pulled away, another car pulled into the slot next to hers and a man got out. Campbell swiped a credit card and pushed the nozzle into the opening of her gas tank.

The man in the next bay was watching her. There was something familiar about his face, but in the glaring overhead lighting, she wasn't sure she'd ever seen him. He hadn't removed the hose from the gas pump.

Her throat tightened. She set the tab on the nozzle so the gas would continue to pump while she got back in her car.

"Stop," the man said.

She whirled toward him.

He held a pistol in his right hand. "Come over here and get in."

KEITH HUDDLED OVER HIS COMPUTER, agonizing over every word he typed. He had to get this warrant application right. He probably wouldn't get a second chance if the judge turned down his bid to tear up that hotel's garage floor.

His phone rang, and he pounced on the receiver.

"J.J. Chase rented a car in Nashville," Officer Ferris told him, and he gave Keith the license number.

He looked at the time on his screen. "Great. Do we know where he is now?"

"Not sure. We've got a squad car watching his parents' house."

Keith didn't like that. He wasn't ready yet for J.J. to know the police were aware he'd flown home from California.

"Can we make it an unmarked car?"

"I'll see. Jackson may be able to handle it."

"Thanks. And give the state police a bolo on that, okay? I don't want them to stop him, but I want to know where he is."

CAMPBELL STARED AT THE MAN. Why hadn't she stayed with the hose? She could have sprayed him with gasoline. She looked past him toward the empty attendant's booth. Wasn't someone supposed to be out here on duty? Where was that guy?

"Get over here now."

"No."

He strode toward her over the concrete island between the gas pumps with heavy, angry steps. She tried to swing the car door open, but he grabbed it and shoved it closed.

"I said now." He reached for her arm.

She jerked away. "But my car—"

"Leave it!" He seized her wrist and dragged her toward his own vehicle.

An SUV rolled past slowly. Campbell let out a yelp, but it kept going and turned at the next corner. The man twisted her arm, and she clenched her teeth against the pain.

"Quit the drama and get in."

KEITH PUNCHED a button on his phone. "Yeah?"

"I told you the state police ID'd the rental car in Cadiz?" Ferris asked.

"Yeah."

"Well, he didn't come across the LBL. He stayed on 24, and Jackson picked up the tail in Draffenville. Looks like he's heading straight for Paducah."

Keith frowned. "Why?"

"Dunno. Maybe someone told him to go up there."

"Okay, thanks." He'd barely put his phone away when it rang again.

"This is Carol," said one of their second shift dispatchers. "Detective Jackson just called in. He said to tell you that Chase has stopped for gas just outside Paducah. He's going to swing around and get in position to follow him when he moves again."

HALFWAY BACK TO MURRAY, Campbell realized who her abductor was. He looked like a younger Jared Chase. He sat slumped in the passenger seat with the gun aimed toward her. He'd forced her to drive, and the key fob and paperwork on the dashboard told her the car was a rental.

"You're J.J., aren't you?"

"Who wants to know?" He sneered at her.

Her pulse picked up. Alana had been J.J.'s friend, of sorts. What exactly had she written about him in her journal?

"I expect everyone in Murray knows you," she said, trying for a bit of bravado.

"You should've thought twice before coming here," he said.

"I heard you were in California."

"Says who?"

"Does it matter?"

"I flew in this afternoon." He shrugged.

"Huh. Nashville? St. Louis? Or did you catch a flight into Paducah?"

He said nothing but sat there frowning, the gun loose in his hand.

"How did you get a gun through security?" she asked.

"There's a big gun dealer between here and Nashville." He smiled. "I made a quick stop."

"No paperwork?" She frowned.

"Amazing what money will do."

She drove in silence for several minutes, turning things over in her mind.

"You knew Alana Shepherd, didn't you?"

That got his attention. "We were friends. What about it?"

Campbell focused on the road ahead and said evenly, "I saw her diary a couple of days ago. Your name was in it."

He sat up straighter and swiveled toward her. "What'd it say?"

"I was just trying to remember." She shot him a glance. He didn't look happy.

After a long moment, he settled back in the seat. "Just drive. Take the 641 turnoff."

Things weren't adding up, and she said in a conversational tone, "Help me out here. How'd you know where I was? Because this obviously wasn't a spur-of-the-moment thing."

"My family has connections." He laughed. "Apparently, your old man spent a couple hours at the hospital this afternoon?"

"Yeah."

"Suffice it to say someone told my mother you were planning to visit a friend up here in Paducah this evening. I was going to find you at the hospital there, but you made it easy. She gave me your license number—said she got it from the Kroger parking lot—and I spotted your car on my way up Route 24."

Campbell said nothing, but she'd have a lot to say to her father later, if she got the chance. One thing she certainly wanted him to teach her was how to know if she was being followed. That and a few other detective tricks. She wasn't as sharp as he thought she was. Nick probably would have spotted the tail long before he stopped at the gas station. And he sure wouldn't have left himself vulnerable while he pumped his gas.

Twenty minutes later, she pulled slowly into a gravel driveway on the west side of Murray. A commercial site was under construction.

"What's this going to be?" she asked.

"I don't know. A shopping center, I think. Something like that. Park here."

Darkness had fallen, and she didn't want to obey, but he stuck the gun against her temple.

"I said park it."

She complied, her heart racing.

"Now get out."

As she fumbled with the seat belt, a shadow morphed into a person beside her door.

DETECTIVE JACKSON CALLED in person this time. "Keith, we have a problem."

"What's up?"

"Chase stopped for gas and I circled the block. I got out to the street just in time to see him take off east, not west."

"He turned back?"

"Yeah. I was going to pull out after him, but I noticed another car in the gas station was left with its door open. The hose was in the gas tank door, but there's nobody with the car."

"What on earth?"

"I did a quick check on the license plate," Jackson said. "Keith, the abandoned car is Campbell McBride's."

Keith's stomach lurched. "Get after him as quick as you can."

"What if I've lost him?"

"He's probably headed back to Murray now. I'll send a patrol car up 641 to watch for him."

"Okay, got it. Man, how did he find her? It seems like a random pit stop."

"Someone must have tipped him off she was headed that way, and he followed her."

Keith hung up and sat staring at the phone for three seconds. He shoved back his chair and hurried out of the building.

22

T he car door swung open, and Campbell looked up into the woman's face. "Bella."

"We meet again. I knew you were trouble when you came into my store. Get out of the car."

Campbell tried to remember everything she'd ever heard about situations like this. Was it best to stay in the car?

"Get out. Now." J.J. had rounded the hood of the car, and Bella snatched the pistol from him and waved it menacingly at Campbell. "Nice and easy."

Carefully, Campbell swung her legs out and stood. "I don't understand why you're doing this. Your husband is already in jail."

J.J. made an impatient grunt. "Dad didn't do it. Don't you get it?"

Blinking, Campbell looked around at the worksite. Distant streetlights and a near full moon overhead showed her that the concrete had already been poured and some of the walls had been raised. Stacks of lumber and a forklift waited for the crew to resume work. So her body could be disposed of?

"Are they pouring more concrete here tomorrow?" she

asked, hoping she sounded confident and a little brazen. "Because this slab's already poured."

"She's right, Mom," J.J. said. "I told you we should take her over to LBL."

Bella held the gun a foot from Campbell's face. She imagined making a grab for it, but the risk was too great.

"You're as stupid as Alana," Bella hissed. "I thought Jared was having an affair with her, but when I ordered him out of the house, he told me what she was really up to. The little witch was blackmailing him—for something he didn't do."

"Then why was he paying her?" Campbell asked. Bella didn't respond for a moment, so she pressed on. "The police know Jared was making payments to Alana before she died. They'll be asking him about that, and if anything happens to me, they'll be asking you."

"Well, he's innocent," J.J. said.

"How do you know?" Campbell swung around and eyed him sharply.

"Dad didn't kill that girl."

"Shut up, J.J.," Bella said.

Campbell squinted at the young man. Was he talking about Alana or Marni Schliemann? If J.J. wasn't involved in the earlier crimes, his mother wouldn't have brought him back to deal with the situation now. "So your father cleaned up after you, got rid of Marni's body, and now you'll do it for him. But there's one thing I don't understand. Why didn't he bury Alana at one of his construction sites? Wasn't she found dead in her apartment?"

"Her nosy neighbor came to the door," J.J. said. "Dad had to hightail it out the back."

"Be quiet," Bella said.

J.J. laughed. "It's not like she's going to be telling anyone, is it?"

The pieces fit together now. J.J. had killed the exchange student, and his father had gotten rid of the evidence, apparently quite well. But Alana had found out, probably from things her friend J.J. had let drop. Campbell could easily imagine him spilling what he'd done, or hints, especially if he was high or trying to impress Alana, or both. Maybe Alana thought Jared had killed the girl, not J.J. Either way, she started collecting from Jared to maintain her silence.

"I guess the point came where Jared was tired of paying, is that it?" As she spoke, Campbell edged toward a pile of boards. The nearest stack held two-by-fours.

"I told you to shut up!" Bella's voice rose almost to a scream, but she turned away from her son and focused on Campbell. "This is all your stupid fault! If you hadn't come nosing around and trying to root out what happened to Alana, none of this would have happened! Jared wouldn't be in trouble, and I never would've had to call J.J. back here to help shut you up."

J.J. grunted. "Well, thanks, Mom. Nice to know I'm good for something."

"You were always such an idiot." Bella glared at him. "Just keep your mouth closed."

Campbell eased toward the stack and grasped the top stud. It was longer than she liked, and it would be heavy. But if she timed it right ...

With the gun pointed approximately toward Campbell, Bella continued her rant, but her attention was on J.J. "If you hadn't—"

Campbell grabbed the two-by-four and swung it with all her strength. Bella whirled as she moved, shock registering on her face just before the end of the board struck the side of her head. The pistol fired. Campbell jumped, but the bullet went wide. With a gasp, Bella sank to her knees.

The gun skittered across the slab. Campbell dropped the board and made a dive for the pistol. J.J. scrambled for it at the same time, but Campbell won the race. Her fingers closed around the butt, and she rolled away from him and stood.

She put one finger inside the trigger guard, trying not to jerk it or shake too badly.

"Stay back." She aimed the muzzle at J.J., and he rose slowly and put his hands up as high as his shoulders.

"Don't shoot me," he said.

Campbell gulped in air, trying not to think about Bella, who lay ominously still a few yards away. She swallowed hard.

"Take out your phone and call 911."

"What?" J.J. stared at her stupidly. "911?"

"For your mother. She needs an ambulance."

He started to reach for his back pocket, but a deep voice came from the edge of the worksite. "Hold it, Chase. Get down on your knees. Ms. McBride, put the gun on the ground."

Within seconds, J.J. was handcuffed and a patrolman was bent over Bella. Half a dozen uniformed officers swarmed the construction area.

The officer near Bella called, "Got a pulse, Detective."

"Call for a bus," said the man who'd spoken first. He came to Campbell's side. "I'm Detective Jackson. We met briefly yesterday."

She peered at him in the odd lighting, made confusing by the flashing lights of police cars. "Yes, when Nick Emerson was attacked."

"I'm sorry we didn't get here sooner. We had all our mobile units out looking for Chase's rental. Detective Fuller told us to try this site, and he was right on the money. Are you okay?"

"Yes." Campbell's voice cracked. "But Bella—"

"The ambulance is on the way."

More vehicles arrived, and Keith came from out of the darkness. "Campbell! Are you all right?"

"Yes." She reached out to him. "But I'm so glad you're here."

He took her hand and squeezed it, then let it go.

"She done good," Jackson said with a smile. "She got the jump on Ms. Chase and had the gun when we got here. All we had to do was cuff J.J." He held up the pistol J.J. and Bella had used, now enclosed in a plastic bag.

"I was afraid I might shoot someone by accident," Campbell said shakily.

Jackson grinned at her. "No fear of that. The safety was on."

One more thing for Dad to teach me, Campbell thought.

A siren cut through the night.

"That's the bus," Jackson said. "I'll get J.J. over to the station and book him."

"For murder?" Campbell asked.

Jackson paused. "Thought we'd start with abduction."

"He killed Marni Schliemann," Campbell said quickly. "I don't know if he meant to, but he did it, and his father got rid of her body for him."

"And I know just the spot," Keith said.

Campbell blinked at him. "Oh. What about Alana Shepherd?"

"What about her?" Keith asked.

"Bella and J.J. basically said that Jared killed her because she knew about Marni and was blackmailing him."

"They came right out and said it?" Keith asked.

"Well—I—" Campbell broke off and thought about it. "I'll have to go over it in my mind. J.J. said something about Jared not moving Alana's body because her neighbor surprised him and he ran out the back door."

"Okay, once you've calmed down a little, I'll have you write out everything, and you can put down the exact words you remember him using, all right?"

"Sure."

EMTs hurried past them carrying their equipment.

Another officer came over and said to Jackson, "We read Chase his rights and we've got him ready to transport."

"Wait," Campbell said. "Before you take him away, I want to speak to him."

"Be my guest," Jackson said.

The two detectives walked with her out to the roadside, where J.J. was sitting in the back seat of a patrol car. Jackson opened the door so she could speak to the prisoner.

Campbell drew in a deep breath. "J.J., your father cleaned up your mess, didn't he? You killed that girl—Marni Schliemann, the exchange student. Your dad got rid of the body and sent you off to boarding school."

"It was an accident." J.J.'s face was purple in the glare of the streetlights. He shot a terrified glance at the detectives. "I didn't mean to hurt her."

She looked at Keith. This was what she'd wanted him to hear, and she'd figured J.J. wouldn't deny what he'd admitted ten minutes ago with her standing right there. The police wouldn't have to worry about him weaseling out of it.

Keith leaned down and gazed at J.J. "You can tell me your side of it back at the station, Mr. Chase. I want to know exactly what happened."

J.J. nodded and his head drooped. Jackson shut the door.

"I'm glad he didn't kill her on purpose," Campbell said.

"Me, too," Keith said. "But it stopped being an accident when he called his father instead of the police. It's a lot more than that now. Come on. I'll take you home before I get into all this."

Campbell's jaw dropped as she remembered. "My car—"

"We found it," Jackson said quickly. "I notified the Paducah police, and we'll send an officer to bring it back."

"We'll deliver it to your father's house," Keith told her.

"And Bella?"

"They'll take her to Murray-Calloway County," Jackson said, looking toward where the EMTs were working. "If she needs advanced care, they'll send her to Paducah or Nashville."

"I hope I didn't ..." Campbell looked bleakly up at Keith.

"Come on." He put his arm around her waist and turned her toward his SUV. "Time you got home and let your dad pamper you for a change."

CAMPBELL'S FATHER ran down the steps when Keith turned into his driveway, with Mart not far behind. When she hopped out of the vehicle, Bill engulfed her in a bear hug.

"Hey, Dad," she managed.

"Campbell! Thank God! One of my friends on the force called me a few minutes ago. What's going on? I thought you were in Paducah."

"I didn't make it that far. Why don't you or Mart call the hospital and check on Nick? Then I'll tell you everything I know about this crazy mess."

"Okay." Bill started walking with her toward the house but turned back. "Coming in, Keith? We've got coffee."

"Not this time," Keith said. "I've got a prisoner to question and a ton of paperwork to do. And it looks like tomorrow we'll be tearing up some concrete."

Bill's eyebrows shot up. "Have fun."

THE NEXT MORNING AFTER BREAKFAST, Mart brought his duffel bag to the kitchen as Campbell and Bill finished their second round of coffee.

"You sure you want me to come back?"

"Absolutely." Bill rose from his chair. "I'm assuming Nick can't work for a couple of weeks at least, and I'll need help."

"Well, I'll go home and make sure everything's good with the family. I'll plan to come back Sunday and start work Monday."

"Sounds good," Bill said.

His friend was widowed, but he had three grown daughters, and the youngest, Reagan, still shared Mart's home.

"I hope I can take some of the load off Dad in the office," Campbell said.

Mart gave her a concerned frown. "I sure hope you find another position soon."

"Not me," Bill said. "I want to keep her here with me."

Campbell opened her mouth and then closed it. This was not the time to have that conversation. Maybe if she took that job at Murray State, she could room here with her dad for the next school year, but so many pieces of the puzzle had yet to fit together that she'd rather not get into it now.

She and her father stood on the porch together and waved as Mart's SUV moved down the street.

"Going with me to see Nick?"

"Oh, Dad, I don't think you should," Campbell said.

"Why not? I called half an hour ago, and the nurse said he was awake."

"But it's over an hour's drive one way. You need to take it easy."

"Nah. I'm fine." He strode into the house, and Campbell followed him.

"Okay, listen," she said. "How about if I go up and see him? I can give you a full report."

"I want to eyeball him myself. And besides, I need to give him his paycheck from last week."

"Okay." She sighed. "We'll go, but we're not staying there more than an hour. It will tire out you and Nick both."

"You wanna drive?" He smiled and dangled his car keys in front of her.

They stopped at the office, and Bill insisted on listening to the phone messages. Two potential clients had called to make appointments, hoping to hire True Blue for new cases.

"Nobody called all last week, except your usual lawyers and insurance agents," Campbell said in disbelief.

Her father grinned. "Word's probably getting around that I've hired a new investigator and she helped solve three murders in ten days."

"Oh, Dad, nobody knows about all that yet. Besides, without Nick and Detective Fuller, I wouldn't have solved anything."

"Okay, so I admit Keith did a lot of the heavy lifting, but from what you've told me, you did a ton of research and interviewing. And that's good work that led to some very good outcomes."

"Thanks." She shrugged, uncomfortable with his praise. "But let's not forget that without the police being on the ball, I wouldn't be here today."

"And without you being sharp as a tack, I wouldn't be here either. So we're even."

She laughed. "Sort of."

Bill pocketed the memo sheets with his messages, and they headed up the highway. When they got to the hospital, they found Nick's father pacing the large waiting room.

"Hey, Justin."

"Bill. So glad to see you. Are you all right?" Mr. Emerson stepped forward to shake his hand.

"Yeah, I'm great. How's Nick doing?"

"Better. Linda's in with him now. He wakes up for a few minutes and then he's off in La La Land again. The doctor says he may have memory issues. He'll be here a few more days, and then he'll need to take it easy for a while."

"Well, I brought him a paycheck," Bill said. "I figure he'll be out of work for a bit, but I can cover him for a couple weeks."

"That's really decent of you. Thanks," Justin said.

"Have you met my daughter?"

"No. You must be Campbell." Justin reached out, and Campbell shook his hand.

"Glad to meet you, Mr. Emerson."

He glanced at Bill. "Your father has done so much for our boy. I can't thank him enough."

Bill smiled. "Aw, Nick's still got a few rough edges, but he's turning out okay."

"Better than we dared hope for a while." Justin sniffed. "We might have lost him this week. Campbell, I understand you called 911 for him before you even got there."

"I did. I wasn't going to take any chances, not after the violence we'd seen over the past week or so. I sure hope he'll be all right."

"Well, let me go and tell Linda you're here. She can come out, and you can go in. It's only one visitor at a time right now, though."

"We don't want to keep you from seeing him," Campbell said quickly. The restriction told her Nick was still in serious condition.

"I've already talked to him this morning," Justin said. "He'd love to see you both."

"We won't stay long," Bill assured him.

Campbell let her father go in first and stayed in the waiting room talking to the Emersons. Linda was a bit teary-eyed and couldn't disguise her worry for Nick.

"I wish we could take him back to Florida with us," she said. "He's still not himself."

"No, he needs to be right here," Justin said firmly.

"Where are you staying?" Campbell asked.

"We got a very nice hotel, just down the street," Linda told her. "He said we could stay in his apartment for free, but it's so far from here."

Campbell nodded. "You're better off to be close to him." She told them the story of how she and Mart had found her father, and they were still marveling over it when Bill entered the room.

"You're up, Campbell," he said. "He's a little groggy, though. Better keep it short."

She excused herself and found the private room, where Nick lay sprawled in the bed, hooked to an IV line and several monitors. He looked pale, and his tattoo stood out starkly on his arm.

"You look awful," she said with a grin, figuring that would get a rise out of him.

"Hey, you don't look so great yourself, Professor. Your old man just told me you almost bought the farm last night."

"Well, with all the cool detective techniques you taught me, I managed to stay alive." She sat down next to the bed. "But I need some lessons on noticing when I'm being followed."

"Seriously, Campbell, you found Alana Shepherd's murderer, and the exchange student's, too. Way to go!"

She returned his wobbly high five. "Thanks, but you know it wasn't just me. Keith Fuller worked out most of it, and his buddy Jackson found my car and followed us down to the construction site. Those guys were in top form last night."

"I'm glad. Hey, Jackson was here this morning."

"Yeah? Wanting to know if you remembered anything?"

Nick nodded, focusing on the far wall. "And I did remember some stuff. I didn't know the guy that ambushed me, but Jackson said the neighbors saw his truck, and guess what? It was from Jared Chase's company."

Campbell's heart skipped a beat. "But—wait a sec. Was Jared in custody?"

"I'd have recognized him. But they had another clue. Seems I managed to make the guy bleed. Some of the blood the cops found wasn't mine."

"Do they know whose it is?"

"They're pretty sure it's Jared's foreman, some jerk named Crider."

"Crider? I've never heard of him."

"They're thinking Jared put him up to it." Nick scowled. "The doc says I can't work for at least two weeks, maybe longer."

"How do you feel?" she asked.

"My head hurts. When I try to sit up on my own, everything spins. And I'm not real clear on what happened the other day.

Short-term amnesia, they tell me. Who knew? It's really a thing."

"You bet it is. Well, take your time coming back to work."

"Listen to you!" He grinned. "Coming back? Are you staying with True Blue?"

She felt her cheeks warm. "I don't know. Dad's friend Mart Brady is coming over for a couple weeks to help out, while you're under the weather. I'll probably hang around the office and make coffee for them and put out more resumés." She didn't mention the job offer at MSU, because every time she thought about it, she got depressed.

"Is Mart staying at Bill's?" Nick asked.

"No, it's pretty small, and I got dibs on the hide-a-bed. He took a hotel last night."

"He can use my place. I've got two bedrooms, and my folks don't want to stay down there."

"Not even when you get out of the hospital?'

"Oh, they'll go back to Florida then."

Campbell eyed him closely. "They're pretty worried about you."

"They'll get over it." He shrugged. "As soon as they see me up and moving again, they'll forget all about it and go back to the Sunshine State."

She had her doubts, but she nodded. "I'll mention it to Dad. He can ask Mart if he wants to do that."

A couple of minutes later, she stood and gave him a playful but very gentle punch on the shoulder. "Get some rest, big guy. I'll see you soon."

"Not if I see you first." Nick grimaced. "Does that even make sense?"

"I'm not sure." She laughed and, with a sweeping bow, backed out the door.

ON THE WAY back to Murray, Campbell drove her father's car in silence.

"Long thoughts, honey?" he asked.

"Yeah, sort of." She turned off I-24 onto the Purchase Parkway. "After seeing Nick, I'm wondering how Bella Chase is doing. I really clobbered her, Dad."

"She was holding a gun on you."

"I know. And they kept implying they were going to kill me. I felt like I would only have one chance, and I had to make it good."

"You did the right thing." He reached over and patted her shoulder.

"She could have died. She could still die. Then what? Will I be arrested for manslaughter?"

"I highly doubt it. Nobody thinks it was anything but self-defense."

Campbell huffed out a breath. "I keep thanking God that they only had one gun between them."

They went home for lunch and then back to the office. Bill returned calls and lined up appointments, then went over the file Nick had started on the last case he'd been working on. Campbell, meanwhile, set herself a goal of two new job applications a day until her immediate future was settled. She used Nick's desk and had just hit *submit* on one to a private college in southern Illinois when the door opened and Keith looked in.

"Hey, McBrides. This place looks busy."

"Come on in, Keith," Bill called.

He walked in and nodded to Campbell. "I swung by this morning, and nobody was here."

"We went up to see Nick," Bill said.

"How's he doing?"

"He'll live. It might take him a while to get back to a hundred percent, though."

"How's it going with the Chase family?" Campbell asked.

"Progressing. After he heard what J.J. told us, Jared admitted to hiding Marni Schliemann's body and killing Alana Shepherd. And J.J. will be charged with abduction and criminal threatening at the least."

"What about the girl?" Bill asked.

"The D.A. is considering a manslaughter charge for Marni Schliemann's death. The thing is, there are no witnesses. All we have is J.J.'s word on what happened. He insists it was accidental, but ... well, we'll see. They may go for murder two."

"How did she die?" Campbell asked.

"J.J. says she overdosed. We've located her body, and we hope to get some information from the postmortem. But J.J. won't admit to giving her the drugs or anything like that. It's a long shot on convicting him there. But tampering with evidence, yes. The D.A. will have to decide exactly what they think they can nail him for."

"And Bella?" Campbell stood to go to the coffeemaker. "Will she be all right?"

Keith let out a sigh. "She was airlifted to Nashville last night. They're not sure she's going to make it."

Feeling a little woozy, Campbell sank back into her chair.

"You all right, honey?" her father asked.

"It's just ... I didn't want to kill her."

"We all know that."

"Nobody would think you did," Keith said.

"I really thought she'd shoot me. But she's not the one who killed those young women." She remembered Bella's sneer as she leveled the gun at her.

"She helped cover it up, and she was willing to take it a step further." Keith came over to stand beside her. "We'll need to get your complete statement. Can you come down to the station later?"

"I—" Campbell glanced at her father, and he nodded. "Sure. As soon as Dad's free."

"Yeah, I'll bring her over," Bill said.

"Okay. I'll get going." Keith opened the door.

Bill called after him, "We'll see you in a little bit."

"Is that why he came here?" Campbell asked. "To get me?"

"Well, it's best if you give your statement while it's fresh in your mind." Her dad came over and rubbed her shoulders. "You want another coffee before we go?"

"Maybe I should just get it over with."

"It'll be okay." Bill slipped an arm around her. "It's great to have you here, kid."

"Thanks. Even though I'm currently unemployed?"

He cracked a smile. "We'll talk about that tomorrow, too. I'm glad you can joke about it. And I know your head's full of sonnets and classic novels, and you'll probably get a line on a new position soon. But if you want to hang around here for the summer, I'd consider it a treat."

"I'd like to stay," she said. "At least for a while."

"Great. Got everything you need in your room?"

"Well, the mattress on that bed's kind of lumpy."

"Stop by the furniture store tomorrow and pick out a new one," he said. "Hey, get a whole new bed. I just stuck that hide-a-bed in there in case—well, mostly for times you came to visit. But if you're going to be here a while, you'll want something comfy. Get a queen if you want. New bedding, too. We can move my desk out to the living room."

"That's very generous. Thank you. I'll think about it. Of course, I might hear back on one of these applications any day now."

"So quit sending them out. You don't need a new job to make *me* happy."

"Wouldn't you feel like my education was wasted?"

"Are you kidding? Nothing's wasted when it comes to

learning. It'll make you a better detective." He kissed the top of her head. "Come on, let's go make Keith happy and then go home. I'm bushed."

"Me, too." She shoved her chair back. "Keith's a good guy, even if he gets bossy sometimes."

"He's one of the best. And it's part of his job."

She reached for her purse. "So, who's cooking tonight?"

"Nobody. I'll run to Pagliai's for takeout while you write out your statement."

"I like the sound of that." She put her arms around him and held him close for a moment. "Did I tell you how glad I am that you're safe, Dad?"

"Yeah, you did. I'm glad you're okay, too. Real glad."

She pulled away with a sniff and brushed a tear from her cheek.

"Well, let's not get all sentimental about it." He laughed.

"Or maudlin," she choked.

"Or even melodramatic."

"That's a real danger."

His smile broadened, and he touched her hair, where it hung down on her shoulder. "You and words."

"I love you, Dad."

He kissed her temple. "And I adore, treasure, and cherish you."

The End

ABOUT THE AUTHOR

Susan Page Davis is the author of more than ninety Christian novels and novellas in the historical romance, mystery, and romantic suspense genres. Her work has won several awards, including the Carol Award, two Will Rogers Medallions, and two Faith, Hope, & Love Reader's Choice Awards. She has also been a finalist in the WILLA Literary Awards and a multi-time finalist in the Carol Awards. Three of her books were named Top Picks in *Romantic Times Book Reviews.* Several have appeared on the ECPA and Christian Book Distributors bestselling fiction lists. Her books have been featured in several book clubs, including the Literary Guild, Crossings Book Club, and Faithpoint Book Club.

A Maine native, Susan has lived in Oregon and now resides

in western Kentucky with her husband Jim, a retired news editor. They are the parents of six and grandparents of eleven. Visit her website at: https://susanpagedavis.com.

ALSO BY SUSAN PAGE DAVIS

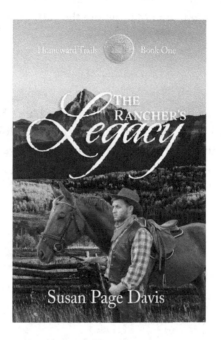

The Rancher's Legacy
Homeward Trails - Book One
Historical Romance

Matthew Anderson and his father try to help neighbor Bill Maxwell when his ranch is attacked. On the day his daughter Rachel is to return from school back East, outlaws target the Maxwell ranch. After Rachel's world is shattered, she won't even consider the plan her father and Matt's cooked up—to see their two children marry and combine the ranches.

Meanwhile in Maine, sea captain's widow Edith Rose hires a private investigator to locate her three missing grandchildren. The children were abandoned by their father nearly twenty years ago. They've been adopted into very different families, and they're scattered across the country. Can investigator Ryland Atkins find them all while the elderly woman still lives? His first attempt is to find the boy now called Matthew Anderson. Can Ryland survive his trip into the wild Colorado Territory and find Matt before the outlaws finish destroying a legacy?

Watch for *Ice Cold Blue*, Book Two in the True Blue Mysteries series, coming October 2021, and *The Corporal's Codebook*, Homeward Trails Book Two, coming from Susan Page Davis and Scrivenings Press in November 2021.

NEW RELEASES FROM SCRIVENINGS PRESS

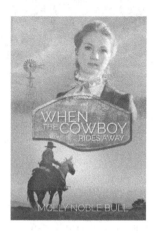

When the Cowboy Rides Away

Historical Romance

Maggie Gallagher, twenty-one, runs the Gallagher Ranch in South Texas and has raised her little sister and orphaned nephew since her parents and older sister died. No wonder she can't find time for romance!

When the Cowboy Rides Away opens two years after Maggie loses her family members. Out for a ride with her sister, she discovers Alex Lancaster, a handsome cowboy, shot and seriously wounded, on her land. Kind-hearted and a Christian, Maggie nurses him back to health despite all her other chores.

How could she know that Alex has a secret that could break her heart?

Ring of Death

Cozy Mystery

Dorey Cameron just wants to do her job. But that's nearly impossible when her dental patients don't show up for appointments. The bizarre accidents causing them not to appear can't be a coincidence. Someone is sabotaging her. But why?

Things take a terrible turn when vandalism, mugging and murder have the police pointing the finger at Dorey. Something in her possession must be worth killing for. If Dorey can't figure out the mystery in time, will she be the next victim?

September Shadows

Book One - Justice, Montana Series

A mystery

After the sudden death of their parents, Jess Thomas and her sisters, Sly and Maggie, start creating a new life for themselves. But when Sly is accused of a crime she didn't commit, the young sisters are threatened with separation through foster care. Jess is determined to prove Sly's innocence, even at the cost of her own life.

Cole McBride has been Jess's best friend since they were children. Now his feelings are deepening, just as Jess takes risks to protect her family. Can Cole convince Jess to trust him—and God—to help her?

Books Afloat

Columbia River Undercurrents - Book One

Historical Romance

Blaming herself for her childhood role in the Oklahoma farm truck accident that cost her grandfather's life, Anne Mettles is determined to make her life count. She wants to do it all–captain her library boat and resist Japanese attacks to keep America safe. But failing her pilot's exam requires her to bring others onboard.

Will she go it alone? Or will she team with the unlikely but (mostly) lovable characters? One is a saboteur, one an unlikely hero, and one, she discovers, is the man of her dreams.

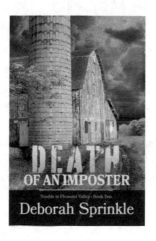

Death of an Imposter

Trouble in Pleasant Valley - Book Two

Romantic Suspense

Rookie detective Bernadette Santos has her first murder case. Will her desire for justice end up breaking her heart? Or worse—get her killed!

Her first week on the job and rookie detective Bernadette Santos has been given the murder of a prominent citizen to solve. But when her victim turns out to be an imposter, her straight forward case takes a nasty turn. One that involves the attractive Dr. Daniel O'Leary, a visitor to Pleasant Valley and a man harboring secrets.

When Dr. O'Leary becomes a target of violence himself, Detective Santos has two mysteries to unravel. Are they related? And how far can she trust the good doctor? Her heart tugs her one way while her mind pulls her another. She must discover the solutions before it's too late!

Stay up-to-date on your favorite books and authors with our free e-newsletters.

ScriveningsPress.com

CPSIA information can be obtained
at www.ICGtesting.com
Printed in the USA
LVHW012139200421
685034LV00017B/1129